This is a very strange world and we have not penetrated very far into its secrets. But we believe it is somehow parallel with our own, though obviously different. Sometime in the past there was apparently a force set into being that could reach into our own world at special places and draw out people. There are many stories in our world of mysterious disappearances.

"Take UFO's, parapsychology, water nixies, the singing of Lorelei, Eve's apple, Merlin, and all the folklore of the British Isles. It sounds improbable but Andre Norton has spun all these themes into HERE ABIDE MONSTERS, an exciting tale of wanderers from our earth who have blundered into the parallel world of Avalon . . . The clash of good and evil escapes the hackneyed and comes out in favor of a plurality of truths."

—*Psychology Today*

Andre Norton

Here
Abide
MONSTERS

◆ ◆ ◆ ◆

DAW BOOKS, INC.

DONALD A. WOLLHEIM, PUBLISHER

1301 Avenue of the Americas
New York, N. Y.   10019

For Bee Lowry,
who suggested that Lung Hsin
be one of the adventurers
in Avalon.

FIRST PRINTING, OCTOBER 1974

1 2 3 4 5 6 7 8 9

◆ 1 ◆

To Nick's left the sun had hardly topped the low trees. It was a ball of red fire; today was going to be a scorcher. He hoped he could make it into the woods road before the heat really hit. Of course he had wanted to start earlier, but there was always some good reason why— Behind the faceplate of his helmet Nick scowled at the road ahead.

Always some *good* reason why the things *he* wanted to do did not fit in with plans, not *his* plans, naturally. Did Margo actually sit down and think it out, arrange somehow ahead of time so that what Nick had counted on was just what was not going to happen? He had suspected that for some time. Yet her excuses why this or that could not be done were so perfectly logical and reasonable that Dad always went along with them.

At least she had not ruined this weekend. Maybe because she and Dad had their own plans, or rather *her* plans. Give Nick another year—just one—and Margo could talk to the thin air. He would not be there to listen to her. That—he relished the satisfaction that thought presented—was the day he was going to start living!

Dad— Nick's thoughts squirmed hurriedly away from that path. Dad—he had chosen Margo, he agreed with Margo's sweet reasonableness. All right, let him live with it and her! Nick was not going to a minute longer than he had to.

The trees along the road were taller now, closer together. But the surface over which the motorbike roared was clear and smooth. He could make good time here. Once he turned into the lake road it would be different. But in any event he would reach the cabin by noon.

His thoughts soared away from what lay behind, already seeking the peace ahead. The weekend, and it was a long one from Friday to Monday, was his alone. Margo did not like the lake cottage. Nick wondered why she had never talked Dad into selling it. Maybe she just did not care. There was plenty else for her to own. Just as she owned Dad.

Nick's scowl deepened, his black brows drawing together, his lips thinly stretched against his teeth. That scowl line now never completely faded, it had had too much use over the past three years. He swayed and adjusted to the swing of the machine under him as an earlier generation would have ridden a horse, the metal framework he bestrode seemingly a part of his own person. The bubble safety helmet covered his head front and back. Below that he wore a tee shirt, already dust streaked, and faded jeans, his feet thrust into boots.

Saddlebags, tightly strapped against loss, held the rest of his weekend wardrobe and supplies, save for the canned food at the cabin and what he would buy at the store going in. He had a full tank of gas, he had his freedom for four days—he had himself! Nick Shaw as he was, not Douglas Shaw's son, not Margo's stepson (though, of course, that relationship was hardly ever mentioned). Nick Shaw, himself, personal, private and alone.

A twisting curve downhill brought him to the store at the foot of the bend, a straggle of houses beyond. This was Rochester, unincorporated, with no "Pop." on the sign Nick flashed past. He came to a stop at the store. A Coke would go good. Ham Hodges always had those on ice.

Bread, cheese, Nick had no list, just had to remember to get things that would not be affected by the bumpy ride in. His boots thumped on the porch as he reached for the knob of the screen door. Behind the screening a black shape opened its jaws in an almost inaudible but plainly warning hiss.

Nick jerked off his helmet. "I'm no Martian invader, Rufus," he said to the big tomcat.

Unblinking blue eyes stared back but the jaws closed.

"Rufe, you there—move away from the door. How many times am I going to tell you if you sit there you're going to be stepped on someday—"

Nick laughed. "By whom, Ham? Some customer pounding in for bargains, or one going out because you ran the prices up on him?"

The cat moved disdainfully back a little, allowing him to pass by.

"Nick Shaw!" The youngish man moved out from behind the counter on the left. "Your folks up for the week-end?"

Nick shook his head. "Just me."

"Sorry your Dad couldn't make it. Larry Green sighted some big ones in the cove. He was just saying to me no more'n an hour ago that Mr. Shaw sure ought to come up and cast a line for one of those. He hasn't been here for a long time now."

Ham was being tactful, but not tactful enough. Nick shifted his feet. They never mentioned Margo, but she was always right there, in their minds as well as his, when they talked about Dad. Before Margo Dad had loved the lake, had been here in the summer and the fall every minute he could get away. How much longer would he even keep the cabin now?

"No," Nick answered in a voice he kept even with an effort. "He's been pretty busy, Ham, you know how it is."

"Don't suppose I can sell *you* any bait—"

Nick managed a smile. "You know me, Ham. I'm about as much a fisherman as Rufus is a dog lover. What I do want is some stuff to eat—what I can carry on the bike without a smashup. Any of Amy's bread to go?"

"I'll see. No reason why we can't spare some baking—"

Hodges turned to the back of the store and Nick moved around to pick other items. A package of bacon from the freezer bin, some cheese. From all the years he had been stopping at Ham's he knew where most things were. Rufus was back on guard at the screen door. He was about the biggest cat Nick had ever seen, but not fat. Instead, in spite of the plates of cat food he could and did lick clean each day, he was rather gaunt. His conformation was that of his Siamese father, though his color was the black of the half-breed.

"How's hunting, Rufus?" Nick asked as he returned to the counter.

An ear twitched, but the cat's head did not turn even a fraction. His interest in what lay outside was so intent that Nick moved up behind him to look out, too. There must be a bird, even a snake—something in the road. But he could see nothing.

Which did not mean that nothing was there. Cats saw above and below the human range of sight. There could be something there all right, something invisible—

Nick wondered just how much truth there was in some

of the books he had read—those that speculated about different kinds of existence. Such as the one that had suggested we share this world with other kinds of life as invisible to us as we might be to them. Not altogether a comfortable thought. You had enough trouble with what you *could* see.

"What's out there, Rufus? Something out of a UFO?"

The cat's attention was manifestly so engaged that it made Nick a little uneasy. Then suddenly Rufus yawned widely, relaxed. Whatever had intrigued him so was gone.

He returned to the counter. There was a paperback turned upside down open, to mark the reader's place. Nick turned it around to read the title—*Our Haunted Planet*—by somebody named Keel. And there was another book pushed to one side—*More "Things"* by Sanderson. That one he knew, he had read it himself, urged by Ham to do so.

Ham Hodges had a whole library of that type of reading, starting with Charles Fort's collections of unexplainable happenings. They made you wonder all right. And Ham had a good reason for wondering—his cousin and the Commer Cut-Off.

"Got you a loaf of whole wheat, a raisin one, and a half-dozen rolls," Ham announced coming into sight again. "Amy says give the rolls a warm-up, they're a day old."

"They could be two weeks old and still be good if they're hers. I'm lucky she can spare so much a day ahead of baking."

"Well, we had some company who was going to come and didn't, so she was overstocked in the bread box this week. Funny about that." Ham thudded the bread and rolls down in a plastic bag before Nick. "This fellow called up last Friday—just a week ago. He said he was from the Hasentine Institute and they were gathering material about the Cut-Off. Wanted to come out here and ask around about Ted and Ben—" Ham paused. "Hard to think of it being all this time since they disappeared. At least it scared people off from trying that road for a while. Only somebody's taken the Wilson place for the summer and, since the new highway to Shockton went in, the Cut-Off's the only road to reach that side of the lake now. So it's getting traveled again.

"Anyway, this fellow said he was doing research and asked about a place to stay. We've that cabin, so we said we'd put him up. Only he never showed up or called again."

"How long has it been, Ham?"

"Since July 24, 1955. Why, you and your Dad and Mom were up here at the lake that summer. I remember your Dad was out with the search party. I was just home from Korea, right out of the army. We sure gave that land a going over—Ted was a good guy and he knew the country like it was his own backyard. Ben was no fool either, he'd buddied with Ted in the Navy and came up for some fishing. No, they just disappeared like all the others—that Caldwell and his wife and two kids in 1946, and before them there were Latimer and Johnson. I made it my business to look it all up. Got out my notebook and read it through this week so I could answer any questions the fellow from the Institute might want to ask. You know, going as far back as the newspapers had any mention of it, there's been about thirty people just up and disappeared on the Cut-Off. Even before it was ever a road, they disappeared in that section. It's like that Bermuda Triangle thing. Only not so often as to get people all excited about it. There's always a good long stretch of time between disappearances so people sort of forget in between. But they should never have opened up that road again. Jim Samuels tried to talk the new people out of it. Heard they didn't quite laugh in his face, but I guess they took it as some superstition us local yokels believe in."

"But if it's the only way to get into the Wilson place—" Nick knew the legend of the Cut-Off, but he could also understand the frustration of outsiders needing an easy access.

"Yes, I guess it is a case of needs drive. You can't get the county interested in laying out a new road to serve just a few summer cabins because there's a queer story about the one already there and waiting to be used. You know, this writer—" Ham tapped the book with a fingertip—"has some mighty interesting things to say. And this one"—he indicated the More "Things" volume—"makes it plain, for instance, that we think we know all about this world, that it's all been explored. But that isn't the truth, there are whole sections we know nothing about at all, mountains never climbed, places where nobody civilized has ever been."

" 'Here abide monsters,' " Nick quoted.

"What's that?" Ham looked up sharply.

"Dad's got a real old map he bought in London last year—had it framed and hung it down in his office. It shows England and part of Europe, but on our side of the ocean just some markings and dragons or sea serpents, with lettering—'Here abide monsters.' They filled up the unknown then with what they imagined might be there."

"Well, we *don't* know a lot, and most people don't want to learn more'n what's right before their eyes. You point out things that don't fit into what they've always accepted, and they say it's all your imagination and nothing like that is real. Only we know about the Cut-Off and what's happened there."

"What do you think really happened, Ham?" Nick had taken a Coke from the ice chest, snapped off the cap, and now drank.

"There's this Bermuda Triangle, only this writer Sanderson says it's no 'triangle,' but much larger, and also they've made some tests and it's only one of ten such places all around the world. Ships and people and planes disappear there regularly—nothing ever found to say what happened to them. A whole flight of Navy planes once and then the rescue plane that went out after them! It may have something to do with magnetic forces at those points. He makes a suggestion about breaking into another space-time. Maybe we have one of these 'triangles' right here. I sure wish that Hasentine guy had shown up. About time some of the brains did some serious investigating. And . . ."

What he was about to say was drowned out by a wild yapping from without. Rufus, his back arched, his tail a brush, gave a warning yowl in reply. Ham swung around.

"Now what the heck's all that about?" He headed for the door.

Rufus, ears flattened against his skull, his Siamese blue eyes slitted, was hissing, giving now and then a throaty growl of threat. The yapping outside was apparently not in the least intimidated.

A car, or rather a jeep, had drawn up, and a girl slid from under the wheel, but had not yet stepped out. She was too busy trying to restrain a very excited and apparently furious Pekingese that fought against her hold, his popping eyes fixed on Rufus.

She glanced up at Ham behind the screen, Nick looking over his shoulder.

"Please," she was laughing a little. "Can you cope with your warrior? I want to come in and I certainly can't let go of Lung Hsin!"

"Sorry." Ham stopped to catch up Rufus with practiced ease in avoiding the claws the big cat had already extended to promise battle. "Sorry, Rufe, you for the storeroom temporarily." He departed with the kicking and growling cat, and Nick opened the door for the girl. She still held the Peke who had fallen silent upon witnessing the unwilling exit of the enemy.

"He's mighty little to think of taking on Rufus," Nick commented. "Rufe would take one good swipe at him and that would be that."

The girl frowned. "Don't be too sure about that! This breed were once known as dragon dogs, lion dogs—they helped guard palaces. For their size they're about the bravest animals alive. Hush now, Lung, you've made your point. We all know you're a brave, brave Dragon Heart." The Peke shot out a tongue and licked her cheek, then stared about him imperiously as if, having chased the enemy from the field, this was now his domain.

"Now what can I do for you?" Ham came back, licking one finger where Rufus had apparently scored before being exiled.

"I need some directions, and a couple of cases of Coke and . . ." She had Lung Hsin under one arm now as he no longer fought for freedom, and with her other hand she pawed into the depths of her shoulder bag. "Here it is," she said with relief. "Thought it might have gone down for the third time and I would have to empty this thing to find it."

She had a list ready now. "If I can just make out Jane's writing. She really ought to print, at least with that you can make educated guesses. That's right, two cases of Coke, one of Canada Dry, one of Pepsi. And she said you'd be holding melons—oh, I should have told you, I'm Linda Durant and I'm picking all this up for Jane Ridgewell—they've taken over the Wilson place. She said she'd call and tell you."

Ham nodded. "She did and I've got it all together. Won't take us long to load it up for you—" He glanced to Nick who obligingly moved away from the counter again.

He was willing to give Ham a hand. Though they should be in no hurry to speed this one off.

This Linda was almost as tall as Nick. A lot of girls were tall nowadays. Her hair had been tied back from her face with a twist of bright red wool, but it was still long enough to lie on her shoulders in very dark strands. Her skin was creamy pale. If she tanned she had not started that process yet this season.

Her jeans were as red as her hair tie and she had a sleeveless blouse of white and blue dolphins leaping up and down on it. Sunglasses swung pendant from another red tie about her neck and she wore thong sandals on her feet. He was not usually so aware of a girl's clothes, but these fitted her as if to complete a picture.

Nick shouldered one of the melons Ham pointed out and took a second under his arm, carrying them out to the waiting jeep. Ham was busy stowing in Coke.

"Wait 'til I get some sacks," he told Nick. "Shake those melons around and you'll get them stove in."

Linda Durant had followed them out. "That sounds," she commented, "as if I have a rough road ahead. You'll have to give directions, Jane's are vague."

For the first time Nick realized that she meant to travel the Cut-Off. He glanced at Ham who looked sober. After what Ham had just been saying—to send a stranger, and a girl, down the Cut-Off—But if there was no other way in now—only Nick had a queer feeling about it.

There was one thing—he could take that way, too. It was really shorter to his own cabin when you came to think about it. And it had been almost his whole lifetime since Ted and Ben had disappeared. This was broad daylight and these Ridgeways must have been up and down there maybe a hundred times since they moved in. So, why look for monsters that did not exist?

"Look here," Nick suggested as Ham reappeared with sacks and newspapers and proceeded to wedge in the cargo. "I'm heading that way. It's rough and we'll have to take it slow, but if you'll match your speed to mine"—he motioned at the waiting bike—"I'll guide you in. I'm Nick —Nicholas Shaw—Mr. Hodges here knows me. My people have had a cabin on the lake for a long time."

Linda gave him a long, intent survey. Then she nodded and smiled.

"That's fine! From what Jane said the road's pretty

rough and I could miss it. I'm very glad of your company."

Ham packed the last of the papers in, and Nick gathered up his own purchases and bagged them in a bundle he could tie over the saddlebags. Several indignant yowls from the storeroom brought an instant sharp response from the Peke.

Linda adjusted her sunglasses and got behind the wheel. But Ham spoke to Nick in a low voice.

"Take it easy now. I have a funny feeling—"

"Not much else we can do—if she's going to get to the Wilson place," Nick pointed out.

As he gunned the bike to life he wondered what looming danger one could watch for along the Cut-Off. No one who had ever met whatever peril lurked there had ever returned to explain what he or she had faced. No, Nick was not going to let his imagination take over. He'd end up seeing a UFO or something lurking behind every tree. He waved to Linda and swung out. She nodded and followed.

They turned off the highway about a half-mile farther on and Nick cut speed, concentrating on the rough surface ahead. He had come this road enough times to memorize every rut and bump, but the heavy rains last week would have done damage, and he had no intention of being spilled through carelessness.

A mile and a half to the Cut-Off. In all the years he had been coming up here he had always looked for the overgrown entrance to what had become a sinister road to nowhere. Could she get the jeep in there at all? But they had been using it, so they must have cleared a passage through. July 24, 1955—he'd been too little then to realize what had gone on. But he'd heard plenty about it ever since. All that searching—the neighbors, the sheriff and his deputies. And not so much as a track to tell them why two young men in the best of health had vanished from a half-mile strip of road one sunny morning.

They had been seen entering, had stopped and talked to Jim Anderson about the best place to fish. Jim had been going to the store. He had watched them turn into the Cut-Off. But they never came out at the lake where a couple of guys were waiting to join them.

Mouth of the Cut-Off—like a snake with jaws wide open to swallow them down.

Nick took firm control of his imagination. If he did not

see Linda to the lake she would go by herself. And he somehow could not let that happen and be able to look at himself in the mirror when shaving tomorrow.

It was only a half-mile, perhaps a little more. They could run it in minutes, even if it were rough. The sooner they got through the better. He wondered what this Linda would say if she knew his thoughts. She'd probably decide he'd been smoking pot. Only when you heard about the Cut-Off all your life—well, you had a different point of view.

He had borrowed a lot of Ham's books, bought some of his own, knew all the things that *did* happen now and then that nobody seemed able to explain. Maybe Fort and those other writers who hunted out such stories had the right of it. The scientists, the brains who might have solved, or at least tried to solve, such puzzles, refused even to look at evidence before their eyes because it did not fit in with rational "facts." There could be facts that were neither rational nor logical at all.

There was the turnoff ahead. And there certainly had been changes since the last time he was here. Looked as if someone had run a bulldozer in to break trail. Nick gave a sigh of relief at the raw opening. There was a healthy difference between wriggling down an almost closed and ill-reputed trail and this open, scraped side road, which now looked as good as the one leading to his own cabin. He flagged the jeep as he came to a stop.

"This is it," he called. Something in him still shrank a little from entering that way, but he refused to admit it. Only he continued to feel that odd uneasiness, which had come to him earlier as he had seen Rufus watch something invisible that Nick had been convinced against his will *was* there.

"Take it slow," he cautioned, also against his will. He wanted to take that road at the best speed they could make. "I don't know how good the surface is."

"Yes." The dark glasses masked her face. She surely did not need them here in the shade of the trees, but she had not let them slide off as she had at the store. The Peke was on the seat, his forepaws resting on the dashboard, looking ahead with some of Rufus' intensity. He did not bark, but there was an eagerness in every line of his small, silky body, as if he wanted to urge them on.

Nick gunned his motor, swung into the Cut-Off, his

speed well down. The jeep snorted along behind him at hardly better than a walking pace. The road crew had run the scraper along, but the rain had cut gullies across, here and there, and those had not been refilled.

The lane was all rawly new, bushes and even saplings gouged and cut out and flung back to wither and die on either side. It looked ugly—wrong, Nick decided. He supposed it had to be done to open up the road, but it was queer the road crew had not cleaned up more. Maybe the guys who had worked here knew about the sinister history of the Cut-Off and had not wanted to stay around any longer than they had to.

That broken stuff walled them in as if it were intended to keep them in the middle of the road, allow them no chance to reach the woods. Nick felt more and more trapped. Uneasiness was rising in him so that he had to exert even more control. This was plain stupid! He must keep a grip on his imagination. Just watch the road for those ruts and lumps so he would not hit something—do that and keep going. They would be there in no time at all.

It was still, not a leaf moved. But the trees arched over well enough to keep out the sun. Probably it was very quiet, too, if the noise of the bike and the jeep had not advertised their coming. Advertised it to what? Nick hoped only to those in the Wilson place.

Right ahead was the turn, a blind one. And this was a narrow road. No place to meet anyone coming the other way. But surely they were making enough noise—

Noise! The Peke had begun to yap, almost as when he had challenged Rufus. Nick heard the girl call out:

"Down, Lung! Down!"

He half-turned his head, the bike hit something and wobbled. Nick had to fight to keep it away from a mass of dying brush. But there was something else, a cloud—like a fog trapped under the trees. It was thickening, coming down like a blanket—fast!

Nick thought he cried out. Behind him he heard an answering scream and a crash. Then he hit something, was thrown, and skidded painfully into total darkness.

✦ 2 ✦

Nick lay with his feet higher than his head, the whole left side of his face smarting. Groggily he levered himself up on his hands and blinked, then shook his head to banish the queer not-here feeling. He could hear a whimpering sound from behind, but at first he was so much occupied with his own aches and pains that it had no meaning.

He looked around.

The bike lay entangled in broken brush into which it must have slammed with force. Nick sat up farther. Bike—the jeep! Where was the jeep? Now the whimpering alerted him to what might be a serious accident. He had no idea what had happened—memory seemed at fault. They had just come around the turn in the Cut-Off and then . . .

Nick got shakily to his feet.

There was no road.

He staggered toward the jeep. That was there, yes, slammed against a tree. A tree that had no business being there at all, for seemingly it had sprung up right in the middle of what had been a newly cleared road.

There was no road!

He reached the jeep, supported himself against it. His aching head still seemed foggy. Fog—mist—cloud—there was something about that he could faintly remember. But that did not matter now. What did was the girl behind the wheel of the jeep.

She was supported partly by her seat belt, partly by the wheel itself. Her eyes were still covered with those sunglasses. With an effort Nick reached over and jerked them off. She was unconscious, he decided.

The whimpering came from the Peke huddled against her, licking at her arm. Lung growled at Nick but only halfheartedly, as he slid in beside Linda.

As far as Nick could see she had no open wounds,

16

but—broken bones? His hands were shaking with a tremor he found it hard to control, as he eased her back in the seat so he could get at the fastening of the seat belt.

"What—what—" She opened her eyes but, though they were turned in his direction, they did not seem to focus on him.

"Hold still!" Nick ordered. "Let me get this open—"

A few minutes later he sighed with relief. She had no broken bones. The side of his face, where it had scraped gravel, was raw, but that was minor. They could have been killed. Looking about him now, with eyes entirely aware, he wet his lips with the tip of his tongue.

Killed—if they had been going any faster—slammed up against these trees. But where—where did the trees come from?

They were huge, giants, and the underbrush beneath them was thin as if their mighty roofing overhead of leaves and branches kept any weaker growth from developing. The jeep was trapped between the one against which its nose was stuck, and a log of a fallen giant behind it, boxed in neatly so there was no hope of getting it out. Impossible, but that was the way it was.

Nick moved slowly around the machine, ran his hands across the top of the log, dislodging moss and fallen leaves. It was very apparent that this had been here, half sunk in the mucky soil, for a long, long time. But—there was the jeep—and—where *was* the road?

"Please—" Linda had edged around on the seat and was looking at him, her eyes very wide and frightened. "Please—where are we—what—happened?" She cuddled Lung against her. Now and then the small dog whined. He was shivering.

"I don't know," Nick answered slowly. Only he suspected what was so frightening he did not want to face the fact that it might be the truth.

"But—there's no road." Linda turned her head from side to side, searching. "We were just driving along and then—*Where is this?*" Her voice slid up the scale; Nick judged she was close to panic.

He was not far from that himself. But they had to hold on, to lose control would do no good. He hurried back to climb into the jeep.

"You—you know—!" She did have her voice under

control now, was watching him narrowly. "What has happened? If you know—tell me!"

But he still hated to face what must be the truth. "I don't know," he said carefully. "It is only a guess." He hesitated. Those trees there were certainly good evidence. What more did he want? They were out of the Cut-Off, in such woods as had not been seen in this part of the country for two hundred years or more when the first settlers had attacked the great forests to carve out mastery of the land.

"Did your friends know anything about the history of the Cut-Off?" he began. How could you explain to anyone what might have happened, something so bizarre, so improbable?

"No." Linda cradled Lung in her arms, murmuring soothingly to him now and again. Her one-word reply was uncompromising. It was apparent she wanted the truth, or what he thought might be the truth.

"Well, the Cut-Off has a history of disappearances— running back as long as records were kept around here—"

("Around here." But surely this "here" was not the "here" of a short time ago.)

"The last time it happened was in 1955, two men going out to the lake to fish. But before that there were others. That's why the Cut-Off wasn't in use. Not until they built the new freeway and closed off the other road in."

"Disappearances to where?" Linda demanded sharply.

"That's it, nobody knows—knew. There are places . . ." Nick paused again. Would she believe him? She had to believe the evidence now before them at least. "Places where people do disappear—like the Bermuda Triangle—a whole flight of Navy planes went there, and the rescue ship after them. There have been planes and ships and people—and on land, in other places, army regiments even." Though he did not want to remember, all the stories he had read flooded back into his mind. "They just flew, or rode, or walked into—nowhere."

Linda sat very still. She no longer watched him. Her gaze was straight ahead at that giant tree trunk against which the jeep was nosed.

"What—what is the theory about it then?" Her voice quivered a little. Nick could sense her effort at control.

"One is that there is a magnetic field like a whirlpool—

that anything caught in it may be thrown into another space-time continuum."

"And—that may be what has happened to us? How do we get back?"

There was no answer to that. There never had been through all the centuries of such disappearances. Nick stared at the tree too now, fiercely willing it to vanish, for them to be back in the Cut-Off.

"There is no return." Linda made that a flat statement rather than a question. "We—we're trapped in this—this *place!*"

"No!" Nick exploded. "We're not sure of that! Anyway we can try—we can always try—but"—he regarded the dim, shadowed places under the trees uneasily—"let's get out of here. On to the lake—"

He had a feeling that they were under observation, not that he could detect any movement, any sign they were not alone. To get out of this place of trees, where a man was dwarfed and lost, into the open was a desire goading him to action.

"We can't take the jeep." Linda stated the obvious.

"No, but I can the bike—push it now—and we can ride if the road gets better and you are willing to hold on."

"Yes! Yes, let's get out of here!" Her reply was feverishly eager.

She opened her shoulder bag, took out a leash she hooked to Lung's collar. "My bag—it's small." She reached into the back of the jeep, pulled out a canvas duffel bag. Then she laughed, though that sound was a little ragged. "All that stuff back there for the party tonight. Jane—Jane may have to wait some for it."

Nick's foreboding lightened. Linda was taking it well. Did she really believe him? Did he believe himself? But his first panic had subsided. And action drew him. Maybe if they could just find the lake, a familiar landmark—Don't think of any future beyond the next few minutes, he warned himself.

Mentally he inventoried the contents of his saddle-bags—first-aid kit, sweater, swimming trunks, matches, a hunting knife, flashlight, chocolate bars, water canteen, two shirts, tool kit for the bike—transistor radio—Radio!

He was out of the jeep, hurrying back to the bike. Radio—if they could hear anything on that—Nick fumbled with the buckles of the saddlebag as Linda joined him.

"What is it?"

"My radio—if we can pick up anything—"

"Oh, hurry!" She shifted from one foot to the other impatiently as he untangled the gear and brought out the small transistor.

Three stations, he flipped the switch from one to the next. Only silence. Then—A gabble of sound, not static, more like speech. But not in any language he had picked up before.

"There! Turn it up!" Linda urged. "You've got something!"

"But what?" Nick asked.

"But what" was right. This sounded like gasps, clicks, and even a gabbled singing, but it made no sense. He thumbed the set off.

"Whatever that was, it was no broadcast of ours," he said bleakly.

"But somebody was broadcasting," Linda pointed out. "Which means we aren't alone here. Maybe if we can find people they will be able to help us."

Nick was not too sure. The language, if language that had been, was far removed from anything he had ever heard in his life and he had monitored a lot of foreign broadcasts with Gary Langford when Gary had his ham outfit. But Linda was right about getting out of here. He had the small compass and the lake was northeast—or it should be—if there was still any lake at all.

They could not keep to a straight line, but the lack of heavy underbrush was a help. And with the compass to steer by they wove a path among the towering trees, rounding boles that the two of them together could not have hoped to span with out-stretched arms.

The bike seemed uninjured, but Nick had to wheel it along, walking beside it. There was no opening through which they dared ride. Linda carried her duffel bag slung over her shoulder by its cords and had let Lung down to patter along over the thick layers of countless years of fallen leaves. The little dog seemed to have lost his fear. But, while he sniffed at a moldering branch now and then, or snuffed into a pile of last season's leaves, he made no effort to pull to the end of his leash, staying close to Linda.

Though the trees about them were awe inspiring, there were sounds in this forest familiar enough to allay some of their distrust. For there were not only birds to be heard and sometimes seen, but those winged inhabitants appeared unusually fearless as well as curious about the intruders.

Intruders Nick felt they were. This was a place that did not know man and had no idea of his species' destructiveness. The barked giants about them had never felt the bite of axe and stood in arrogant pride. Had it not been for that gabble from the transistor Nick would have suspicions that the phenomena, which haunted the Cut-Off had brought them to a space where his kind had never existed at all.

"It—it is so quiet." Linda moved closer, laid one hand on the bike near his. "Except for the birds. I never saw woods like this before. The trees—they are huge! When I was little my aunt had an old copy of *Swiss Family Robinson*—there was a tree in it that they turned into a house. You could do that with most of these."

Nick had one eye on the compass. They had had to make a good many detours, but they were still heading for the lake. Only here among all these trees it was hard to judge distance. Surely they couldn't be too far away from it now. But—what if there was no lake here?

He wanted that lake, he *had* to see it. The body of water was a promise of security somehow—without the lake they would be lost entirely. Nick hardly heard Linda's comment, he was so intent on willing the lake to be waiting for them, hoping that the stand of trees would soon thin so they could glimpse it.

"Nick!" Linda's hand flew from the bike to his wrist, tightened about it in a convulsive grip.

But he had seen it too.

They closed ranks, the bike between them. Lung lunged to the full length of his leash, set up a frenzied barking, not unlike that with which he had challenged Rufus. It was plain what he saw he resented.

Where it had come from was a minor mystery. For it was such a shimmering, dazzling white in this greenish gloom that it caught and held the eye almost at once. Yet they were so suddenly aware of it that it might have emerged from the tree against whose bark it was now framed.

"I—don't—believe—" Linda's voice trailed away. She saw it, Nick saw it. And so did Lung, still dancing on two hind feet at the farthest reach of his leash, jerking the strap in her hands, waving his forepaws in the air with his furious desire to be at this new enemy.

"What do you see?" Nick's wrist was still in her tight grasp. They had both taken knocks back there in their rough transition into this alien world. Perhaps this was a collective hallucination. Only—would the dog share it?

"A unicorn," she answered. "Don't—don't you see it, too?"

The creature was about the size of a large pony, not a horse, Nick thought. Its coat was that dazzling white, almost a source of light. The mane and tail were also white. But that single spiraled horn set just between and above the creature's wide dark eyes was golden. And it, too, glowed. This was certainly the fabled unicorn, as Nick had seen it in reproductions of medieval paintings.

It stared back at them and then tossed its head, so that the forehead fringe of mane about the base of the incredible horn lifted. Then the creature pawed the earth with one slender hoof, lowered its head, and snorted at Lung as if replying to the Peke's shrill challenge. To all appearances, Nick thought it real enough.

Once more it tossed its head and then turned and paced away among the tree trunks, its white glow speedily lost.

"But unicorns—they are not—they never were alive," Linda said in a voice hardly above a whisper.

Something he had read came to Nick's mind then. All the old legends of dragons and griffins, the People of the Hills, the very core of folklore and myth—men had believed in them for a long time, had sworn oaths in court that they had seen such, had had converse with the more humanlike figures of an unnatural, magical world. Could it have been that, just as he, Linda and Lung had been caught up in some force that had deposited them here, some of the creatures native to this world had been dropped into theirs? But a unicorn! Now that it was gone Nick had already begun to doubt what he had seen, to try to rationalize it.

"Wait here!" he ordered Linda and started for the place where the animal had stood. There he went down on one knee to examine the thick leaf mold. Then he wished he had not, for it was cut and patterned by tracks. Something had been there, unicorn or not.

Nick hurried back to Linda and the bike. They must get out of this woods as quickly as they could. For that

sensation, which had come upon him earlier was back full
force. They were under observation—by the unicorn? It
did not matter. Nick was aware they were invaders in this
place. And sometimes intruders meet with active retalia-
tion.

"I did see a unicorn," Linda was repeating, apparently
to herself. "It was right there, under that tree. I have to
believe that I saw it—believe that or—I just have to believe it!" She had picked up Lung, holding him high on her
breast so his silken head was right under her chin. The
Peke had stopped barking and was licking her face, or as
much of it as his tongue could reach.

"Let's get going." Nick's tone was rough. They must get
away—out into the open, if they could find any open.

The compass did bring them out a few minutes later
into a space where the giant trees ceased and brush took
their places. They pushed through the thinnest section of
this and came to an expanse of tall grass, which in turn
gave way to reeds bordering the lake—or a lake.

Along the shoreline, they could see no cabins, though by
now Nick had ceased to hope to find those, or any sign
that their own species had ever been there. Wading
through the shallows were several herons that paid no attention to the newcomers. And in a rough pasture farther
to the south animals were grazing. They were so light of
hide Nick wondered if they had chanced upon a small
herd of unicorns. Then one raised its head and showed
branched antlers. But who had ever heard of silver-gray
deer?

"There're no cabins—" Linda loosed her hold on the
bike, let her duffel bag thump to the ground. "Nick, what
are we going to do?"

He shrugged. "I don't know." He was no superman, no
use in her turning to him as if he could get them out of
this by flexing his muscles or something like that. "If you
want to know the truth, I'm hungry. We might as well
eat."

By the angle of the sun it must be close to noon. And
he *was* hungry. It appeared that even a jump across time
(if that was what had really happened to them) was not
enough to subdue one's appetite.

"Hungry!" Linda repeated. Then she laughed, even if it
was a small and difficult sound. "Why, I guess I am, too."

The grazing deer paid no attention to them. And, here in the open, nothing could sneak up on them without attracting attention. Linda moved on to a place where the grass did not appear as tall.

"Here's a good place." She beckoned as if this were an ordinary picnic. But Nick thought now about food. Not of how hungry he was, but of the meagerness of the rations they carried.

He had been depending on the store of canned goods at the cabin, and all else he had was what he had picked up at the store. That would not last long. Then they would have to live off the country. But what if they could not?

Even in the countryside of his own world he did not know much about what could be eaten in the way of berries (if any could be found) or other growing things, except those from gardens. There were survival books supposed to explain just how you could live off the wild, but such knowledge had never appealed to him and he had never read one. No, they would have to go light on their provisions. Back in the jeep—if they could find their way back—were the two melons and all those cases of drinks. But that was not much.

He squatted down on his heels, facing Linda who had settled cross-legged in the grass.

"Listen—about food—I don't have much. You have anything in that?" He pointed to her bag.

"You mean—" He could see from the expression on her face that she understood. Then she went on, steadily enough. "You mean we might not be able to find anything to eat here?"

"Well, there might be fish in the lake. And there are blackberries—at least there were blackberries near our cabin. But this isn't our lake. We had better go easy with what we have until we know the score."

Linda pulled at the knotted drawstring of the duffel bag. "I don't have much, but I was taking two boxes of peanut brittle up to Jane, and a tin of English toffee—Jane loves peanut brittle and Ron has this thing about toffee—the rum-flavored kind. There're the melons and all that Coke and stuff back in the jeep. But it's heavy to carry. I don't think we can pack it along with us. Nick, where will we go? There're no houses here, and beyond there"—she pointed to the far side of the lake—"it looks like more woods."

She was right. There was a dark rise of trees over there, matching that from which they had just emerged. In fact, as far as Nick could see, though the lake curved farther south and that end of it was now hidden, the water was ringed by forest. Suppose they did work through that, and they had no idea how many miles of it there were, what lay beyond? He had a hazy idea, from a novel he had read concerning the early American wilderness, that such growth could extend across a state with very few breaks.

"I don't know," he said frankly again. "But I'd rather be here in the open than under the trees. We can move down to the end of the lake—there's an outlet—the Deep Run—there, if this is like our lake. Maybe we could work out of the woods using that for a guide." He was rather proud of himself for remembering that.

"*If* this lake is like the one you know," she commented. "Does it look like it, really, Nick?"

He stood up, shading his eyes against the glare of the sun, which was hot now, but not as hot, he thought, as it might have been in their world. Slowly he studied the part of the lake visible from here. It was hard to equate this untouched, wild land with that where cabins and small docks were visible. But he was almost certain the contours of the shoreline were not too dissimilar from those he had known since he was small. And he said so.

"Do you suppose," Linda asked, "that we have gone back in time—that we're in the country that existed long before our people came into it? That—that we may meet Indians?" She shot another wary glance at the woods.

"That would not explain the unicorn. Nor gray deer—" Nick indicated the peacefully grazing herd. "We could be in an alternate world." He was unrolling the package of food from the store, but now his hands were still as he thought of what he was saying. Alternate worlds, time travel—such things did not exist! They could not—not for Nick Shaw a very ordinary person who only wanted a quiet weekend for himself. He *was* Nick Shaw, he *was* alive, yet this was happening! Unless, of course, he had really knocked himself out back there with the bike and maybe now was in a hospital with a vivid dream—

"Alternate world? But unicorns—they never existed at

all. They are only fairy tales." Linda shook her head. "Nick!" For the second time her voice soared up and she caught at him. "Nick, look there! Isn't that smoke?"

She pointed south beyond the deer and he followed her finger with his gaze. She was right! From somewhere in the brush beyond the meadowland a beacon of smoke was rising. And smoke could mean only one thing—people! Ted and Ben—trapped here all those years! Nick's thought flew first to them. But company—company to help them, to let them know they were not alone in a nightmare!

Hastily he repacked the food, put the bag back on the bike. He wished they dared ride, but it would be folly to try. And they had better be careful about getting around those deer. The animals looked harmless enough but that was not saying they would remain so if alarmed.

They wanted to run, but the grass tangled and pulled at their feet and the bike wheels, so that they floundered along at little better than a walking pace. Also, at Nick's insistence, they made a detour around the edge of the open space where the deer were, putting a screen of brush between them and the animals. And they froze once as the stag that was the leader flung up its head and stared straight at the bush behind which they happened to be.

Nick felt very naked and exposed then. He had heard that if you were absolutely still animals would lose interest in you and he scowled a warning at Linda. She nodded, holding her hand about Lung's muzzle. But the Peke appeared to understand and did not fight for his freedom and a chance to bark.

The stag watched them, or at least Nick thought they were its quarry. But after a time when the two dared hardly draw a full breath, the stag grunted and trotted toward the lake. When it was what seemed to Nick a safe distance away they hurried on.

But this closer sight of the deer presented another puzzle. Surely these gray animals were larger than those of Nick's own world, differing in size as they did in color. He wished he knew more, could get enough hints to answer some of his questions, if those might be answered at all.

They moved on, around the curve in the lake. Yes, there was the opening to Deep Run. So this place did follow the general pattern of their own world. And the

smoke rose near the mouth of the Run. Nick felt some return of satisfaction at being proved right on one point of
geography. But his triumph was speedily dashed.

"Stand where you are, chums!"

◆ 3 ◆

Lung broke into a wild barking, facing the bush screen from behind which that order had come. Nick halted, though Linda took a step or two as if the plunging of the now aroused Peke pulled her ahead.

Nick touched her arm with one hand, with the other he steadied the bike.

"Who are you?" he demanded of the bush and was inwardly glad his voice was so even and controlled. Ted—Ben? Some other who had preceded them into this alien world?

There was a moment of silence, so prolonged that Nick wondered if the challenger had faded into deeper cover, tricking them into a halt while he withdrew. But why would anyone be so elusive? The stranger in hiding could certainly see they were harmless.

Then the bushes parted and a man came into the open. He was very ordinary looking, a little shorter than Nick, but broader of shoulder, his bulk of body enhanced by the garment he wore, a coverall. Perched on his head was a helmet rather like an inverted basin, and he had on thick boots.

His face was round and there was a thick brush of moustache, grayish red, half hiding his mouth. In one hand he carried—

A slingshot!

Viewing that, Nick could have laughed, except there was something in the stranger's attitude that did not permit such a reaction to his childish weapon. And there was a very faint stir of memory deep in Nick's mind. Somewhere, sometime, he had seen a man wearing just such clothing. But where and when?

As yet the newcomer had given no answer to Nick's question. Instead he eyed them narrowly. Lung, straining to the very end of his leash, was sniffing, his barking hav-

28

ing subsided, sniffing as if to set this stranger's scent deep in his catalog of such odors.

If the stranger intended to overawe them with such a beginning, Nick refused to yield.

"I asked," he said, "who are you?"

"And I heard you, chum. I ain't lost the use of m' ears, not yet. I'm Sam Stroud, Warden of Harkaway Place, if it's anything to you. Which I'm laying odds, it ain't. There's just the two of you?"

He watched them closely, almost as if he expected them to be the van of a larger party. Linda broke in:

"Warden! Nick, he's dressed like an air raid warden—one of those in the picture about the Battle of Britain they showed in our history course."

English! That explained his accent. But what was an Englishman in the uniform of a service thirty years in the past doing here? Nick did not want to accept the suggestion the discovery brought.

"Is she right?" He added a second question to the first. "You are that kind of warden?"

"That's so. Supposin', m'lad, you speak up now. Who are *you?* An' this young lady here?"

"She's Linda Durant and I'm Nick Shaw. We're—we're Americans."

Stroud raised a thick hand and rubbed his jaw. "Well, now—Americans, hey? Caught right in your own country?"

"Yes. We were just heading for a lake—like this lake—then suddenly we were here. Where is *here?*"

Stroud made a sound that might have been intended for a bark of laughter, except there was very little humor in it.

"Now that's a question, Shaw, which nobody seems able to answer. The Vicar, he's got one or two ideas—pretty wide they are—but we've never been able to prove them one way or another. When did you come through?"

"Not too long ago," Linda answered. "Is that your fire making the smoke? We're awfully hungry and we were just going to eat when we saw it and came along . . ."

"You have some supplies?" Stroud rammed the slingshot back under the belt of his boiler suit. "All right, come ahead." He turned a little toward the bush from which he had emerged, put two fingers to his lips and gave a low, but carrying whistle. "You ain't bait as far as I can see."

"Bait?" Nick did not like the sound of that.

Again Stroud gave his crow of laughter. "Bait, yes. You'll learn, m'lad, you'll learn. This way now, an' mind the bushes . . ."

He pushed ahead and they followed in a way which to Nick's eyes used all available cover. But if there was such a need to hide, why then did they allow smoke to rise like a banner in the air? Only a moment later, he realized that they were not heading toward the site of that fire, but well to the left of it.

Linda must have made the same discovery, for now she asked:

"Aren't we going to your camp?"

"Right ahead—" Stroud's deep voice reached them. "Mind this vine, enough to trip a man up it is."

Nick had to mind the vine, a tough cover on the ground, with attention. It caught at the bike, as well as at his feet, with such persistence one could almost believe it a set trap. Twice he had to stop and untangle it, so that Stroud and Linda had disappeared and he had only the marks of their passing to guide him on a trail that took them farther and farther from the site of the fire and then curved again toward the Run.

He came out at last in a clearing walled by what seemed a solid siding of thick brush. And there he found Stroud, Linda, and three others. Two were men, the third a woman. They had been facing Linda, but, as Nick pushed his way through with a crackling of brush, they turned almost as one to stare at him.

The men were in contrast to each other as well as to Stroud. One was elderly, very tall and gaunt, his white hair in a fluff about his head as if it were too fine to be controlled. He had a great forward hook of a nose that was matched by the firmness of the jaw beneath. But his eyes, under the shadow of bushy brows, did not have the fierce hawk glare Nick expected. They were intelligent and full of interest, but they also held an acceptance of others, not the need for dominance that the rest of his face suggested.

He wore a dark gray suit, much the worse for hard usage, and a sweater underneath its coat that did not come high enough to hide a clergyman's roundabout collar. On his feet were rough hide moccasins, which were in strange contrast to the rest of his clothing, shabby as that was.

The younger man was an inch or two taller than Nick and, like Stroud, he was in uniform, but not that of a warden. His blue tunic was much worn, but there were wings on its breast, and he had pushed to the back of his blond head a pilot's cap.

Their feminine companion was almost as tall as the pilot and she, too, was in uniform, with badges Nick did not recognize on the shoulder. A helmet like the Warden's crowned a mass of unruly dark hair. Her figure was almost as lean as that of the clergyman, and her face, weathered and brown, made no pretense to good looks. Yet there was an air of competence and authority about her that was impressive.

"Americans," she commented. "Then," she spoke to the clergyman, "you were entirely right in your surmise, Adrian. We did travel farther than we thought in that cage."

The blond pilot also fingered a slingshot. "We'd better shove off." His eyes had gone from Nick to the brush. He had the attitude of one listening. "No use watching the trap any longer—"

"Barry is correct," the clergyman nodded. "We may not have had the kind of success we hoped to obtain. But by attracting our young friends here we have excellent results."

"Better introduce ourselves," the woman said briskly. "Adrian Hadlett, Vicar of Minton Parva." The clergyman gave an old-fashioned and rather majestic inclination of his head. "Pilot Officer Barry Crocker, and I'm Diana Ramsay—"

"Lady Diana Ramsay," Stroud growled as if that was important.

She made an impatient gesture with one hand. The other, Nick noted, held a third slingshot.

"There're a couple more of us," she continued. "You'll meet them at the camp."

Once more, this time with Nick and Linda in the midst of this energetic group, they pushed on, to come out on the bank of the Run. And not too much farther on was their camp.

Logs had been rolled into place and reinforced with rocks, forming what was half-hut, half-cave. Lung set to barking as a huge, gray-furred shape, which had been sunning by the entrance, reared back and showed a brush of

tail. With ears flattened to its skull, the cat faced the excited Peke with a warning hiss that deepened into a growl.
Linda dropped her bag to catch up the willing warrior,
holding him despite his struggles.

"Now then, Jeremiah, m'dear, that be no proper way to
say good day, not at all it ben't."

From the door issued a small woman, to catch up the
cat, a hefty armload, and soothe him gently with hands
crook-jointed by arthritis, patched with the brown spots of
age. Her hair, as white as the Vicar's, was twisted into a
tight little bun above a round face with a mere knob of a
nose that gave very precarious perch room to a pair of
metal-framed glasses.

She lisped a little as she spoke, perhaps because her
teeth seemed uncertainly anchored in her mouth, but there
was a bright and interested welcome in the way she regarded the newcomers. Her dress was covered in part by an
apron of sacking and an old macintosh which swung
cloakwise from her shoulders. On her feet were the same
kind of crude moccasins as the Vicar wore.

"Jean," she called back over her shoulder. "We've got
company."

The girl who came at that summons was perhaps only a
little older than Linda herself. She also wore a dark blue
uniform, though over it she had pinned apronlike a piece
of dingy cloth, as if she hoped so to protect the only clothing she had. Her hair was brown and sprang in waves
about her tanned face, a face that was pretty enough to
make a man look a second time, Nick thought.

"Americans." Lady Diana again carried through the ritual of introductions. "Linda Durant, Nicholas Shaw. And
this is Mrs. Maude Clapp and Jean Richards, who is a
WREN."

"WREN?" repeated Nick, a little bewildered.

The girl smiled. "Women's Royal Naval Service—I believe you call yours WAVES."

"Well now, didn't I tell you that the dream I had me
last night was a true one?" Mrs. Clapp's voice was cheery
with open friendliness. "Company comin', that it was. An'
we've fish all ready to fry out nice'n crisp. Couldn't have
been luckier, now, could it?" she asked of the company at
large, but not as if she expected any real answer. "Jeremiah here, he won't take at your little dog, Miss, if the

dog don't take at him. Jeremiah, he ain't a quarrelsome beast."

"I hope Lung isn't." In Linda's hold the Peke had become quiet. Now she swung him up so she could view him eye to eye. "Lung, friend, friend!" She spoke with emphasis, then turned the dog around to face the big cat whom Mrs. Clapp had put on the ground once more. "Friend, Lung!"

The Peke flashed his tongue across his own nose. But when Linda set him down he settled by her feet, quiet, as if he had not been only moments earlier in a frenzy against a tribal enemy.

Nick offered his own supplies.

"Bread!" Mrs. Clapp opened the bag and sniffed ecstatically at its contents. "Fresh bread! Lands, I almost forgot what it smells like, let alone tastes."

Nick had grounded the bike. Now he stood a little to one side glancing from the pilot Crocker to the girl Jean, then on to Stroud in his warden's uniform. Crocker, unless Nick was a very poor judge of ages, was in his early twenties, Jean even younger. They could *not* be as old as Stroud's uniform suggested. But—

"Something bothers you, my boy?" It was the Vicar. And without thinking Nick asked his question baldly:

"Do you mind telling me, sir—how long have you been here?"

The Vicar smiled wearily. "That—that may be impossible. We tried to keep a record in the beginning, but after they captured us and brought us here—" He shrugged. "By a matter of seasons, I should judge about four years. The raid hit Minton Parva the evening of July 24, 1942. I think we all have reason to remember that. We were in the crypt shelter of the church. Mrs. Clapp is, was, my housekeeper. Lady Diana had come to see me about the hospital fund. Jean and Barry were on their way down to the station to take the train back, they were both returning from leave. And Stroud had come to check up on our supplies—when the alert sounded and we all went into the crypt. There was a sound—frankly, Shaw, we all believed it was the end. And then—somehow we were out of the church, out of even the England that we knew . . ."

He hesitated. Those tired, but very keen eyes had been watching Nick's face. Now the Vicar's expression changed.

"You know something, don't you, my boy? Something that is disturbing you. What is it?"

"Time, sir. You say you think you have been here about four years. But today is—was—July 21, 1972."

He expected the Vicar to challenge him on that. It was not believable, not if Hadlett had been speaking the truth. And Nick was sure he had.

"July 21, 1972," repeated the Vicar slowly. "No, I do not doubt you, my boy, as I think you are expecting. It is too apt, it bears out all the old tales. But—1972—thirty years— What happened there—thirty years back?"

"Thirty years what? . . ." Crocker lounged over to them. He had been more intent on the motorbike than he had on their conversation, but now he looked at Hadlett alertly. "What is this about thirty years?"

"Tell him your date," the Vicar said to Nick as if his saying it would make the deeper impression.

"The date today—it's July 21, 1972," Nick returned. Hadlett had accepted that without question, but would the others?

"Nineteen seventy-two," repeated the pilot blankly. "But—it's impossible—Padre, it's about 1946, unless we counted wrong, and a man can't tick off thirty years that way without knowing it!"

It was Lady Diana who had listened this time. "Adrian, then you were right. It's like the old tales, isn't it? Thirty years—" She looked beyond them to where the water curled around the stones in the even flowing Run. "Eighty-five—but I'm not, Adrian, I'm no older—"

"That, too was part of those same old tales, Diana," he said.

"No!" Crocker protested. "This kid has it all wrong, he's one of *Them* maybe. How do we know—" He was backing away from Nick, the slingshot again in his hand. "He's working for *Them,* sent to break us down with a story like that!"

"Here—what's goin' on?" Stroud bore down on them. "What's this talk about *Them?*"

Crocker burst out with his accusation. And there was open anger in his voice as he turned on the Warden. "We brought these two here—next *They* will be coming! Tell us that we've been here thirty years! That's a lie no one's going to believe."

"Now, then." Stroud's hand was on Crocker's shoulder.

"Take a reef on that there tongue of yours, Barry. These don't smell like the Herald do they? An' when did the flying devils use bait? They zooms right in an' takes what they wants, no frills about it. All right, you say it's 1972 back there—what happened to the war?"

Stroud's rumble had drawn them all. They made a semi-circle, looking at Nick, some with speculative, Crocker with accusing, eyes.

"That ended in '45." Nick searched memory for an account of the conflict that had ended before he was born, but that to this handful was still vividly a threat.

"Who won?" demanded Crocker angrily, as if by his answer Nick would be judged.

"We did—the allies. We invaded and took Germany from one side, the Russians came in from the other—they got Berlin. Hitler killed himself before they got to him. And we dropped the atom bomb on Hiroshima and Nagasaki—then the Japanese surrendered that same year."

"Atom bomb?" Crocker no longer sounded angry, but rather dazed.

"Yes. Wiped out both cities." Nick remembered the accounts of that and hoped he would not have to go into details.

"And now—?" the Vicar asked after a pause, while his companions stared at Nick as if he were speaking a foreign language.

"Well, there's still trouble. The Korean War and now the one in Vietnam, we're standing off Communist expansion. China has gone Communist, and Russia still has half of Germany under control—the eastern part. But we've made two manned landings on the Moon." He tried to think of what had been progress and not just dreary wrangling. "And now we are planning to put a station into space. But—I can't tell you everything that happened. England—they've given up the Empire, and they had a Labor government for a long time—it's been tough over there—awfully high taxes and slipping back—"

"Thirty years, yes, a lot can happen." The Vicar nodded. "And still wars—"

"Please." Linda broke into the quiet that followed his comment. "If you came here from England and we from Ohio— Did you get across the ocean some way? Or is this all just one country?"

The Vicar shook his head. "No, the general contours of

this world seem geographically aligned to those of our own. This continent and England appear much as they must have in a very remote past before men began to tame the land. We were brought to this continent as prisoners. Only by the grace of God were we able to escape. Since then we have been trying to devise a way to return. Only I fear that this world has no ships to offer us. But ours is a very long and complicated story and I would suggest we tell it by degrees, perhaps over some of Mrs. Clapp's excellently cooked fish. Shall we?"

Perhaps it was the return to tasks they all knew and had shared for some time that relieved the tension. They got ready for the meal. And passing around the bread Nick had brought apparently made this a feast.

Hadlett turned a roll about in his fingers. "You never know how much you miss the small things of life"—he used a cliché to express the truth—"until they are taken from you. Bread we cannot produce here. Though Mrs. Clapp has experimented with ground nuts and seeds from a wild grass not unlike oats. It is good to eat bread again."

"You said you were brought here as prisoners." Nick wanted to know the worst of what might now menace them.

"Ah, yes. It is best that you be warned." The Vicar swallowed a bite of roll. "This is a very strange world and, though it has not been for want of trying, we have not penetrated very far into its secrets. But we believe that it is somehow parallel with our own, though obviously different. Sometime in the past, we do not know how far past, there was apparently a force set into being that could reach into our own world at special places and draw out people. There are many stories in our own world of mysterious disappearances."

Nick nodded. "More and more of those have been collected recently into books. We came from a place that has such a reputation—many disappearances over the years."

"Just so. And our church at Minton Parva was situated near a fairy mound—"

"Fairy mound?" Nick was startled. What was the meaning of that?

"No, I am not trying in any fashion to be amusing, my boy. In Britain we have a very long history—considered today to be legend—of disappearances near such sites. People 'fairy taken,' who sometimes reappeared years, even generations, after their disappearances, with an explanation of spending a day, or a month, or a year in another world, these are common in our folklore."

"Then," Linda broke in, "we can go back!" She had been holding Lung, and perhaps her hands closed too tightly on the small dog, for he gave a whine of protest.

"That," the Vicar told her gravely, "we do not know. But our own efforts have failed. And—we have seen enough here during our wanderings to suggest that such escapes, or returns, must be very exceptional."

Linda, still holding Lung in her arms, was on her feet. She stood so for a moment, her glance sweeping from face to face, ending with Nick. And it was to him that she spoke directly, as if she was prepared to believe him over whatever the others might say.

"Do you think we can get back?"

He had the choice of lying, of trying to be easy with her. But somehow he could not do it.

"No one ever went back through the Cut-Off that we knew of." In his own ears his voice sounded harsh.

Her face was blank of expression. She turned abruptly and began to walk away, her walk becoming swifter as she went. Nick got up to start after her.

"No." She did not turn to look at him, but it was as if she knew he would follow. "Let me alone—just let me alone for a while!"

And such was the force of the way she spoke that he stopped, uncertain as to whether he should force his company on her or not.

"Jean." It was Hadlett who spoke. "See that she is safe, but let her be. We must all face our truths as best we can."

The English girl passed Nick. He turned to the others.

"See that she is safe?" he repeated. "And you were prisoners. Who and what do you have to fear? Let's have it straight!"

"Good enough." Stroud had been eating stolidly. Now he leaned back against one of the logs helping to form their shelter. "We're not alone here, you must have guessed that. And as far as we've been able to find out there's three kinds of people—or things—or whatever you want to name 'em.

"There's some like us who have been caught. We tried to make talk with a couple of crowds like ours—or we think they're like us. But they don't understand. The last time it was soldiers, an' we got shot at. Not our soldiers—they looked Chinese.

"Then there's the Herald an' those who listen to him an' change—" He spat out that last word as if it were some obscenity. "The Herald—he may always have been here, native to this world. He has the cities an' the People with him. He wants us. Soon as he finds out about you two he will come snoopin'. All we know is if you take what he has to offer, then you change. After that you're not a man or a woman any more, you're something different. We aren't havin' any of that. You won't either, if you have sense.

"Third—there's the flyer hunters. They ain't o' this world anymore than we are. Only in their flyers they can get in an' out. One of their planes winks into the air an', 'fore you know it, they have you netted. I don't know what they do with the poor devils they catch, outside of, shut 'em up in cages like we was. But we were lucky. The ship that caged us, it got something wrong. Made a crash landin' here an' we escaped 'cause the crew were wiped out. That's when we found out they'd brought us out of England."

"But your smoke—you talked about bait. What—or who—were you trying to catch?"

Stroud grunned. "Not the flyers or the Herald, you can bet. No, we came across some tracks yesterday, mixed, women an' children. We got to thinkin' it was another crowd we could meet up with an' not get shot at. Of course, they might be dream things. But we figured it wouldn't do no harm to set up a signal an' see what came lookin'."

"They set traps," Crocker commented. "We thought we'd try one, but not for *Them*."

"You meant the hunters?" Nick was confused. After Stroud's story of the flyers he wondered that these people wanted to pull such a menace down on them.

"No, either the other drifters, or else the changed ones—if they were changed an' not just born that way."

"We saw—or thought we saw," Nick said slowly, "a unicorn when we were back in the woods. Was that what you mean by changed ones?"

"Not quite," the Vicar answered him. "We've seen a

good many strange beasts and birds and things that combine two or more species. But such do not threaten us, and we believe they are native here. Perhaps from time to time in the past they strayed into our world to leave legends behind them. We have yet to meet a dragon, but I would not swear that none exist here. The changed ones—they are human for the most part in general appearance. It is the small details—certainly their 'powers,' which is the best word to use for their abilities—that betray them. The People of the Hills are very old."

"We stay near the woods"—Stroud nodded at a stand of trees not more than a few strides away—"because the flyers can't get in under those to reach us. So far we haven't seen many of 'em. They come in waves like—we'll have a sky full of them for a few days—then they're gone. An' as long as we keep away from the cities we're all right. The flyers got a hate for the cities—try to bomb 'em."

"Not bomb, I told you, Stroud!" Crocker cut in. "They don't bomb. In fact I don't see what they do—though it must be some type of raid the way they come over. Whatever they try to accomplish, it doesn't cause any damage—none that we can see. The cities are safe."

"For them as wants to be changed," Mrs. Clapp observed. "But we ain't them."

Nick felt as if his head was spinning. It would seem that life here was complicated past even the many perils that now threatened his own time and space. This band, which had continued existence together as a group, displayed great hardiness and determination. Undoubtedly he and Linda had been lucky in this meeting. What if they had wandered on, on their own, to face all these threats without warning?

He tried to express his relief at their good fortune, and the Vicar smiled gently.

"You, yourself, have a part in your future, my boy. You have managed to adjust to a situation that might indeed have threatened your reason. We have seen the pitiful ending of one man who could not accept his transition. Acceptance is necessary."

Nick saw Linda and Jean coming back along the bank of the Run. So much had happened. Had he really accepted as Hadlett said, or was this all some kind of crazy dream from which he could not wake? Would there come a time when it would hit him as it had Linda, and he must make his peace with what seemed insanity?

◆ 4 ◆

Outside the rain was falling steadily. It had begun at sunset and had continued. Nick could hear the even breathing of those asleep around him in what was now a crowded shelter. But he could not sleep, rather lay close to the door staring out into the dark, listening.

The sound had started some time ago, very faint and far away. But it had caught his attention and now, tense, he listened with all his might, trying to separate that rise and fall of distant melody from the gurgle of the Run, the rain.

Nick could not tell whether it was singing or music, he could not even be sure it had not died away upon occasion and then begun again, faint, far away—drawing— For, the longer he listened, the more he was caught in a net of desire. A need to answer moved him, in spite of the rain, the utter dark of the night in a hostile land.

Sweet—low—but now and then clear and true. Nick thought he could almost distinguish words. And when that happened his inner excitement grew until he could hardly control it. Run—out into the night—answer—

Nick sat up now, his breath coming faster as if he had already been running. There was movement behind him in the shelter.

"Lorelei—" Hadlett's precise, gentle voice was a whisper.

"Lorelei," Nick repeated and swallowed. He was *not* going, he dared not. Caution born of his basic sense of self-preservation was alert, warning—He dared not.

"A lure," the Vicar continued. "The rain appears to produce it. Or else the proximity of water. There is this you must understand—part of those who are the permanent inhabitants are well intentioned toward us, or neutral, others are merely maliciously spiteful. A few are blackly evil. Since we cannot guess which are which, we must be

41

ever on guard. But we have proof of the Lorelei—we witnessed the results of its—feeding. Oh, not on flesh and
blood—it feeds on the life-force. What is left is an empty
husk. Yet its lure is so strong that, even knowing what it
may do, men have gone to it."

"I know why," Nick said. His hands were balled into
fists so tightly that his nails, short as they were, cut into
his skin. For even as Hadlett had been talking that sound
swelled. Now, in growing fear, he raised his fingers to his
ears, plugged out the melody.

How long he sat so, or if the Vicar continued to talk to
him, Nick did not know. But at last he allowed his hands
to fall, dared to listen again. There was nothing now but
the rain and the stream. With a sigh of relief he settled
back on the pile of dried stuff that formed his bed. Later
he slept and dreamed. But as important as those dreams
seemed, he could not remember them past waking.

For two days thereafter they might have been camping
out on a normal countryside with no sign that they shared
the land, untouched as it was by ax, uncut by road. Fishing was good, and in addition there were ripe berries and
a variety of headed grass close to the grain of their own
world, which could be harvested. Nick learned that this
shelter by the river was not the permanent base of the
party, but that they had a cave farther north they considered their headquarters. They were engaged now in making a series of exploratory trips.

Using the compass on the second day Nick managed to
guide Stroud and Crocker back to the jeep.

"Tidy little jumper." The Warden considered the machine regretfully. "No getting it out of that pinch though."

Nick had gone straight to the cargo, those cases of
drinks and the melons. But someone or something had
been there before him. All that remained were a couple of
smashed bottles.

"Pity," Stroud commented. "Not a pint of the old stuff,
maybe, but we could've used it. What do you say,
Barry—who nosed in ahead of us?"

The pilot had been inspecting the leaf mold around the
stranded jeep.

"Boots—army issue, I'd say. Those Chinese maybe.
They could have drifted down this way. But it was in the
early part of the evening, maybe the afternoon." He
squatted on his heels, using a twig to point out what he

could read stamped into the ground. "There's been a slinker here, its pads cover one of the boot marks, and those don't go prowling until dark. Anything else worth taking?"

Stroud was searching the jeep with the care of an experienced scrounger.

"Tool kit." He had unrolled a bundle that he had found under the seat to reveal a couple of wrenches and some other tools. "That's all, I'd say."

Nick stood near the tree against which the jeep nosed. This had been the middle of the Cut-Off. Yet looking around now he could not believe it.

"What caused it—our coming through?" he asked, though he did not expect any answer.

Stroud had rewrapped the tools, his face mirroring his satisfaction in the find. Now he looked up.

"There was a talk I heard—about our world running on electromagnetism. This brain who was talkin', he said we were all—every one of us, men, animals, trees, grass, everything—really electrical devices, we vibrate somehow. Though most of us don't know it. Then he went on to say as how we have been using more an' more electricity an' how now some small thing like a radio or such can throw out force enough to stop a much larger power source without meanin' to.

"He was warnin' us, said we were usin' forces we didn't fully understand, without carin'. An' something might just happen to lead to a big blowup some day. Maybe these places we come through work that way. The Vicar, he thinks a lot about it, an' he said that once."

"But we've been using electricity only close to a hundred years, and people disappeared this way before that. Right here." Nick pointed to the trapped jeep. "We had records of people disappearing here going as far back as when the white men first moved in, and that's about one hundred seventy years. According to your Vicar it goes much farther back in your country."

Stroud shrugged. "Don't know what works the traps. But we're here, ain't we? An' we'll probably stay, seein' as how we ain't goin' to get back across the ocean by wadin'. An' what about you, Shaw, any chance of your findin' a way back from here?"

Nick shook his head. The solidity of the tree he could touch, the scene about him, was manifest. And no one had ever returned from the Cut-Off once they had gone. The sudden realization of that closed in on him as it must have on Linda earlier. He wanted to scream, to run, to allow his panic some physical expression. Somehow he did not dare, for if he lost control now, he was sure, he could never regain it.

His fingers dug into tree bark. No—he was not going to scream—was *not* going to break!

There was a sharp sound from the jeep. Stroud threw himself flat on the seat. Crocker went to earth as quickly. Nick stared, not understanding. Then he saw it lying on the ground. A spear— They were under attack. He crouched, sought cover.

Nick listened for another sound, warning of an outright attack. He had no weapon, not even a stone, with which to defend himself. The quiet was absolute, no birdcall, not even a rustle of breeze in the foliage above them. Stroud and Crocker had their slingshots—but what use were those here?

Nick studied the spear. It had made a dent in the side of the jeep. That he could see. But the weapon was outside his own experience. In the first place the shaft was shorter than he would imagine it should be. The point was metal with four corners united. He knew next to nothing of primitive weapons but he thought it was not American Indian—if Indians did roam this world.

The spear, the silence— Nick found himself trying to breathe as lightly as possible. This waiting—when would come the attack? And from which direction? They could be completely surrounded right now. His back felt very naked, as if at any moment another of those weapons might thud home in his own body.

He could see neither Stroud (who must have squeezed himself to the floorboards of the jeep), nor Crocker. The pilot must have had training in such warfare, he had gone to earth so well. What did they do, just sit here and wait for death to come out, either silent, or in a wild roaring charge they could not counter with bare hands?

Nick's mouth was dry, his hands were so sweaty he wanted to wipe them on his shirt, yet dared not move. What were *They* waiting for?

What did break the silence was the last thing he expected to hear—laughter.

So this enemy was so sure of them it could laugh! That cut through his fear, made him angry. Funny was it?

Laughter and then a voice calling out in some incomprehensible tongue. A demand for their surrender, a listing of what would happen to them when they were overrun and taken? It could be either, but Nick noted that neither of his companions made any response to it. He could only follow their lead, hoping that their hard-learned lessons might in turn teach him some answer to the local perils.

Again laughter, light, mocking— But was it threatening? It seemed rather to have the spirit of mischief in it. Something in that tone made Nick less tense. So he was not startled when again a voice called, this time speaking his own language:

"Out of hiding, fearful men! Did you believe the Dark Ones were upon you? Scatter and hide, is that the way to greet us, you who came tramping into our land without asking? No courtesy?"

Nick watched Stroud heave his bulk out of concealment. Apparently the Warden was willing to accept the harmlessness of the questioner, or else there was a truce on. Crocker crawled out also, and, still wanting some reassurance, Nick was shamed into joining him in open sight.

He was beginning to wonder how good the aim of the unseen might be. That spear had struck well away from any of them. It could have been intended as a warning, a drastic announcement of arrival.

"We're waiting." Stroud's voice held a very audible note of exasperation. Nick could believe that the Warden was angry at his own reaction moments earlier, though Nick would think it was better in this country to cling to caution.

"No courtesy—yes," countered the unseen. "So you are waiting. What if we make a wall of waiting to enclose you, spin a cage?" Now the voice was sharp in return.

Nick stared in the direction from which it appeared to come. There was space there between the massive trees, but the speaker could well be concealed behind any trunk. He could detect no movement.

Shroud shrugged. "I don't know who you are, or what you are. You offered attack—" He was making a visible effort to reply calmly, not to cause any more annoyance to the concealed speaker. "We've shown ourselves—now it's your move."

"Move, move, move!" the voice repeated in a rising

chant. "A game—the heavy-footed stumblers would play a game, would they?"

Out of nowhere flashed a ball of light. It almost touched Stroud, then halted in midair, bobbed up and down in a wild dance around him. The Warden stood still, his hands loose at his sides. Though he blinked when the ball seemed ready to dash into his very face, he did not try to dodge its swift flurries of seeming attack.

"A game—you play then, stumbler. Take your courage in your thoughts and play!" The ball went into a dazzling flurry of movement, becoming nearly too blinding to watch.

With a sudden leap it abandoned Stroud, made the same threat of attack about Crocker, who presented a like impassive front. Now it changed color with eye-searing rapidity—green, blue, yellow, violet, and all shades rippling in between. Never red, Nick noted, nor any shades of yellow bordering on that color, nor did it reach pure white.

"You do not care to play then? But the sport would be poor with you, stumblers!" The ball withdrew, bobbed up and down vertically some distance away. The glow increased so its movement wove a pillar of light, a light that continued to hold when the ball itself disappeared.

Now the column of light winked out as a blown candle flame, leaving a small figure. Perhaps he did not top Nick's shoulder, with even the upstanding feather in his cap, a feather that quivered with every slight movement. But he was completely humanoid in form, and by his appearance an adult male. His face was smooth, young, and yet about him was the feeling of age and boredom. He wore dull green breeches, the color of the leaves. They were very tight-fitting breeches and they were matched by calf-high boots of the same color, only visible because they were topped with wide turn-over cuffs.

His tunic, which laced up the front and had no sleeves, was green also and exposed his small muscular arms. The lacings were glinting gold, as was the elaborate buckle of his belt, and the clasp that fastened his cloak, which was flung back over his shoulders to allow his arms full freedom.

The cloak was scarlet, lined with green, and his cap was of the same shade. Fair hair fell to his shoulder. And the hair held a light of its own, surrounding his head with a gleaming mist. He had well-cut, handsome features, only Nick saw, where the locks of hair were swung back be-hind his ears, that those were large out of proportion, ris-ing to very discernible points.

There was a short sword, or long knife, sheathed at his belt, and he carried a second spear, twin to the one lying by the jeep. His expression was one of malicious amuse-ment. But he did not speak. Instead he pursed his lips to whistle. And there was movement behind him, shadows detached themselves from the tree boles to flit forward.

Humanoid the little man might be, but the force he captained was not. There was a shambling bear that sat up on its haunches, its forepaws dangling, its red tongue loll-ing between only too-evident teeth. Beside that crouched a spotted cat—but what was a leopard doing in these woods? Those two of the company Nick could readily identify—but there were others—

What name did you give a creature with a catlike, spotted body, but with four limbs ending in hooves, a canine-inclined head, bearing great upstanding twin fangs in its lower jaw and double horns sprouting at the beginning of a horse mane just above its wide, fierce eyes? There was a second beast beside it that might be very remotely related to a wolf, save that it had a more fox-like head, a very slender body, the talons of a giant bird in place of fore-paws; the hind paws and bushy tail normal enough, if any-thing might be termed normal in such a mixture.

The four creatures sat at ease, their glowing eyes, for even the bear's eyes glowed red, intent upon the three by the jeep.

"You see," the small man with a graceful wave of his hand indicated his hoofed and clawed, and pawed com-panions, "our strength. Now we ask of you your absence. This is our domain and you have not asked our permission to enter it."

To his own surprise Nick found himself answering:

"We did not want entrance. We came without it being our will." He pointed to the jeep. "One minute that was on a road in my own world—the next it was here."

The small man lost the smile that was close to a taunt. In fact all expression faded from his face. He held out his hand and the spear he had flung earlier arose in the air, went to him, fitting its heft neatly into his grasp. If he made some sign to his company Nick did not catch it. But

the four oddly assorted animals arose and faded away into
the gloom, where they were instantly lost as if they had
turned into nothingness.

"You are, being what you are," the stranger said slowly,
"not for our governing. But I say to you, get you hence,
for this is a forest under rule and not a wild wood open to
wanderers."

He lifted the spear once again as if about to cast it. But
it would appear that was only to underline his order. For
a moment he held it so, then the blaze of his cloak, the
mist about his hair billowed out like smoke from a fire,
clouding his body to hide it utterly. The vapor drew back
again on a center core, then vanished. They were alone.
Nick turned to his companions.

"Who—what—?"

Stroud reached back into the jeep and jerked out the
bundle of tools, hurrying so fast to unwrap it again that
he almost dropped it. He drew out a small wrench and a
screwdriver. Crocker grabbed the latter, holding it at chest
level as if it were a weapon or shield. Stroud thrust the
wrench at Nick who accepted it with surprise.

"Hold that in plain sight," the Warden ordered.

"Why? What—what was that?"

"Why—because it's iron. An' iron is out an' out poison
as far as the People are concerned. If we'd had this in
sight he wouldn't have dared even sling that toothpicker at
us. As to who or what he is—you'd better ask the Vicar.
We've seen his like a couple of times before. People of the
Hills, the Vicar calls 'em—the Old Ones who have always
been here according to what he says. They can get at a
man alright—not with those spears an' swords of theirs—
but in his mind—makin' him see whatever they want him
to. An' if they say this place is theirs they mean it. We'd
better get out—"

Stroud was already two strides along the back trail,
Crocker matching him. Nick hurried to follow. The others
did not look around. If they feared any ambush they
showed no sign of that. He would be governed by them.
Iron—iron was poison, was it? He held the wrench in
sight. Good enough—if showing this was a form of protection he was willing to comply.

He could not draw level with the others until they were
well away from the jeep. Nick himself kept looking
around suspiciously, certain at one time or another he

would catch a glimpse of one of the animals slinking behind to make sure they were leaving what was a haunted
forest. Yet he never saw anything except the trees. Not
even a unicorn this time.

When he finally joined Stroud he had another question.

"What about the animals? I can understand a bear—
though leopards are African animals. But those other
two—they weren't real—they couldn't be—"

He heard Crocker grunt. "You tapped it right there,
Yank. But it doesn't matter how 'real' they are, you know.
Here they'll be real enough to tear your throat out if that
Green Man back there gave the order. You'll see worse
than them. You heard him mention the Dark Ones? Those
nobody wants to see! They have most power in the dark
as far as we can tell—" He turned his head to look full at
Nick, his face haunted by some memory. "Iron beats
them, too. Ask Jean and Lady Diana sometime. They
were berry picking and came upon a tower—it looked like
a tower. That was late afternoon an' a cloudy day, so perhaps those in there were more active than they would
have normally been. Jean saw one—full on—an' she, well,
we had to wake her up at night for awhile. She had nightmares that near sent her around the bend! We've learned
a lot—mostly the hard way—about what you can an' can't
do here. An' you've just had your first lesson—when you're
warned off you go!"

In spite of their zigzag path they made far better time
getting out of the forest than Nick and Linda on their first
journey. But when they came out into the comparative
open Crocker gave a cry of alarm.

"Down!"

Seeing Stroud throw himself belly flat and half roll under a bush almost large enough to give him complete cov-
erage, Nick tried to follow suit, though his own hastily
won protection was smaller and thinner than that which
sheltered the Warden. He saw Crocker a little beyond,
also flat, but with his head supported on his crooked arm,
looking out and up over the water.

"No—not a flying saucer!" Nick's protest was said
aloud. And a vengeful-sounding hiss from his left reminded him to keep his mouth shut. Only he could not believe
what he was seeing. Somehow this was harder to accept
than those mixed up beasts in the forest.

The thing—machine—illusion—whatever it was—hung

silver bright and stationary well above the surface of the water. It was saucer shaped in part, though the upper half swelled to near dome proportions.

Unmoving, it hung. Then, from the south, there sped another sky craft of an entirely different model. This one was cigar shaped and moving at such speed it arrived almost in the wink of an eye. It swooped at the waiting saucer and from it shot a brilliant beam that should have struck full upon the swelling upper half. Instead the beam hit an invisible wall a good distance from the skin of the vessel.

The cigar backed off in another of those incredibly swift maneuvers, rose over the stationary craft to strike from a different angle. This was not a duel, for the saucer made no attempt to retaliate. It merely hung there in the open, well protected by whatever shield it carried, while the other craft in a frenzy of effort, aimed its weapon-beam from various angles. Nick could imagine the frustration building up in the attacker—to launch his—or its—greatest power and not even awaken a slight response from the attacked must be infuriating.

Finally the cigar climbed directly above the saucer and hung there as motionless as the craft beneath it. There were no rays stabbing downward from it now. Instead there was an instant of sparkling light, a flash that was gone so quickly Nick could not even be sure he had sighted it at all.

Slowly the cigar began to descend, straight down on the saucer. What this maneuver might be Nick could not guess, nor had he any help from his companions. So slow was the descent that it was plainly ominous. The pilot of the upper ship now must be using the ultimate weapon at his command.

Down, down—was he going to ram the other—as did the Japanese pilots of World War II who died willingly to take an enemy plane or battleship with them? Down—

Nick saw a tremor in the lower ship. And then—

It was gone!

Exploded? But there had been no sound, no shock wave, no debris. It was just gone.

The cigar lurched, gave an upward jump. It circled the lake twice as if trying to make sure the enemy was no longer there. Once more it returned to hover over the site of the attack. Then it left, streaking away with a speed that took it out of sight in seconds.

Crocker sat up, holding his screwdriver in one hand before him as a worshipper in church might hold a candle.

"Fun and games," he commented. "So they're out to burn each other down now. That good or bad for us. I wonder?"

"What was he trying?" Nick wanted to know. "Coming down on the saucer that way?"

"I would guess, and it's just a guess, mind you, that he was going to use his force field against whatever one that other ship had. The flyers—they're years—centuries ahead of us with their technology—just as the People are with their 'magic.' Anyway the other plane decided it couldn't take it."

"I know one thing"—Stroud crawled on hands and knees between them—"that's plain now, m'boyos. We're gettin' out of this here country. With the Nasties back flyin' overhead, this ain't a healthy place for us to be. An' we've been warned out of the woods so we can't go kitin' in there to be safe. Get started out as soon as we can." He was on his feet, his pace near a run, as he headed up the open land toward the river camp. Yet even if it were needful to make speed, Nick noticed, he kept as much as he could to cover, as did Crocker. And Nick copied their caution.

◆ 5 ◆

Nick ran his hands along the handlebars of the motorbike. To leave it here would be like closing the door yet tighter on any chance of return. But Stroud was right, he could not take it through rough country ahead and it would be worthless anyway when the gas was exhausted. He wheeled it to the back of the shelter and there concealed it as best he could.

They had waited until close to dawn of the next day before preparing for their trek back to what the English party considered their best haven of safety. But the night had not been an easy one. They had taken guard duty by turns, alert for any sky sign to prove the hunters' return, or any noise at ground level to suggest they were watched.

There had been a moon and the night was cloudless. And the light had drawn strange shadows, to look upon, which stirred the imagination, Nick believed, in a manner that did not allay uneasiness.

He had not been helped to confidence when, during his watch, an hour after midnight, the furred shape of Jeremiah flowed past him into the open just beyond his reach. Out there the big cat sat down, his tail stretched out straight behind him, his attitude one of listening. Then, without warning, the tail lashed from side to side, and there was a low growl. The sound never arose to that squall meaning a challenge, but kept on a low note, while the tail beat the sandy soil.

Nick wanted to use the flashlight he had taken from his saddlebags. But, though he longed to see what had so affected the cat, he did not want to run the risk of drawing the attention of what might be prowling out there.

He could hear nothing at all except what were, as far as he could tell, normal noises of the night. What Jeremiah could see, or hear, remained lost to his less efficient senses.

The cat cowered to the ground, tail still. He no longer

growled. Across the sky something large and dark moved silently. There was a slow, single flap of wings, and it was gone. Jeremiah streaked back, leaping Nick's knees to reach the interior of the shelter.

But the sound that followed his return— Was it laughter? Not loud, hardly above an evil chuckle, it sounded. And it seemed to Nick to come out of the air, not from ground level. That flying thing? Nick drew on logic, reason—though logic and reason from the past had little to do with this world. How much was real, how much imagination?

Now that it was morning and they were preparing to leave, he found disbelief easier.

"Too· bad you're havin' to leave your fine big bike." Mrs. Clapp was inducing Jeremiah to enter a woven basket, a form of imprisonment he was protesting. The cat turned his head suddenly and seized her hand between his jaws, though he did not apply the pressure of a true bite.

"Now, now, would you be left here, old man?" She scratched behind Jeremiah's ears. "Get in with no more fuss about it. It is me who'll have the carryin' as you well know. An' when have I ever made it the worse for you?"

She closed the lid, fastened it with quick efficiency.

"Yes." She spoke to Nick again. "A fine big bike an' one that cost you a good penny too, if I have eyes in m' head to guess. This country's not for ridin' though—less'n we get ourselves some of the white ones—"

"White ones?" He slung his saddlebags together over his shoulder and turned his back on the bike, trying to put it out of mind.

"Them what belong to the People. Ah, a fine proud sight they are, ridin' on their white ones. Horses those are, or enough like horses to give 'em the name. We've seen 'em twice at their ridin', always between the goin' of the sun an' the comin' of dark. A fine sight." She reached for a small pack to one side, but Nick had his hand on it before her fingers closed on its carrying loop.

"You have enough to look after with Jeremiah," he said.

Mrs. Clapp chuckled. "That I have. A big old man he is—ten years about. No. . . ." Her round eyes showed a trace of distress. "Thirty years back—that's how you said it now, didn't you? Thirty years—that I can't believe somehow. Ninety-five that would make me, an' I'm no

granny in front of a fire. An' Jeremiah—by rights he'd be
long gone. But he's here an' I'm as spry as ever. So I ain't
goin' to believe in your thirty years."

"Why should you?" Nick returned. "It's a time that does
not hold here, that's certain. I read something once—does
time pass us, or do we pass it? And we can add to that
now—how fast or slow?"

"Slow, I'll speak up for the slow!" She smiled. "Ah,
now, hand me over m' collectin' tote. I'll just have that
handy. It's a good lot of things to fill the stomach snug,
like you can find just marchin' along. Drop 'em into a
stew an' you'll be smackin' your lips an' passin' up your
bowl for more."

She slung the woven grass band supporting what was a
cross between a basket and a tote bag made of reeds, over
her stooped shoulder. And, with Jeremiah's basket firmly
in hand trotted out, Nick following.

They all carried by shoulder bands, or knapsack fashion, similar bags. And Nick noted each also kept close to
hand the iron defense, either in the form of one of the
small tools from the jeep, or, in the case of Stroud, a
small knife, blade bared.

Linda had Lung on a leash again. The Peke kept close
to his mistress, but he held his head high, turning it from
side to side as if he were defining and cataloging the various scents of the land.

The Run's bank was their road. And along it they went
in an order that apparently was customary to them,
Hadlett and Stroud to the fore, then Mrs. Clapp and Jean
Richards, with Linda, Crocker and Lady Diana playing
rear guard. Nick joined the latter.

"Running water." Lady Diana looked down into the
Run. "That has more than one use here, young man. You
drink, you wash, and it can be a barrier for some of the
Dark Ones."

Crocker grunted. "Except you never know with a new
type whether it's water-shy or not."

"There's that of course," Lady Diana agreed. "But here
everything's really a matter of luck or chance. We've had
more than our share of luck so far. There have been very
difficult times—"

Again Crocker had an addition. "That's one way to see
it. I'd say we've just squeaked through, more than once.

I'd thought we'd used up all our luck when we walked away from the crash."

"What is *that?*" Nick had been only half listening, more intent upon the land around them than the conversation. He was staring with stark amazement at what lay half on the bank, half in the Run on the opposite side of the water.

A boat, canted over a little so its lower deck was awash on one side. But such a boat! And how had it come into the Run, which was manifestly too narrow and shallow to give it water room?

Now that they were closer he could see that it had been nearly gutted by fire, which had eaten in places into the great stern wheel that had been its method of propulsion. But how had it come here—and when?

He had seen a cruising sternwheeler on the Ohio River that took passengers for nostalgic rides during the summer. One such caught now in time?

"It's too big for this stream—" He protested against the evidence his eyes supplied.

"Not in flood time." Lady Diana carried a stout staff and with this she pointed to evidence, higher up the bank they traveled, that some time in the past there had indeed been a far greater rush of water here.

"We went over that coming down the first time," Crocker supplied. "Looks as if there had been an explosion. Hadlett said those things often blew up if they were pushed too hard. If there were any survivors"—the pilot shrugged—"they must have gone off. It's been here for some time."

"This stream must join a larger one farther south." Lady Diana nodded. "It drains the lake and flows southeast. If they came through and were lost, they could have turned into it, hunting—" she shook her head. "Panic came, and they pushed the engines harder all the time—then the end here."

"Those were in use," Nick had no desire to view the charred hulk closer, "more than one hundred years ago."

"We've seen stranger than that." Lady Diana strode along at an even pace Nick was trying hard to match. "Overseas." She did not enlarge upon her statement and Nick did not ask questions.

About a mile beyond the wreck of the sternwheeler, their party turned aside from the riverbank, to shortly after climb a rise overlooking fields. There Nick had his second shock of the morning.

For there were lines bisecting this open land. They were straggling and in some places nearly gone, but this had been walled once, with fieldstone divisions into recognizable fields! And down the slope, directly before them was evidence of a road, drifted with soil, overgrown by grass, yet still a road that had once run straight between those deserted fields.

Stroud's arm swung up. In instantaneous answer the whole party dropped, flattened themselves in the shrubs growing here. From across the fields came another band of wanderers.

There were horses, undersized when compared to those Nick knew—some bearing riders, others running loose, herded along by the same riders. Behind them crawled an object so totally beyond his experience that he could not put name to it. On a platform to which had been hitched a massive team—if you could refer to some twenty straining animals as a "team"—was a domed construction. The vehicle was awkward, yet it did cover ground, a guard of horsemen around it reining in their restive mounts to keep pace with the lumbering wagon.

The band had turned into the road, avoiding the walled fields which would be an obstruction it could not hope to overcome. Nick was thankful the whole caravan was heading away. He marked the bows and lances that equipped the horsemen, who presented so barbaric a sight he could not believe they would make comfortable fellow travelers.

"Mongols." Lady Diana lay shoulder to shoulder with him. "True Mongols—a clan or family perhaps."

"You mean," Nick demanded, "the people of Genghis Khan—*here?*"

The sternwheeler had been a shock. But a Mongol party was almost as severe a dislocation of logic as the strange animals of the wood. And they had not the awesome feeling of the forest to cloak them with the air of being where they belonged.

"That is a yurt—one of their traveling houses," Lady Diana continued.

He glanced around. Her weatherbeaten, strong-featured face was alive with interest.

"Here the past comes alive." She seemed to be talking

to herself. "Perhaps those warriors down there really did ride with the Great Khan. If we could talk to them—"

"Get a lance through us if we tried it," Crocker replied. "If I remember rightly they had a talent as bowmen, too."

"They were good enough," Lady Diana agreed, "to wipe out half the chivalry of Europe. And they could have mastered the whole continent if they had pressed on."

"I'd rather," Nick commented, "see the last of them now."

But they had to lie in their hastily found hiding places (which perhaps would be no shelter at all should one of the horsemen choose to come scouting) for some time until the Mongols passed out of sight. How many more remnants of the past had been caught here?

"Those fields, the road—" Nick strained to see how far he could trace that highway. "Who built those?"

"Who knows?" Crocker answered. "There are a lot of such places. We've seen a complete castle. And there are the cities of the People."

"Cities?" Nick remembered mention of those before. "The ones the flyers bomb?"

"Not bomb." Crocker sounded exasperated. "They fly over and hover and shoot rays down. Not that that seems to accomplish anything. But it's not bombing as we know it. I can testify to that."

"The cities," Lady Diana mused, "they are different. Our own cities sprawl. You ride for miles through gradually thickening masses of little box houses swallowing up the country, you see less and less open. These cities are not like that at all, they have no environs, no suburbs, they are just there—in the open."

"All towers," murmured Crocker, "and such colors as you wouldn't think people could use in buildings. No smoke—all light and color. But if Hadlett's right—they're traps. And traps can be attractive—we're in no mind to prove that."

"Traps?"

"We believe," Lady Diana explained, "that the Herald comes from one. And that can be the source of energy or whatever it is that draws us—all of us—from our own world. Whatever governs our coming has been going on for a long time."

"We saw a Roman cohort. If that wasn't one of *their* dream spinnings," Crocker said. "You can't be sure of what is real and what isn't, not here with the People around."

Stroud rose to his feet, and the rest came out of hiding. They used what cover was available to cross the road where the ruts left by the yurt and the hoofprints were deep set, coming into the fields. At the edge of a small copse they laid down their packs to rest and eat.

"That's an orchard over there." The Vicar pointed to another stand of trees a field away. "Apples, I believe— perhaps early ones."

He glanced at Stroud inquiringly. It was apparent that, on the march at least, the Warden was in command.

Stroud squinted into the sun. "We've got to make the farm before dusk. And with them around"—he glanced in the direction the horsemen had vanished—"it's a risk to stop."

"Not too big a one," the Vicar answered. "We'll be under cover of the trees."

"The wall"—Lady Diana stood, measuring the distance ahead as if this was something she knew well how to do—"runs along to the trees. And it grows higher all the way."

"We could do with some fruit." Mrs. Clapp patted her harvest tote as if she already felt it lumpy with plunder.

"All right," Stroud decided. "We set guards though an'—"

"I am afraid that we shall do nothing now," Hadlett cut in. "Look there."

As usual Stroud had steered them to cover. If they kept near to ground level they would escape sighting from any distance.

Bearing down from the same general direction that the Mongols had come was a second party. These were on foot and Nick could see they moved with the caution of those who expected either ambush or attack. They were in uniform and some had rifles, though the majority were not so armed. Their clothing was a dull, earth brown, ill fitting, and he could not identify them.

"The Chinese," Hadlett said softly.

Those in the woods watched the cautious advance, as the newcomers went along the same route as the Mongols. Nick wondered if they were in pursuit of the former band. If so, he was not sure of their chances when or if they did catch up. Somehow those rifles looked less efficient than the bows of the horsemen who in their time, as Lady Diana had observed, had accounted for armored knights.

"The whole country," commented Crocker, "is getting a little too crowded."

"Yes. And what is the reason for all this activity?" Hadlett added.

"It's got a nasty kind o' smell to it," Stroud broke in. "The sooner we get undercover, I'd say, the better. Maybe there's a huntin' party out."

They spent no time in a fruit harvest. As soon as the Chinese squad was well gone, they broke from the copse and traveled at a jogging pace along the protection of a wall, pushing to reach a ridge about a mile and a half away. Nick thought that most of them could make that effort without difficulty, but he wondered about Mrs. Clapp and the Vicar. He saw Jean fall in beside the older woman and take Jeremiah's basket, to carry herself.

There was a straggling growth of vegetation in the fields, resembling self-sown grain, though its like was new to Nick, for the ripe heads were red with protuberant seeds or grains. It also possessed narrow leaves studded on the edges with tiny hooks that caught at their clothing with amazing strength so they had to constantly jerk free.

Nick swallowed. He was thirsty, but he had no time to drink from his canteen. The need for speed was so manifest in the attitude of the others that he kept steadily on. Linda had taken Lung up to carry him, though the Peke had walked most of the morning.

Luckily the rise of the ridge was a gradual one, but it taxed their strength after that trot across the open. Stroud signaled a rest. There was plenty of cover and from here one could see some distance.

"More drifters!" Jean and Linda were on either side of Nick, and the English girl indicated at a distance too far to see details of clothing or accouterments, another band of travelers.

Stroud and Crocker, Nick noted, had flopped over, shading their eyes against the sun, studying not the country beyond but the sky above.

"No sign of 'em," the Warden said.

"Not yet. But there's too much movement. If a big hunt was on—"

"We stay flat an' under cover until dusk," Stroud decided. "Yes, that's pushin' it," he added at an exclamation from Lady Diana. "But I don't see how else we can do it—'less we spend the night right here."

"How far are we," Nick ventured to ask, "from your place?"

"About three miles straight. But keepin' under cover adds to that. We've seen more drifters today than we have in weeks before—"

"And now we see something else!" the Vicar interrupted. "The Herald—we are not too far from the city."

There was no concealment, no hunting for cover by that colorful figure below. As the Mongols, he was mounted. But he did not bestride any rough-coated half-pony. The animal bore a general resemblance to a horse right enough, save that its legs were longer and thinner. And its white coat had about it a halo of light such as had been cast by the hair of the Green Man in the forest.

Mounted on this creature, which skimmed the ground at so swift a pace as made Nick stare, was a man, or at least a humanoid. His clothing was as dazzling as the brilliant coat of his steed, a kind of patchwork of bright colors centering in a stiff and sleeveless tabard that flared out over his hips as if boned. Under that were breeches such as the Green Man had worn. And on his head was a four-cornered cap, the points of which projected.

Unlike the forest man, his hair was short, sleeked to his head. And what little showed was very dark. On his face, a line of hair, as fine as if it had been drawn on with a delicately handled brush, crossed his upper lip, to bracket either end of his mouth.

There was purpose in the way he rode, in the wide, ground-covering strides of his horse. And then, watching their going more carefully, Nick perceived what he had not at first sighted. The "horse" was not hooved, but had clawed paws not unlike those of a hound.

And—they did not touch the surface of the ground over which it passed. The thing galloped as if it followed some invisible pathway some inches above the foundation. It did not swerve or even appear to leap as it came to one of the walls about the fields. Instead it simply rose higher in the air, crossing the obstruction, climbing a little more with each pace, heading for the ridge some distance away.

Up and up, always well above the ground now. The paws worked evenly, without effort. It was gaining altitude steadily, ready to cross the ridge. Now Nick heard a whining hum—from the rider?

No, that came from overhead.

"Hunter!" Stroud warned.

They cowered within their cover as there appeared, as suddenly as if the sky parted to drop it through, a flyer. This was like the saucer they had witnessed in battle beside the lake, but very much smaller. And from its bubble top a ray of light shot groundward.

Nick felt a choking sensation. He could not move, was rooted to the ground on which he lay. There was a tingling close to pain through his body.

The ray held steadily on the climbing-horse thing and its rider. But neither looked up to their attacker. Nor did the gallop of the beast fail. The ray increased in intensity. Nick heard a whimper from Lung, a growl from the cat basket. Yet neither animal protested more loudly.

However, the beam was centered on the rider, strengthening until Nick had to glance away from that searing brightness. When he dared look again it was to see the rider slowly descending on the other side of the ridge. Whatever weapon the flyer used had no effect on the Herald. He continued to speed on, completely disregarding the attack as if the alien had no existence.

Yet the saucer followed, training the beam on the Herald, as if by the persistence of its power it could eventually win. When both were well gone, the Herald only a spot of color rapidly disappearing into the distance, the saucer relentlessly in his wake, Nick discovered that he felt better. He hunched up to watch the strange hunt go out of sight.

"A hunter, but it didn't get him," Crocker said. "And he's heading for the city. Defense, not attack—"

"What do you mean?" Nick wanted to know.

"Just that. The hunters try to break down the cities, but the cities never retaliate. They don't let off ack-ack, never send a bolt back. It's as if they don't care, as if the hunters can't touch them, and so they needn't bother to fight. You saw the Herald—he never even looked up to see who or what was strafing him! If we only had a defense like that—"

"We can accept their offer," the Vicar said quietly, "You know that, Barry."

"No!" The pilot's return was violent. "I'm me, Barry

Crocker, and I'm going to stay me. Even if I have to run and hide all over this country!"

"What happens if one accepts a Herald's offer?" pushed Nick. "You said that one changes—how?"

Crocker did not allow the Vicar to answer. He scowled at Nick.

"You just change. We saw it in Rita." And he closed his mouth as if he could not be forced to add to that.

"You see," Hadlett answered slowly, gently, as if there was some emotion here he feared to awaken fully, "there was another one of us once, Barry's fiancée. She met the Herald before we understood, and she accepted what he offered. Then she came to us to urge us to do likewise—"

"She was better dead!" Crocker pushed away from them.

"But what happened to her?" Nick persisted. "I think we, Linda and I, have a right to know—if the same choice should be offered to us."

"It will be," Lady Diana replied sharply. "But the boy's right, Adrian. Give him the truth."

"There were"—the Vicar hesitated as if he found giving that truth a difficult, almost painful matter—"certain physical changes. Perhaps those could be accepted. But there were mental, emotional ones also. To our belief, Rita—the Rita who returned to us—was no longer human. Men have an inborn fear of death that very few of us are able to overcome, we shrink from even the thought. This change is like a kind of death. For the one who accepts it crosses a division between our life and another. There is no return. We have in us such an aversion to what they become that we cannot stand their presence near us. I am trying to find the proper words, but in reality this change must be faced to be fully understood."

The Vicar met Nick's eyes, but all the rest, save Linda, looked away, almost as if they were afraid, or ashamed of what he said. The Lady Diana spoke again, a rough note in her voice:

"Well, Stroud, do we sit here much longer?"

◆ 6 ◆

In spite of the cover about them Nick felt exposed, helplessly defenseless before whatever might come from the sky, or pad across the land. Yet the way he could overlook from the ridge was far too open. Down there he thought they had no way of passing unseen.

Stroud was making a careful survey of the same territory.

"We can work along there." His finger indicated the slope of the ridge far to the right. "When we get that far we can see better what's still ahead—"

The journey along the ridge was a rough one. They had to take part of it on their hands and knees, scuttling from one patch of brush to the next. It was hardest on Mrs. Clapp. But she made no complaint and the rest took turns by her side, giving what unobtrusive help they could. At least they did not witness the return of the hunting saucer, nor did they see any more drifters in the country below.

However, by the time they reached Stroud's halting point, the sun was well west. Mrs. Clapp's face was deeply flushed and she breathed in small gasps. Her hands, as they lay across her knees, were shaking. Privately Nick thought she would never make it without a good rest.

"We wait 'til dusk," Stroud said. "Eat and wait."

Nick's canteen and another Stroud carried made the rounds and they ate from their supplies. To all sighting, the land below appeared deserted now. But, as the sun crawled down the sky, Nick became aware of another light radiant in the northeast.

He was sharing the watch with Jean. Now he touched her shoulder lightly and pointed to the glow.

"The city," she answered his unasked question. "At night it is all alight—you have never seen anything like it."

He wondered if he detected a wistfulness in her voice.

"How close have you seen it?" The mysterious city, or

63

cities, intrigued him. Apparently they were secure havens of safety for their inhabitants.

"Close enough," she returned, "close enough to be afraid." For a moment she was silent and then she added:

"What the Vicar said about Rita—is true. She was—different. But she was crying that last time she tried to come to us. She didn't mean us any harm—she wanted to help—"

Her voice was uneasy, as if in some way she felt guilt.

"But you all turned her away." Nick regretted his words the moment he spoke.

Jean turned her head to look straight at him. "We sent her away," she said harshly.

Nick was disconcerted. Why had he said that? These people knew what they were doing, what they had to do to survive here. And what he had voiced sounded like an accusation.

Jean had turned away again to watch the dusk creeping across the land. Though she lay within easy touching distance, Nick sensed that in one way she had totally withdrawn.

"If we go on"—he wanted to break that silence—"how can Mrs. Clapp make it? She is exhausted—"

"I know." Her tone was remote. "But she will have to try and we can all give her a hand. We must get to a place we can trust before nightfall."

"See anything?" asked Stroud from behind them.

Jean shook her head. "It's been clear. The city's turned up tonight."

The glow in the sky strengthened as the natural light failed.

"But the far ridge will cut that off." Stroud appeared satisfied at that thought. "We'd best be gettin' to it."

The descent from the ridge was gradual. Jean again had Jeremiah's basket. And Linda, carrying Lung, had closed in on Mrs. Clapp's left. When they hit the more level country Stroud set a brisk pace and the Vicar dropped back to the three women.

They took breaks at intervals, and Mrs. Clapp made no complaint. But it was plain to see that only her determination kept her going. Even her collecting tote now swung from Linda's shoulder to balance her own duffel bag.

Lady Diana moved in, setting her hand firmly, without any word, under Mrs. Clapp's arm. What they would do when the full dark came Nick could not tell. Luckily this was the season when twilight held. And the land also had light from the glow in the sky.

The night was not quiet. Nick's tense nerves twitched in answer to the sounds. There were cries, sometimes wailing. None of the sweet, beguiling singing such as he had heard the night of the rain. Rather these held an abiding terror to feed one's fears, made one look at intervals over one's shoulder to see what sniffed along one's trail. He longed to ask what this or that noise meant. But as his companions accepted them he would not.

"We're well along," Stroud announced at one halt. "We've only a short bit now, then we'll lie snug."

They were out of the fields, nearly at the foot of the ridge above which blazed the radiance of the city. As Stroud led right again, they followed a smoother path between more tumbled walls—this could be a lane.

So they arrived at a black bulk of building, its walls. also stone, though now the twilight was so subdued Nick could not be sure just what it was like. With the ease of familiarity Stroud opened a door and entered.

"Praise be," Nick heard Mrs. Clapp's breathy voice. "Not one minute too soon for these old legs o' mine. Just get me in, m'lady, an' let me sit a little. Then I'll be as right as right again. I'm a mite too old for all this scramblin' about, that I am."

"Nonsense!" Lady Diana propelled her forward with a right good will. "Don't you forget, Maude, we all took a dose of that hunter's ray back there. That doesn't do anyone any good."

There was a glimmer of light in the doorway. As Nick crossed the threshold, Crocker behind him thudded shut a stout door to close out the night. The light was feeble, but it showed the American most of a single big room with a fireplace double the size of any he had ever seen, a bench, some stools and a table—all made of wood and massively heavy.

Mrs. Clapp dropped rather than sat on one of the stools, and Jean hastened to put Jeremiah's basket down beside her. There was a pleading mew from the cat. Mrs. Clapp fumbled with the fastening to allow him out. He shook himself vigorously and then looked about, sniffing at the fireplace, and beginning a cautious exploration of the room.

There were windows, Nick could see, but each was covered with an inner barred shutter. Crocker had just dropped into place a similar but thicker bar across the door. Their light came from a bowl on the table where a cord burned in liquid. There was a pleasant scent from that burning and, in the room itself, an aura of peace and security that was relaxing.

"What is this place?" Linda put Lung on the floor and he flopped flat at once, his chin supported by his paws. "Somehow—it feels—good!"

The Vicar seated himself on the bench not too far from Mrs. Clapp. He smiled at the girl.

"A place of rest, yes, and more than rest, recruitment for the spirit. We have found several such. Some are the work of man's hands—others are of nature. But from them you may draw peace of mind and relaxation from all tensions. This was perhaps built by one who was an exile here, even as we are. We believe it was once a farm—in days when this land was not so troubled as it now is. There is iron set into the door bar and across the windows—which means that those who built were of our kind. But how they brought into their building this spirit of contentment, that we cannot tell. Perhaps all emotions are heightened in this time-space. We meet terror in some places, this blessed quietude in others. While in our own world, if such exist, our senses are not attuned to recognize them."

Stroud had subsided on a stool, his thick legs stretched out before him, his craggy face only partially lighted by the lamp.

"We could stay, weren't it so close to the city. At least we can hole up for now."

That feeling of peace lulled them all. Nick's legs ached, he could not remember when he had walked so far. And, while the pressure of the need to escape had kept him going, now that that was removed his fatigue settled all at once, bringing every ache and pain of misused and seldom-used muscle with it. A little later he was glad enough to stretch out flat on one of the heaps of dried leaves along the wall to which Crocker pointed him. And sleep came quickly.

There were dreams, not frightening, but rather the kind one longs to hold onto, to prolong. Even when he drifted awake and knew he was awake, he held his eyes shut and reached again for the dream. However, it was not only gone, but he could not remember it at all.

"Nick! Oh, why doesn't he wake up! Nick!" A fierce whisper, a hand on his shoulder.

Reluctantly he opened his eyes. Linda crouched by him. Though the lamp was out he could see her face in the thin gray light that came from a small opening very high in the walls.

"Nick!" She shook him harder.

It took a great effort of will to answer her.

"Yes—"

"Be quiet!" She leaned closer. "You'll wake one of them."

The urgency in her tone was enough to make him sit up. It banished the peace of this place.

"What is it?"

"Lung—he's gone!" Now that he showed himself fully aroused, Linda withdrew a little. "There was a whistling and he went!"

"Went how? The door's barred—" It was true. The bar Crocker had put there last night was still firmly in place.

"In the other room—" She jerked at his arm. "There's an open window. Lung ran—I got there just in time to see him squeeze through—"

He followed as silently as possible in her wake. Around him he could hear snores, the heavy breathing of those deep in slumber. Linda's hand reached back for him, drew him on. They passed the fireplace and turned right. There was a brighter glimmer of the gray light.

Here was another room, the door to it a little open. Inside there was no furniture, but there was the square of an open, barred window, set quite low in the wall. Nick did not have to be told that the bars were iron.

Linda dropped his hand, ran to the window, her hands gripping those bars as she pressed against them, striving to see out into the light of pre-sunrise.

Perhaps time had eaten away the strength of that metal barrier, or perhaps there was some concealed catch the girl's weight activated. The crisscross of bars swung outward and Linda half fell, half scrambled through.

Nick hurled himself after her. "Linda, don't be a fool! Come back here!"

If she heard him she was not about to obey. As he banged into the lattice that had fallen into place again, Nick could see her moving out into the yard calling Lung softly. The bars now seemed solid, but he beat his fist against them, and once more the lattice gave and he went through.

"Linda!" He shouted. If it awakened the others, all the better.

He could see her by an opening in the wall.

"I see him," she called back. "Don't follow me, he's being naughty—he'll run again unless I can coax him. And he certainly won't come if he sees you."

There was no way Nick could reach her in time. Unheeding of her surroundings, she was already through that gap, now calling again.

"Lung—here, Lung—Lung—Lung—"

In spite of her admonition, Nick pushed open the window bars again and went after her. Maybe what she said was true and, seeing him, the Peke would be wary. But he had to reach her, make her understand the danger of wandering out this way. If necessary she would have to abandon Lung for her own safety.

However, even as he knew the logic of that, Nick also realized he could never make Linda agree to it. It might take physical force to return her to safety.

"Lung—Lung, you bad, bad boy! Lung—" Linda crouched in the lane, her hand out, her voice coaxing. "Lung—" With her other hand she dug into the big patch pocket on her jeans. "Lung—goodies—the kind you like—goodies, Lung!"

Nick could see the Peke. He had stopped, was looking back at Linda. Nick slowed to a halt. If Linda could coax him to her—

"Goodies, Lung—" She spoke as if this was a game she had had to play before.

Lung turned a little, his pink tongue showing, as if he already tasted what she had to offer.

"Goodies—" Linda made the word a drawn-out drawl.

One step, and then two, the Peke was returning. Nick held his breath. As soon as Linda could get her hands on Lung it would be his turn to hurry them both back to the house.

"Good—good—Lung—" The Peke was almost within reaching distance of her hands now. On the palm of one were some broken pieces of brown biscuit. "Good Lung—"

Sharp, shrill, a whistle.

Instantly the Peke whirled, looked toward the stand of trees to their left, from which the sound had come. He barked and was gone in a flash.

Linda cried out, stumbled to her feet, and dashed after him, aware of nothing but the running dog. Nick called, and then went after her, prudence thrown away, knowing that somehow he must stop Linda before she met whatever summoned Lung.

The Peke was still barking. And Linda shouted in return, calling his name at the top of her voice. Nick kept silent. No use wasting breath when she would not listen.

He might have caught her, but a stone half-embedded in the ground proved his downfall. As the toe of his boot met that, he sprawled forward, hitting the ground hard enough to knock the breath from his body.

It was a moment or two before he could claw his way to his feet again. Linda had gone, only a swinging branch guided him. But he could still hear the barking and her calls. The little fool—stronger names came to his mind as he went on. Doubtless his folly was as great as hers in following. But if he went back for help she could be lost. He would have to take the chance as it was the only one he had.

Thrusting his way through bushes at the cost of bloody scratches. Nick won to an open space under the trees. Though the direction of those barks and calls might mislead, they were all he had to guide him. And somehow the sounds were reassuring, at least they were both able yet to make them.

"Lung—Lung!" Between those two words there was a change in tone. The first utterance had been a call, the second—what? A protest?

Nick pushed on at the best pace he could, and, without warning, stepped into an open, treeless glade. Before him stood Linda, but she was making no effort to capture Lung.

The small dog was still barking, sitting up on his haunches, waving his forepaws excitedly in the air. While she whom he was wooing with all his might smiled and enticed him with something held tantalizingly in her hand.

Linda moved just as Nick caught up with her. Before he could reach out to restrain her—

"No!" she shouted. Her hand swept through the air to strike at the other's.

Swept out—and passed through!

Linda screamed. The other shrank back. But Linda threw herself to the ground and seized the Peke who struggled wildly in her hold, actually snapping at her in fury.

Nick pushed her behind him, confronting the other—perhaps a phantom.

There was a nebula of light about her, seemingly thrown off by the unusual white skin of her face and hands. In part that light misted her, made her from time to time harder to see. But, in spite of what had happened when Linda had tried to strike the morsel from her hand, she seemed to be entirely real and solid. And she looked more human than had the Green Man.

Her hair was a warm chestnut brown, reaching a little below her shoulders. She wore breeches of forest green, with matching boots and shirt, the sleeves of which showed from beneath a tabard like the Herald's. Only hers was not multicolored but also green, bearing across the breast glittering embroidery, in silver and gold, of a branch of silver leaves and golden apples.

"Who are you?" Nick demanded. "What do you want?"

But the stranger continued to back away, and, as she went, the mist about her deepened, clung tighter to her body, until all that could be seen was her face. There was nothing there of threat. Instead from her eyes came the slow drip of tears. And her mouth moved as if she spoke, only he heard nothing. Then the mist covered all of her, dwindled again to nothingness and they were alone.

"She wanted Lung!" Linda still held the dog to her with tight protectiveness. "She tried to take Lung!"

"She didn't get him," Nick pointed out. "Get up! We have to get out of here quick."

"Yes." For the first time Linda seemed to realize how far they might have ventured into danger. "Nick, she tried to take Lung!"

"Maybe—"

"Maybe? You saw her! She was going to give him something—You *saw* her!"

"She was teasing him with it. But she might have had a bigger capture than Lung in mind. You followed him, didn't you?"

"Me?" Linda stared at him. "But she didn't even look at me—it was Lung she called—"

"Could it be she knew you would follow him?" Nick persisted. Looking back he could not swear that the girl had seemed any menace at all. But he had no way of evaluating the many traps this world could offer. At any rate Linda had better be well frightened now so that she would not be so reckless again.

"Do you really believe that, Nick?"

"More than I can believe she was only after Lung. And—"

He had been looking ahead, his grasp on Linda's arm hurrying her along, intent on regaining the safety of the house with all possible speed. But now he realized that he was not sure of the direction. Though it was much lighter than when he had set forth, he could sight nothing here as a landmark he remembered. As he studied the ground he hoped for some mark there to guide them.

Yes! His momentary uneasiness passed—here—and there— He need only follow those quite distinct marks and they would lead them back to safety.

Odd, he would not have believed they were so far from the house. It had seemed, remembering, that he had not been too long under the trees before he had caught up with Linda. But the tracks were plain enough to keep him going.

Until they pushed under the last tree, past the last bush to face not the building, but an open meadow with knee-high grass and tall spikes of yellow flowers. There were more trees a distance away, but to Nick all of this was totally unfamiliar.

He had retraced their own tracks—then how— *Their* tracks? A small chill grew inside him—*whose* tracks? Or had those been tracks at all? As the lure of the singing, and the whistling that had drawn Lung, had those been signs deliberately made to draw them on, away from safety?

"What are we doing here, Nick?"

Linda was caressing the now subdued Lung. Perhaps she had not even paid attention to where they had headed.

"I thought we were headed for the house. We must have been turned around back there."

The only thing to do, of course, was to return in the opposite direction. But he had the greatest reluctance to do that. Fear of the ill-omened glade made him unwilling to voluntarily enter it again. What was happening to him that he was afraid—actually afraid—of the woods?

"We'll have to try to go through it." He spoke his thoughts aloud, more than to her. Nick was determined not to yield to that growing aversion to the necessity for retracing their way.

"No, Nick!" Linda jerked back when he would have drawn her with him. "Not in there."

"Don't be silly! We have to get back to the house."

She shook her head. "Nick, are you sure, absolutely sure, that you can?"

"What do you mean? This is no forest. We got through it one way, and that didn't take us hours. Sure we can go back."

"I don't believe it. And I won't." It was as if she braced herself against his will. "I won't go back in there!"

Nick was hot with exasperation. But he could not drag her, and he was sure he would have to if they went in that direction.

"We've got to get back to the house," he repeated.

"Then we'll go around." Linda turned her back on him and began to walk along the outer fringe of the brush and trees.

Nick scowled. He could not leave her here alone, and short of knocking her out and carrying her—

Kicking at a clod of earth, though that hardly relieved his feelings, he set out after her.

"We're going to have to go a long way around."

"So we're going the long way around," Linda snapped. "At least we can see where we are going. Nothing is going to get behind some tree to pick us off as we go by. Nick, the woods—had things in it besides *her!* I could feel them, if I couldn't see them."

"The tracks." He brought into words his own fear. "They led us out here—perhaps to trap us."

"I don't care! I can see anything that comes here."

But she was willing to hurry, Nick noted. And they followed the edge of the woods, heading south, at a pace that was close to a trot. He hoped this detour would not take long, he was hungry and he was also worried as to how the others would accept their absence. The English might believe that he and Linda had cut out on their own.

No, they had left their bags, everything they owned

now. A little reassured at that thought, Nick decided that the others would not clear out and leave them. Maybe right now they were in a search party, hunting. Suppose he called?

But he could not. If Linda was not just running from her own imagination, they could be watched by things from the trees. Or hunted by those to whom his calls would serve as a guide. Though the grass was so tall it was hard to tramp through, he thought he saw ahead the end of the woods.

"Nick—there's water." Linda angled to the left across his path.

The hollow was not a pond, but rather a basin that the hand of man, or some intelligence, had had a part in devising. For the water trickled from a pipe set in a wall about a hollow. Then that was cupped in a rounded half-bowl and fed once more into a runnel that ran on out into the meadow and disappeared.

Linda knelt, loosing Lung, who lapped avidly at the basin. She flipped the water over her flushed face and then drank from her palms cupped together. Seeing the water, Nick was struck by thirst, just as an ache within him signaled hunger. But he waited until the girl had drunk her fill, standing on guard, his attention swinging from woods, to sky, to open fields, watchful and alert. As Linda arose he ordered:

"Keep a lookout." He went down in her place, the clear, cold water on his hands and face, in his mouth, down his throat. He had never really *tasted* water before. This seemed to have a flavor—like mint—

"Nick!"

◇ 7 ◇

He choked and whirled about, water dribbling from the side of his mouth. One look was enough.

"Get back!" Nick forced Linda, by the weight of his body and his determination, into the brush fringe of the woods.

"Keep Lung quiet!" He added a second order.

They were no longer alone in the meadow. Two figures had rounded the rising bulwark of the ridge, were running, or rather wavering forward desperately. They were dressed alike in a yellow brown that could easily be seen against the vivid green of the grass. But they did not try to take cover. It was as if some great terror, or need, drove them by the most open ways where they could keep the best speed they could muster.

Both staggered, as if they kept erect and moved only with the greatest of efforts. One fell and Nick and Linda heard him call out hoarsely, saw him strive to pull up again. His companion came to a wavering halt, looked back, and then returned to help. Linked by their hands they went on.

"Nick—in the sky!"

"I see it. Keep down, out of sight!"

A small saucer craft, such as the one that had hunted the Herald, snapped into view. Now it was almost directly over the runners who may or may not have had an instant or so to realize their peril.

Both men continued forward, their agonized effort plain. It might have been that the grassy meadow had been transformed into a bog in which sucking mud held them fast. Then they wilted to the ground and lay very still.

The saucer hung motionless directly above them. From its underside dropped a mass of gleaming cords looped and netted together, lowered by cable that remained fastened to the ship. And swinging down that came another figure.

The saucer man (if man he was) was small, dwarfish. But little could be seen of him save a silver shape. For he wore suit and helmet not unlike those of an astronaut. A second such joined the first and they busied themselves with the net and the inert men on the ground. At a signal the net swung up, heavy with the runners, the suited crewmen riding with it.

The craft swallowed up captives and captors. But it did not disappear as Nick hoped desperately that it would. He began to fear that those on board had knowledge of their presence also. Who knew what devices the hunters might operate?

"Nick—!" Linda's whisper brought a warning scowl from him.

Her hand went to her mouth as if she needed to physically stifle her fear. Lung crouched beside her shivering, but he did not utter a sound. Dare they try to move? Edge farther back into the woods where they were more protected by the trees? Nick was not sure they could make it—not now. It could be that they were needlessly alarmed. Still the saucer did not go.

Lung whined.

"I told you, keep—" Nick began hotly.

What he saw stunned him into silence in mid-sentence.

Between the bushes where they lay and the open meadow flashed a slender line of light. It broadened, became a mist, forming a wall before them.

Out of the saucer in turn came such a ray as had followed the Herald during his ride. It was aimed at them and once more Nick felt that sickening tingling. Where the ray met the vapor wall, the mist balled into a fiery spot. And from the centering of energy ran out lines of fire.

"Quick! This protection cannot be held. Into the woods!"

At that cry Nick did not hesitate. When he reached for Linda, his hand closed on emptiness, she was already retreating, fighting her way into the shadows of the trees. It was not until they were well under that leaf cover again that Nick demanded:

"Who called to us?"

"Nobody!" Linda leaned against a tree trunk as if she

could no longer trust her own feet. "It—it was in our heads. Somebody—something—*thought* at us!"

He shook his head, not altogether denying what she had said, but as if to clear away the disorientation brought about by the realization that it was true. No one had shouted that order, it had rung in his mind!

Linda turned her head slowly from left to right and back again.

"Please, whoever—wherever you are"—her voice was low and not too steady—"we're grateful—"

But need they be? Nick's wariness was back full force. It might only be that they had been marked down as prey by one power who thus had defended them against another.

Something flashed into his memory as clearly as if he still saw the scene before him.

"She was crying," he said.

"Who?" Linda was startled.

"The girl with Lung. She was crying when she disappeared."

"You think *she*—" Linda was, he saw, prepared to protest.

"It might be. But why was she crying?"

Linda pressed Lung so closely to her the Peke whined. "I don't know. Maybe she wanted Lung so much—"

"No, it wasn't that." Nick shook his head again. That queer sensation frustrated him. It was as if he had been on the very edge of learning something important and then a door slammed, or communication was sharply broken, leaving him ignorant. "I don't think it had anything to do with Lung at all."

"She whistled him to her," Linda snapped. "Nick, what are we going to do? I don't like this woods any better than I did before, even if it shields us from that saucer."

He agreed with her. There was a feeling of life around them that had nothing to do with trees, or vines, moss, or the rest of the visible world. Which was the lesser of two evils—the unknown of the woods, or the open and the hunting saucer? Somehow, of the two, he was more inclined now to risk the woods and he said so.

Linda looked dubious and then reluctantly agreed.

"I suppose you are right. And we would have been netted just like those others if something hadn't interfered. But which way?"

There Nick was at a loss. The compass on which he had depended before was back at the house with the rest of his gear. And he no longer trusted his own ability to set any course, not after what had happened before.

"Too bad Lung isn't a hound—he might guide us—"

"But he might! Oh, why didn't I think of that?"

Linda actually seemed to believe the Peke could guide them, and Nick was amazed at her obsession with the dog.

"His leash! I need his leash—" She had put Lung down between her feet, was looking about her as if what she sought could be materialized out of the air by the strength of her desire.

"Wait—maybe this will do." She caught at a vine running along the ground. It was tough and resisted her efforts to wrench it loose.

Nick grabbed a good hold on it and jerked. He had no false optimism about Lung's ability to take them out of the woods, but perhaps Linda knew more about the Peke than he did.

Linda stripped off the leaves and small stems and fastened one end to Lung's collar. Then she picked up the small dog and held him so his slightly protruding eyes were on a level with her own.

"Lung—home—home—" She repeated that with solemn earnestness as if the small animal could understand. Lung barked twice. Linda put him down. Again she repeated:

"Home, Lung!"

The Peke turned without hesitation and headed into the woods. Linda looked back impatiently as Lung pulled at the improvised leash.

"Are you coming?"

Nick could refuse, but at the moment he had no alternative to offer. And there could be a chance she was right about Lung, that he might find the way back. Nick followed.

Apparently Lung had utter confidence in what he was doing. He wound his way among the trees never hesitating at all. And the very certainty of his steady progress promised something, Nick decided. But he was still only partly able to accept the fact that the Peke had such ability as a guide when they came out of the woods (it must have been a narrow tongue at this end) and could see, some distance to their right, the farmhouse.

"I told you!" Linda had such a note of triumphant relief

in her voice that Nick guessed she had not been so firmly confident of Lung's abilities after all.

Now she ripped off the vine leash, picked up the Peke, and ran for the building that was more than ever a promise of safety. Nick halted for a moment to check the sky. The saucer people might have foreseen this move, could be cruising overhead, or snap suddenly into view—

But Linda was running faster, too far ahead for him to catch and suggest prudence. He set out after her. As they entered the space immediately before the door Nick saw it was not, luckily, barred to them but stood ajar. Did that mean that the others were gone—?

Linda crossed the threshold, he was now only two or three paces behind her. And Nick had hardly cleared the space of the door swing before that was clapped to and the bar clanged down.

The transition from sunlight to this darkened room was such that Nick could not see clearly. Someone seized his arm ungently. He knew Stroud's voice.

"What d'you think you're doin'?

"I ought to give you a good one!" the Warden continued, and his grasp tightened into a painful vise. "You haven't even the sense of a coney— not you!"

"Get your hand off me!" Nick flared. All his fears, frustrations, his anger against Linda for her foolishness, was hot in him. He struck out at the man he could only half see.

"Sam!" The Vicar pushed between them as the Warden ducked that badly aimed blow with the ease of one trained in such business.

Stroud loosed his grip, but Nick, breathing hard, did not draw back.

"You keep your hands off me," he said again between set teeth.

"Stop it!" Linda cried out. "Nick only came after me—"

"And what were you doing out there, girl?" Lady Diana asked.

"I went after Lung. Someone whistled and he went out—through the winow in the other room. I had to go after him. It's a good thing I did or she would have had him!'

"She?" It was the Vicar who asked that. Nick's sight had adjusted to the gloom now. He saw that they were ringed by the rest of the party.

"The shining girl in the woods. She was going to give Lung something—something to eat, I think. When I tried to knock it out of her hand," Linda's voice faltered, "my—my hand went right through her arm!"

She stopped as if she thought she would not believe her and for the space of a breath or two she was met by silence. Then Crocker spoke, a roughness in his voice close to that which had hardened Stroud's when he accused Nick.

"What did she look like—this ghost girl of yours?"

"She—she was about my height," Linda said. "I was so afraid for Lung I didn't see her much to remember. I think she had brown hair and she was wearing green. Ask Nick—he saw her better than I did. When my hand went through her arm—" As her voice trailed into silence Nick saw them all turn to him.

"She—well, she had brown hair, only it had some red in it, too. And it was shoulder length." He tried to remember all the details he could. Crocker had pushed ahead of Stroud, was as intent upon what Nick said as if this was of utmost importance. "She wore green—with a coat like the Herald's—a silver and gold apple branch on it. And she was pretty— Yes," memory suddenly provided him with another small point, "she has a little dark mole, right about here." He touched his own face near his mouth. "You could see it because her skin was so very white."

He heard Crocker's breath hiss as if the pilot gasped.

"But—" Nick added what seemed to him to be most important, "when she faded away she was crying."

"Rita!" Crocker pulled away, his shoulders hunched, his back to them.

"Or an ullusion," Hadlett said quietly. "We have seen illusions, many of them, Barry."

Crocker did not look around, his hands were covering his face.

"An illusion would be intended for us, we knew her. These two didn't! So what would be the purpose of feeding them an illusion?" His voice was low, toneless. Nick thought he fought to control it.

"Barry is right," Lady Diana agreed. "Unless the People want us to try and find her—and provide such an illusion to get us out of here."

"Which they won't, not that way!" Crocker replied. But

he still did not look at them. "We let her—it—know that long ago—"

"What else happened?" Hadlett took over the questioning.

Nick supplied the account of the mist-hidden departure of the illusion (he thought the Vicar had the right identity there), their following the wrong tracks out into the open. As tersely as he could he gave them an account of the capture of the fugitives by the saucer, the strange wall of light that undoubtedly saved them from a like fate, and their return with Lung's aid.

Hadlett was more interested in the defense that saved them from the saucer than all else, and he took Nick through as full a description of that as he could give for a second time.

"Definitely a force field," the Vicar commented when he had pried every possible detail out of Nick. "But the People have never interfered before, not for one of us."

"Rita would—" Jean said. "I don't care," she added. "He said she was crying, and Rita did cry that last time. I believe it was Rita, not just an illusion sent to trap us. And I believe she did save them from the hunters."

"She's one of *them!*" There was ugly violence in that sentence Crocker hurled at Jean.

"Yes." Her agreement was bleak as if he advanced an argument no one could deny.

"We do not know," Hadlett commented, "how much of the human remains in those who accept. If Rita remembers us I do not believe it is in anger. We did what we had to do, being what and who we are. It seems plain that something well disposed to these two young people did save them this morning. And that is no small action."

"That's all past," rumbled Stroud. "What we've got to think of is that there's hunters here—not too far away. Something in the woods wanted you two free, but that don't mean that it's goin' to keep on fightin' for us. We can hole up here—for awhile—but not long. No supplies to keep us goin'. We've got to get back to the cave."

"We've the bolt hole," Crocker said as if he welcomed the change of subject. "That'll put us on the other side of the ridge."

"An' a sight too near that city for my thinkin'!" Stroud answered. "But it may be we won't have much choice."

They scanted on the rations they shared for breakfast.

Luckily they did not lack for water, for in the far corner of the big room a round stone could be heaved up and there was a well below. It would seem, Nick decided, that the original inhabitants of this place had built to withstand sieges.

Stroud held a council of war, to which Nick and Linda could add very little. That they had returned safely from the morning's venture, now seemed to Nick to be better fortune than they deserved. But perhaps some good had come from it by their witnessing the capture by saucer, a warning of the trouble now hovering aloft. It was finally decided that they would wait out the day where they were, since their position here was safe. With dusk they would move again, this time through a secret exit of the house.

Hadlett suggested the advantages of resting all they could, since once they were on the move again they would have heavy demands made upon their strength. It was then that Mrs. Clapp spoke up.

"You are all goin' to listen to me now." She spoke with the same firmness as Stroud showed upon occasion. "The Vicar, he has the right of it when he says as how this is goin' to be a hard pull. Me, I ain't put by in a chair with a pap bowl under m' chin an' two shawls around me—not as yet. But I'm stiff in m' legs, an' when it comes to a spot o' runnin', I ain't no gal in m' teens, as it were. This is a safe place, as we all know. Best I bide here an' you take off where m' old feet won't be no hindrance to you. This is only proper sense an' you all know it!" She glanced from one to another, her face stubbornly set.

"Maude." The Vicar spoke gently. "This is something we decided long ago—"

"Not the same at all, it ain't!" she interrupted him. "It weren't no matter then o' one o' us havin' to lag so badly that she was a botheration an' handicap to put all the rest in danger. You can't make me be that, sir, you can't!"

"Perhaps not, Maude. But do you want to lay a worse burden on us then? To go and leave you and remember it?"

She stared now at the hands twisted together in her lap.

"That's a hard—hard thing to say—"

"Would you go, Maude? If I broke a limb and could not travel, if Lady Diana, Jean, Sam, any of us said what you have just said, would you agree?"

He paused, she made no answer. Then he continued:

"From the first we said it, and we mean it—we stay together, no matter what comes—"

"It ain't fair—sayin' that. Me an' Jeremiah, we're old, an' we're safe here. You could come back when it's safe again."

"*We* shall make it, Maude." Lady Diana moved up behind the stool on which Mrs. Clapp sat. Now her hands closed on the rounded shoulders of the older woman, and she gave her a small shake that had a rough caress in it. "We've been through a lot, and we've always made it."

"There's always a first time not to, m'lady. An' I don't want to be a burden—"

"*You*, Maude Clapp? What would we do without your knowledge of growing things? Remember how you pulled Barry through that fever when we had all given up? We can't do without you!"

"And don't forget what we owe Jeremiah." Jean knelt beside the stool, her brown hands laid over the gnarled, arthritis-crooked fingers clasped so tightly together. "He always knows when the People are around and tells us. You and Jeremiah, we couldn't do without either of you, and we're not going to!"

"It ain't right." Mrs. Clapp held to her view stubbornly. "But, if I say you 'no,' you're like to try to carry me. I wouldn't put it past your stuffin' me in a basket"—she smiled a little—"an' draggin' me along. An' a good hefty bit of draggin' I would make for the one who tried that, I'm tellin' you, should you have a thought in that direction."

"You'll go out on your own two feet, along with all of us," Hadlett assured her. "I foresee more skulking and hiding in our next journey than running. Is that not so, Sam?"

"You have the right words for it, Vicar. With them flyin' devils out an' bein' so close to the city, an' all. We go out through the bolt hole an' then we take to the country like Jas Haggis used to."

"Seein' as how we ain't no poachers nor night hiders like Jas," Mrs. Clapp commented, "I don't believe that for one minute, Sam. Me, I'm more used to a good comfortable kitchen than all this trampin'. Get back to the cave, I will, an' then you're goin to have a good hard argufyin' on your hands do you talk about doin' this again."

Jean laughed. "I shall remind you of that, Maude, the

next time you get down your herb bag and start talking about what you think may be waiting to be popped into it if you only have the chance to go and look."

"You do that, m' gal." Mrs. Clapp chuckled. "You just remind me about m' perishin' feet, an' aching back, an' all the rest of it. An' like as not I'll be a homebody as quick as I could scat Jeremiah—not that I am like ever to do that. Am I now, old man?" The gray cat had come to her knee and now stood on his hind legs, his forepaws braced against her, looking intently into her face as if he understood every word she said.

"So we wait and rest." The Vicar spoke briskly. "And go at dusk."

"Seems best," Stroud agreed.

But if the others could rest, Nick found that the day dragged. There was more light in the room, but it was stuffy, for the small slits under the eaves that admitted the light did not do the same for much air. The door to the room with the barred window was open and he could see the sun on the dusty floor there.

They had all retired once more to their beds, and he thought some were asleep. But he was sure that the pilot, whose pile of leaves adjoined his own, was not one of them. Crocker turned restlessly. Nick believed he heard him mutter once or twice. But his words were obviously not addressed to the American and the latter dared not break the silence between them.

Rita—Crocker's girl who had accepted what the Herald had to offer and so was no longer human. Nick would never forget seeing Linda's hand pass through the other's outstretched arm. Illusion, but, if so, created by one who knew Rita well. And why had an illusion been crying? Was that so he, Nick, could carry such a tale back here?

His head ached, the stuffiness of the room was unendurable. With as little noise as possible he got up, went into that other chamber and to the window guarded only by the grill, being careful not to touch the iron lattice. There was actually a breeze here and he filled his lungs gratefully with fresh air.

From this point he could not see the front lane nor the woods. That was east, this faced south.

Color—a shimmer of color at first. Then it—hardened was the only word Nick could supply for the process. Shaped, fully three dimensional, he saw brilliant details.

A man stood there, his eyes on the house, searching.
Somehow Nick thought this stranger knew just where he
was, even if the window's shadow might hide him. Out of
an angle of the wall paced a white animal, its legs stilt
thin, pawed where they should be hooved. But this time
flat on the ground, not inches above the surface.

The stiff material of the Herald's tabard was divided by
pattern into four sections, each rich with embroidery.
Nick could guess where the English had gotten their name
for the alien—the tabard had a strong likeness to a quar-
tered coat of arms, a true "coat" since it was worn.

Herald and horse, interested in the house. Nick wondered if he should give the alarm. But, as he hesitated, he
saw the Herald swing up on a saddle that was hardly more
than a pad.

The "horse" took an upward leap, soaring as if it had
spread wings. And, though Nick now pushed against the
grating, he held the two in sight for only a second or two.
As long as he could see them, the steed was still rising.

◆ 8 ◆

"What is it, my boy?"

Nick started. He had been so intent upon the disappearance of the Herald that he had not been aware of the Vicar's coming up behind him.

"The Herald was out there. Then he mounted, and his horse flew over the house." The rising of the mount that was able to climb in thin air still astounded him.

"The Horse of the Hills—" Hadlett joined Nick at the window. There was nothing to be seen out there now but part of the wall in the full sun. "Do you read Kipling, Shaw? He is not so fancied nowadays—the new thinkers hold his 'white man's burden' against him. But there is a bit in one of his tales about the People of the Hills out on their steeds in a stormy night—Kipling knew the old legends, perhaps he believed in them a little, too. You need only read his *Puck of Pook's Hill* to know how much the Old Things of England captured his imagination. Yes, the People of the Hills, and their airborne mounts. There were others before Kipling who knew—Thomas the Rhymer for one.

"In Britain they lingered, as in all the Celtic realms. You find them also in Brittany, which is akin more to Celtic Britain than to Gaulish France. There must have been dealings in the old days between our world and this one—"

"Sir"—Nick looked from the window to the old man's hawk face framed by that silver-white hair—"is the Herald, or what he represents, as much our enemy as the saucer people?"

Hadlett was not quick to answer. Nor did his eyes meet Nick's at that moment. Rather they looked beyond the American, out the window. When the Vicar did reply, he spoke slowly, as if he wished to be very sure of every word.

85

"The saucer people, as you call them, they threaten our bodies, and I do not dismiss that as a minor thing. But the Herald comes to us not in open threat, but as a tempter. If we accept his offer of alliance, or absorption, then we are truly absorbed. We become other than ourselves. There would—there could be no return to our present state. It would be an abdication of all our beliefs. Those who accept are as divorced from our state as if they were not our blood kin. It is, as I have told you, a type of death."

"Rita—if that was Rita we met . . ." Nick had heard the warning notes in the other's voice not to pursue this subject, but he could not let it alone, though neither could he understand what worked in him to so question. "She—she was crying. And it may have been she who saved us from the saucer."

"Yes. She wept also when she came to us the last time and Crocker would not look at her. In her, through the change, there lingered ties. That, too, exists in the legends. Fairy men and fairy maids and the mortals they loved. But never was there any happiness at the end, but sorrow, loss and defeat.

"But you say the Herald was watching the house. Which means he is aware of you and Linda, that he will offer his bargain. Be warned of that, my boy." Hadlett placed his hands on the window frame as he looked out.

"So fair and smiling a land. He who built here must have had untroubled years, for he was able to work these fields, sow his crops, raise this house as a bulwark against the night and that which prowls it. How long ago was that, I wonder?"

Nick was forced to accept the Vicar's change of subject. Hadlett being what he was, the American could not push further on a topic plainly so distasteful.

"Have you seen any places such as this where people live now?"

"No. This is a land under a blight. Perhaps it is the flying hunters who have made it so. The cities seem to flourish and stand intact. But the open land is full of traps. Not all the People were ever of a friendly or neutral nature. We have our tales of ogres, giants, black witches, trolls. And there are traces here of dark malignancy seen and unseen, though not to the extent we found them in England before we were captured. This is perhaps a younger land, one in which such inhabitants have not spread far. Still we have seen ruins—towers, a castle—that are certainly not of the America you must have known. This has been a fruitful, well-populated country. Now there are only the cities and such places as this. In the open move bands of drifters—in the sky, the hunters."

"Do the cities, or the Herald, control our coming here?" Nick had a need to know as much of the truth as Hadlett could or would tell him. He judged that the Vicar was the only one of the three men who might have tried to seek out the causes for action. Stroud was intent on a problem immediately at hand, and as yet Nick knew very little of Crocker.

"If we can accept old legends as a guide," Hadlett replied, "the People do have a manner of control. But according to all accounts they exercise that by appearing in our world, to achieve their purpose by forms of enticement or outright physical kidnapping. While our type of transference is different. Undoubtedly the cities represent a high form of what we might call, for want of a better term, technology. Though when you look upon them you cannot rationally identify them with our civilization. They may generate forces to operate a drawing power at certain sites."

"And if we could discover how they brought us in, we could reverse that?" Nick persisted.

Again the Vicar hesitated. "You are forgetting the time element, that your own arrival here made clear to us. We have counted seasons to reckon four years—you tell us it has been thirty in our own world. Again there were legends of men who returned, to age and die quickly as they passed from one state of existence to another."

Nick counted days—three—no four—since they had found themselves here. How long back there—weeks—months? He shivered because that was so hard to believe. But doggedly he returned to the subject at hand.

"But the cities are safe against the saucer hunters—"

"Yes. Twice we have witnessed an aerial attack. You yourself saw them try to bring down the Herald. There appears to be a great anger or fear working in the flyers—not only for the cities but for all that pertains to them—such as the People."

Nick digested that. The cities were safe, the open countryside was an invitation to danger. What if they could get into a city, without accepting the Herald's bargain? He asked that.

Hadlett smiled. "But of course that is logical, and so do not think, my boy, that that idea did not present itself to us early during our existence here. Only, it cannot be achieved. For one must enter in the company of a Herald, or else there is no way in. Around each city there is an unseen wall of force. And the price for entrance is too high. The Herald will come sooner or later, he will offer you that choice. It will then be your decision to accept it, or refuse. But at that moment you will know what one of our blood must do."

To be told a thing is one matter, to experience it another. After another word or two the Vicar returned to the larger room. But Nick remained. This insistence on the frightening change in those who accepted the Herald's offer continued to interest him. The English apparently agreed it should not be done. Yet all their words could not bring home to Nick what was so horrible. To him the saucer hunters were the greater menace—perhaps because he could understand them better.

Looking back now he believed that Rita had offered them no threat. He could not erase his memory of her tears. In fact every time the scene came again to the fore of his mind it was clearer. Nick could recall more and more details. And he was willing to accept the fact that Rita's intervention had saved them from capture.

The safe cities—that could only be entered in the company of the Herald. In the company of the Herald—that repeated itself. Could one take the Herald as hostage?

But surely the English must have considered every possible angle. None of them were stupid, and the need for survival sharpens the wits, bringing to the fore all one's native abilities. Yet he kept returning to that idea. Were the Herald's powers such—and in this world no powers whether improbable or incredible could be dismissed as impossible—that there was no possible way of capturing the air-riding messenger, or warden, or whatever he was? Nick knew so little, except that the cities were safe, and he had a desire to find safety.

He slept awhile in the long afternoon on the floor by the window. When he roused it was to find Jeremiah beside him, an enigmatic, unmoving statue of a cat, his tail tip folded neatly over his paws, his green eyes unblinkingly

set on Nick's face. There was something in the regard that
made the young man uneasy. He had the impossible idea
for a moment that the cat knew exactly what he was
thinking and was superiorly amused, as one might be
amused at the fumbling of a child striving to master some
problem too adult for his comprehension.

Nick had always liked cats. He had had old George for
twelve years. And one of the stoutest stakes in the barrier
between him and Margo had been her having George "put
to sleep" when Nick had been in New York a year ago.
George was old, he had had to have checkups at the vet's,
he was a "nuisance." So George went, with a surface-
sweet explanation of how wrong it was to prolong life that
was a burden for an old and ailing animal. But Nick knew
that George could have been saved. He had never answered her, never given her the satisfaction of knowing his
raw anger at that new defeat. George was gone, he could
do nothing about that. But Nick could remember as he did
now—in every detail.

Jeremiah growled, his ears folding down to his skull, his
eyes still intent on Nick's. And Nick's breath hissed between his teeth, almost with the sound an angry or alarmed
cat might make.

The cat—knew! Jeremiah was reading his mind! Nick
was as certain of that fact as if Jeremiah had spoken
aloud. But it was Nick who spoke.

"You know." What he expected in reply, he did not
know. Would Jeremiah give some sign of complete understanding? But the cat made no move, did not utter a sound.
And Nick's certainty of that exchange began to fade.
Imagination— Yet he could not altogether accept the fact
that he had been wrong. One did not deny the idea of
telepathy nowadays, of the paranormal talents some people possessed—the gift for psychometry, precognition, all
the others. And animals were supposed to be psychic, es-
pecially cats. All the rational explanations for what he believed had just happened came to mind now. Yet they did
not quite explain it—and *he* was not psychic in the least.
So how could Jeremiah have read his thoughts, his memory, and reacted?

Whether Jeremiah could understand him or not, Nick
went on speaking softly to the big gray cat.

"George didn't look like you. He was long-legged, and
no matter how much he ate, and George was an eater all

right"—Nick smiled at the memory of George enjoying a plate of turkey—"he never fattened up any. You'd have thought we kept him on short rations. He was a hunter, too. And he liked to sleep on beds, but he didn't want you to turn over and disturb him, he could make that plain."

Jeremiah still watched him. Then the big cat yawned, stood up and walked away, his boredom plain in every movement. Nick felt foolish. It was so obvious that Jeremiah was no longer interested in the least. His disdain of George, undoubtedly an inferior type of feline, obvious in every small flirt of his upheld tail as he went. Do not regale *him* with accounts of other cats, he seemed to be saying; there was, naturally only *one* Jeremiah!

For the first time since his arrival in this world Nick laughed. Jeremiah could communicate alright—after his own fashion. And even if the cat had read Nick's mind, he still had the standards and logic of his own species. Nick could question, but he must also accept what he saw and not close his mind.

Their party made the move at dusk, having eaten. Nick's bread was long since gone, but some of the cheese and bacon were left. And the English carried small hard cakes made of ground nuts and dried berries pressed together, with strips of dried and tough meat.

The exit, Nick discovered, was via the fireplace. That was a cavern of an opening, the largest he had ever seen. At its back four great stones, fastened together, could be pulled out like a door. He tendered his flashlight and Stroud accepted it at once.

"Wait for me to beam up now," the Warden ordered. "These steps are tricky."

He disappeared and Nick caught sight of the beginning of a narrow stairway leading down. It was laid into the back of what must be a very thick chimney. They waited until from below a bright beam reached up. Then Lady Diana squeezed through with Jeremiah's basket, followed by Mrs. Clapp, Jean and Linda carrying Lung. Hadlett went next, and he was hardly through the low door before Crocker nudged Nick.

"Now you. I'll have to set the blocks back."

It was a narrow squeeze alright. Mrs. Clapp and Stroud with their greater bulks, must have found it almost painful. But it was not too long. Then Nick was in a level passage, also stone walled, elbowed aside by Stroud who still held the light steady for the pilot.

Crocker did not come at once. They caught a couple of mutters to suggest he was having difficulty in fitting the door back into place. At last he joined them and Stroud sent the light ahead, taking the lead in a passage that kept them going singly, but was wider than the cramped staircase.

Little of the light filtered back as far as Nick. The air was dank, the walls sweated drops of moisture, and there was an ill smell. The passage appeared to be endless as they tramped along. There were no breaks in the walls, the way did not give access to any cellar, or side passage. Nick wondered how those with whom he now traveled had ever come to discover it. They called it the "bolt hole" and that seemed apt. But much hard labor had gone into its making, which suggested that those who had fashioned it had felt the need for such a hidden exit to the outer world.

After a while the stone walls changed to upright stakes set close together with earth packed behind them, a cruder piece of work. Nick glanced up overhead and saw a crisscross of similar stakes, thick beams to support weight. He trusted that time and decay had not damaged them.

Then, after what seemed a very long time, the light revealed another flight of stairs, these far less finished than those in the chimney, resembling a crude ladder. Up these Stroud climbed. In a few moments the light swung down to show the hand- and footholds for those who would follow. Nick watched Hadlett and Lady Diana assist Mrs. Clapp all they could and it was a lengthy process.

But the way was then clear for the younger members of the party who made the climb with more agility and speed. They emerged in another stone-walled place. Above their heads, well above, was an opening to the night sky, with a star or two winking there in reassurance; and the fresh air felt good after that passage.

Before Stroud snapped off the light, Nick caught sight of the charred remnants of what must once have been beams protruding in places from the wall above, marking the sites of perhaps two upper floors. And there was a mass of fallen debris underfoot so they linked hands in the dark and moved with caution toward the open arch of a door.

Vegetation masked the ruin rankly on the outside. Bushes Stroud had been holding aside snapped back when the last person was through the door, covering the door from sight. Nick saw the rise of the ridge now at his back.

Outside the tower they had more light than the natural night offered. It sprang rainbow hued from some ground source ahead, hidden by the trees and brush which so well cloaked the ruin.

At Stroud's order they kept close together. If the Warden was no trained woodsman, he did his best, as did the others, following his example, to keep their passage as noiseless as possible. They were angling right, and with every step they took, the growth about them thinned, the light grew brighter—until at last there was only a thin screen of branches through which Nick saw the city.

The wonder of that sight stopped him short so that Crocker bumped into him. But he paid no attention to the pilot, he was entranced by what he saw.

It arose abruptly, without any outlying clusters of buildings, even as they had said. And it towered until he thought that its spires might well dispute the stars. For it was all towers and spires, reaching shafts like longing arms held up to the wonders of space.

What might be the material of those distant buildings Nick could not begin to speculate. He could not equate stone with the constant play of color. For that blaze of brilliance, which radiated from the walls to light the night, was not constant in any one place. Rainbow-mixed shades, light and dark, rippled and flared, to die down, before once more flaming up.

Strange as the city was it did not seem alien to the ground on which it rested. There was the green of woodlands in its sheen, the gold of meadow flowers, the rust red of bark, the blue, the silver gray of water, the pale pink of blossoming fruit trees, the ruddy, heavy splendor of that same fruit come to full ripeness. It was all the colors of the earth mingled joyfully together.

For the city did not frighten, it did not awe. The emotion that filled Nick as he gazed upon it was happy excitement. Something that had long been sought, that had been glimpsed imperfectly, perhaps in a dream, now stood proud and magnificent before him.

"Come on, you fool!" Crocker caught him, gave a jerk

hard enough to break Nick's daze. "What's the matter with you?"

"It's wonderful!" Nick wanted to run straight across the open to the city.

"It's a trap!" The pilot was uncompromising, harsh. "They set it for us. Don't look at it."

Was Crocker right? Nick could not believe him. But the distant towers did draw him. And now that he had passed his initial wonder, he distrusted that longing a little.

Yet it was still with reluctance that he moved on, edging always to the east after Stroud and the rest. Crocker matched step with him as if he feared that Nick might suddenly take off.

They had not progressed far before Stroud hissed a warning and they halted. To the west, figures came into the light. There was no mistaking the long-legged creature that paced ahead of that group—a Herald "horse."

But there was no one on its back, rather the brilliantly coated one who was the creature's master walked behind. With him were three others, a strangely assorted group.

There was a man wearing the drab uniform of those Nick had seen netted, and behind him—surely that was one of the suited aliens from a saucer. Yet here they walked as if they were not enemies, both with their eyes fixed on the Herald. The third was a woman.

"Rita!" Crocker cried.

Nick would have thought the party too far away for any to be recognized. But he could read on the pilot's face the conviction that the green figure was his lost friend.

A sharp noise in the sky. This time it was not one of the saucers that appeared out of nowhere, rather one of the cigar-shaped craft.

It shot earthward as if about to bury its nose in the soil. From it pulsated sharp bursts of light. They struck around the advancing party—who paid them no heed—bringing wisps of smoke from charred stretches of ground. The rays were obviously deflected and struck at angles to either side or the rear of those on foot.

Overhead the flyer made reckless darts, as if its pilot was determined to stop the others if he had to ram his craft into them. But in every one of those dives the ship wavered from side to side and the effort with which the pilot maintained control was manifest.

All this time it would appear that the four people and

the "horse," were entirely oblivious to the attack. They did not turn from the straightest route to the city. And Nick could imagine the frustration of their attacker.

At length the flyer's pilot must have accepted defeat. The craft skimmed back toward the ridge, streaking off at incredible speed. But the party on foot continued their even-paced way, unruffled and undaunted.

Nick was impressed. He had a real safety blanket, did the Herald. With such protection he could travel anywhere and not worry. If a man could just discover how that worked! Nick watched the Herald speculatively, wondering why he now walked instead of rode. Was that so his protection covered those he led? If they only had his secret!

The Herald and the city, one or the other was the key. And Nick was sure they merited a detailed study. The Herald went out of the city, so he would be easier to check on. A man could not enter the city without the Herald—but could a Herald be held for ransom?

That might be utterly impossible. They had just had a demonstration of how impervious the Herald and those under his protection were to force. And there was no use in trying to talk the English into such an attempt—not until Nick had a plan that had an even chance of working. But he would continue to think about it.

The pace of the Herald's party must have been swifter than it seemed, or else the city was closer, for they were almost there now.

"That *was* Rita!" Crocker said. "She's helping them set their traps for poor fools, marching them in!" He balled one hand into a fist, struck it into the open palm of the other with force. "She's *helping* them!"

"Why not?" Jean asked. "She is one of them now."

She stood to the other side of Crocker, not looking at the pilot, but rather at the city. When she spoke again it was in a lower voice that embarrassed Nick for he could not move out of hearing and he knew it was not meant for him.

"She is gone, Barry. And you cannot bring her back—let her go. You won't be whole again until you do."

"Let me alone!" Crocker flung out his arm. He did not quite touch Jean, but the force of his voice was close to a blow. "I know she's gone—but let me alone!" He plunged past her and there was a stir among the rest where they huddled. Stroud started them moving to the east, and a little later they began to lose the glow of the city in a darkness that seemed twice as heavy and drear because it was away from the strange glory—the promise behind.

Nick caught at that half-conscious thought. No, he must not allow his momentary enchantment at the first sight of the city to influence him now. There were traps aplenty here without allowing himself to be beguiled by such an obvious one.

◇ 9 ◇

"We've never seen it like this before."

That "safe" stronghold, the one place in this alien and threatening land that they could call home, held them at last, had sheltered them now for several days. But conditions, Nick was quick to discover, were far from what the English had earlier faced. In the pile of thumbled rocks that masked the entrance to their hideout they had a sentry post. He now shared it with Crocker.

"We can't hunt or fish—not now," the pilot continued.

For the land was no longer seemingly deserted as the refugees had led Nick to believe was generally the case. It was rather as if a sweep was coming from the north, bringing past their place of concealment a tide of drifters.

Though they expected to see the drifters harassed by the saucers, there had been no sighting of those. Just the bands, which moved with unslacking determination as if they fled from fear. And the sight of them made the watchers uneasy. Yet they were not ready to desert their own stronghold.

The foundation of their refuge was a natural cave but it had been enlarged, embellished by the hand of man or some other intelligence. Walls had been smoothed. On their surfaces were incised lines, some filled in with ancient paint to make the designs fully visible.

There was light, too. A kind that puzzled Nick more than the rock paintings, for such as those were to be found in his own world. But these rods, based in the native stone, yet bearing on their tips flares of blue light, were of a civilization far more advanced technically than one that would have used caves for dwellings.

These lights were oddly controlled also. There was no apparent switch—one *thought* them alight! You need only face one of the slender rods, wish for a light, and the flames, like those of giant candles, flared aloft.

The patterns on the walls and the lights were the myste-
ries of this world. The rest was what the refugees had
brought—beds of dried grass and leaves, a fireplace of
small rocks, wooden bowls and spoons Stroud had carved,
having the knowledge a hobby supplied. They were cave
dwellers surrounded by the remnants of a vastly more advanced civilization. But so easily defended was the way
into their stronghold, so safe its atmosphere, they clung to
it.

If the land continued so occupied, Nick could understand Crocker's concern. Food supplies were dwindling,
even though they had stocked up well in the days when
this land had been their own. One could not hunt or fish
and be constantly alert for attack.

They had been pent-up for two days now, unable to
venture out because of the drifters. Those did not appear
even to rest at night. Twice in the one just past they had
witnessed flickerings of lights out there. Nick was impatient. They ought to do something—find out what was
going on.

He had depended upon the English for guidance. Only
an utterly stupid person would plunge ahead without
learning what he might have to face. But, within the past
few hours, he was sure they were just as baffled as he, that
this mass migration was new.

Ill assorted, the drifters were. It was, Nick thought, like
watching the flow of history stirred into a weird mixture.
He had seen Indians once. And later three men with
long-barreled rifles and the fringed hunting shirts of the
early colonial frontier. But there were others—a party of
bowmen with steel helmets accompanying two armored
knights. And another band, this one with women (who
were always rare), also in armor but of a far earlier
period, the helmets topped with brushes of red-dyed bristles,
bronze-embossed shields on their arms.

Stroud had slithered out that morning, using rocks and
brush as cover. The Warden was, Nick gathered, the only
one who appeared to have the ability to scout, limited as
that might be. It was his intention to reach the river to the
east and judge the traffic around it.

Though the cave had been their headquarters ever since
they had first chanced upon it and they had other refuges,
such as the camp by the lake and the farmhouse, they had
never intended to make any of these a permanent base.

Their plans had been to reach the sea and, if possible
(which sounded hardly probable), find transportation back
to their own land. In pursuit of this general plan they
had begun work some time ago on a raft at the river, but
had been forced to hide the results of their labor when
there had been sudden saucer activity near that point.

Now Stroud was to discover if that section were still pa-
trolled, or if they could hope that the movement of
drifters had drawn the flyers after them. If so, and they
could not wait out the migration, then the raft on the
river might mean escape. It seemed a very slender hope to
Nick, but he knew that they held to it.

The city continued to haunt his own thoughts. If one
could just learn the secret of getting in—

"I'm going to the back post and relieve Jean," Crocker
said. "Lady Diana will be here shortly."

The pilot was gone, Nick was alone. He was glad of
that. Crocker was alright, but Nick knew that the pilot did
not warm toward him, any more than Nick himself would
have sought out Crocker back home. It was plain that the
Englishman had problems, which kept him in a sullen,
brooding state, and he did not welcome strange company.

Now the Vicar—Nick could warm to him. And he understood Stroud. The Warden reminded him vividly ·of
several men he had known, the last being Coach Heffner
at high school. Mrs. Clapp—he smiled—and Jean—but he
was sure Jean had an eye only for Crocker. He wished her
well in that direction but success seemed dubious.

Lady Diana was manager whether they welcomed it or
not. She was one you would have to reckon with if you
crossed her.

Linda—he thought about Linda. Before they met the
English, they had drawn together. Afterward, she had become more quickly absorbed in the other group than he
had. And, following their adventure in the wood, she had
avoided him. He had made no attempt to close the gap
she had opened. Linda was alright, but he certainly was
not going to make any effort to know her better. Just because they were fellow victims did not mean they were
thereby joined in a relationship.

Nick tensed—movement out there, a shaking of bush
not caused by any wind. During his sentry tours Nick had
seen animals on the move also, disturbed by drifters.   ·

And the animals had sometimes been grotesque. There

were the light-colored deer, and twice wolves, giant ones as large as a small pony. Rabbits of a very ordinary type had come and a flock of wild turkeys. But there had been a pair of nightmare forms as weird as the two he had seen with the Green Man. Each had four limbs and a body not unlike that of a giant cat, though the fur was more like deerskin, and a long neck ending in the head of a beaked bird, an eagle, scaled instead of furred or feathered. From the shoulders had sprouted membranous wings like those of a bat, plainly too small and weak to support the bulk of the body. In the open the creatures stretched their wings with a clapping sound.

He described these two to Hadlett, and the Vicar nodded as if he recognized such an impossible mixture of bird and beast.

"An opinicus—"

"A what?"

"A fabulous beast used in heraldry. Just as the two you met in the forest were a yale and an enfield."

"But—" Nick was completely bewildered. He had an idea that heraldry had something to do with shields, coats-of-arms, the designs used in the Middle Ages to identify knights in battle, and used nowadays as a form of snobbery to make wall plaques, mugs, designs on stationery. But living animals—

"Yes," The Vicar continued. "Imagined beasts do not roam the countryside. But here they do! They are allied to the People and show no interest in us, unless they are directed to do so. Fortunately that seldom happens."

Now as Nick watched the movement down slope he speculated as to what might appear, a normal animal he could name, or one of the weird companions of the People. But what flowed out, with the sinuous grace of his species, was Jeremiah. The cat was experiencing some difficulty, having to keep his head at an angle unnatural for him, for he had mouthed and was drawing along a large bird. Twice on his way up the slope he had to pause to take a fresh hold. But his determination to bring in his catch never faltered.

He finally reached Nick and dropped his burden. His eyes fixed upon the man, he gave a warning growl. The limp bundle of now dusty feathers was vividly colored. Some of the long tail pinions were bent and broken. It seemed about the size of a chicken, but its plumage was far removed from the barnyard fowls Nick had known.

"Good catch," Nick observed. "You're a better hunter, Jeremiah, than we've been lately."

The cat lay down on his side, his forepaws outstretched. Now he dropped his head on these and gave a visible sigh. It was plain his endurance had been taxed by the effort of bringing home the fruits of his hunting. Nick put out a hand toward the bird, watching Jeremiah for any sign of resentment. But the cat merely watched him, did not again assert ownership.

He had killed the bird cleanly, there was not even any outward sign of a wound. Nick smoothed out the bedraggled plumage in wonder. The colors were as brilliant as those of a parrot, yet blended into one another in a subtle fashion. He was reminded of the glory of the Herald's tabard.

The Herald—holding the bird Nick no longer saw it. He was rather remembering that long moment in the farmhouse when he was sure the Herald had known he stood behind the window. And his thoughts moved to his own— well, you could not call it a plan—idea of somehow getting the Herald to use as a key to the city.

But the trouble was he would have to know so much more about the Herald himself. And Nick was well aware that such discussion was taboo as far as the English were concerned. Only Hadlett had given him bits and pieces, never as much as he needed to know, always changing the subject when he tried to find out more about the enigmatic master of the city. *Was* he master there, or a servant messenger? The status of the Herald could have a distinct bearing on what Nick wanted to do. If he only knew—

Hadlett had warned him that he and Linda would be the target for an offer. But so far that had not happened. And holed up here as they were now, how could it? If Nick could meet the Herald, perhaps he could learn for himself— But if a saucer attack could not trouble that alien, what could he do?

The need for action continued to gnaw at him. He did not believe they could indefinitely hide out here in the present state of the country. And what if whatever was driving the drifters south did arrive? The very flimsy hope of escaping via the raft was no hope at all, he was sure, rather a delusion that might prove fatal. No, the city was safe—

Nick was so certain of that that his very surety was a surprise. He had played with the idea ever since he had seen those glittering towers, but this was absolute conviction.

A soft rub against his hand. Jeremiah must want his trophy. But when Nick looked down at the cat, the animal had not reached for the bird at all. Rather he rubbed his head back and forth against Nick's hand and arm, and he was purring.

"Good boy!" Nick scratched behind the gray ears, rubbed along the furred jaw line. "You agree with me, don't you?"

The question had been asked in jest, but at that moment he knew he spoke the truth. Once more Jeremiah had reached into his thoughts, and the cat was agreeing in the way he could best express himself.

Nick's hand slipped gently under the jaw, urged Jeremiah's head up, so he could meet those wide eyes straightly. "How much do you know—understand—Jeremiah?"

The cat's reaction was swift and sharp. A paw flashed up, claws raked across Nick's wrist. He jerked back. Plainly he had taken an unallowable liberty. There was a warning growl and Jeremiah once more mouthed the bird, pushed around Nick, and vanished into the cave. Again Nick was left unable to judge what was the truth, what imagination. He must ask Linda about Lung—did the Peke also give her the impression that here he was able to communicate if he wished?

He was still staring after Jeremiah when Lady Diana scrambled up.

"Anything to report?" she asked directly.

"Nothing except Jeremiah coming back with a big bird."

"That cat! Maude is right under his paw, which is where every cat wants you. Though I will admit he seems able to sniff out any of the People—"

"The Herald, too?" Nick asked.

She studied him. "What about the Herald?" There was a hostile note in her voice.

"Does Jeremiah know when he is around?"

"Now that"—his question appeared to be a surprise—"I don't know. He can point out one of the People whether we see them at first or not. But the Herald—Why are you so interested?"

"It would seem he's such good security, I just wondered."

"Ask Maude, she knows everything knowable about that animal. Your food is waiting, you had better get to it before it's cold."

"Yes, m'lady!" Nick sketched a half-salute, giving her the address Stroud used, and scrambled down into the cave entrance so well masked by the jumble of rocks.

He found Linda on K.P. duty. Mrs. Clapp was some distance away, Jeremiah's trophy laid across one knee, stroking the cat's head and telling him what a brave, smart boy he was. Jeremiah accepted this praise complacently, with a feline's estimate of his own worth.

Nick picked up a bowl and went to where Linda was stirring a pot sitting on a pier of stones over the fire. Lung was beside her, his head cocked a little to one side, apparently intent on watching the flames.

"Linda, have you noticed anything different about Lung?"

"Lung?" She had taken Nick's bowl to fill it from the pot. But she turned her head quickly to look down at the small dog. "What's the matter? Lung?"

At his name he sat up on his haunches, waving both small forepaws in the air, and gave a soft bark.

"Has—" Now that Nick was prepared to ask his question it sounded improbable. He could have imagined Jeremiah's response. No, he had not! Gathering courage from that, he continued. "Has Lung given you the impression that he understands—well, what you are thinking?"

"What I am thinking?" she echoed. Now she turned her attention from the Peke to Nick. "No," she said as if to herself. "You really mean that, don't you? I told you— Pekes have a very high intelligence. He could always make me understand things—"

"That's not what I meant—" began Nick when she interrupted.

"I know. You mean—like telepathy, don't you? Why do you ask? Has Lung been reading your mind?" She might have asked that derisively, but he thought her tone was rather one of deep interest.

"No. But I think that Jeremiah has."

"Jeremiah!" Linda gazed beyond the fire at the cat curled

up now at Mrs. Clapp's feet, and her expression was not altogether approving. "They keep telling me, Jean and Mrs. Clapp, about how wonderful that cat is, how he can let them know when there's any of the People around, or a bad influence, or something like that. You'd think he was a marvel. Now you come and tell me that he can read minds! I think you're all crazy!"

"But," Nick persisted, "have you tried finding out if there is any change in Lung?"

"You mean there might be something in this place that does produce mind reading and all that? But why not us, then, instead of the animals?"

"I don't know." He had to answer with the truth.

"Lung." Linda shoved the filled bowl into Nick's hands. Her attention was on the Peke. "Lung—"

The dog gave another soft bark, put his front paws on her knee as she sat down cross-legged and held out her hands to him. Gathering him up, she held him as Nick had seen her do before, with those bulbous dark eyes on a level with her own. "Lung, can you read my mind?"

Nick watched them. Was she serious with that question, or was it a jeer aimed at him?

Linda was silent, staring intently into the Peke's eyes. The dog made a dart with his head, his tongue went out to lick her chin. The girl gave a muffled exclamation, pulled him tightly against her until he woofed in protest.

"You—you are right. Lung knows."

"How can you tell?" Nick demanded. Now all his own objections to such a belief came to life again. He did not want confirmation, he realized, he wanted denial.

"I know." She did not enlarge on that. "Nick—we have to get away—back home!"

She sounded so afraid Nick was once more startled. It was as if during that long moment of confrontation with Lung she had learned something that made her whole world unsafe.

"We can't very well leave now," he pointed out. "You know as well as I do what we'd run into out there."

"They—" Linda's voice became a whisper. "Their plan for hiding out here—Nick—that can't go on much longer. The food is very low. And as for going down river on a raft—" The note in her voice underlined her honest opinion of that. "Nick, whatever, whoever is chasing all the drifters we've seen, it's got to be something everyone has good reason to fear. If we just stay on here—Nick, we can't!"

Those were his own thoughts put into words. But would she accept his only other suggestion—the city?

"Nick, if we went back—right back to where we were when it all began, do you think we could get back to our own world?"

He shook his head. "There was a history of disappearances in our world for a long time—and no returns. It could not be for want of trying, I'm sure of that."

She leaned forward so her cheek was against the Peke's soft fur. Her hair was tied back with the red yarn still, but a piece of it was loose enough to fall over her eyes like a half veil.

"Nick, I'm scared! I'm scared the worst I've ever been in my life."

"I think we all are. I know I am." He matched her frankness. "But we've got to hold on. I think *here,* if you lose your grip, you're really lost."

"Yes, that's what I'm the most afraid of now, Nick. They—Jean—Mrs. Clapp, Lady Diana—they all seem to be just able to take it and it doesn't matter. Mrs. Clapp—she's old and thinks that this is like a test of her belief that being good will help a person. She's talked to me about it. And Lady Diana, all her life she's been fighting for things—Mrs. Clapp told me about her, too. She's done a lot for the village where she lived. She sort of bullies people into doing what they should. I can't imagine her being afraid. And Jean—you know, Nick, she's in love with Barry. As long as she's near him and all's right as far as he is concerned, then she doesn't care about anything else. All that hurts her is that he still wants Rita—

"But not one of them is afraid the way I am. And, Nick, I'm so afraid I am going to break wide open, and then all of them will despise me." Her head sank lower and the lock of hair now hid most of her features.

"Not one of them will!" Nick tried to find the right words. "You're wrong, Linda. If you *could* read minds, I'd swear to it you'd find every one of them has a limit of control. Maybe they haven't reached it yet—but it's there. You're hinting we ought to go by ourselves? But we have a better chance of sticking it out here, at least for now."

"I suppose so," she agreed dully. "But I wish— No, I can't let myself wish, can I? I have to accept what's here and now and go on from there. But, Nick, we can't possibly stay here and starve. What can we do?"

Before he could control his tongue he answered: "There's the city—"

"The city? What do you mean?"

"That's really safe—at least from the saucers. We saw that proven." Now he was driven to get her reaction to his half-plan. "Suppose we could get into the city—"

"We can, easily enough. Accept the Herald's bargain, as Rita did. But, Nick, the way they talk about that—there must be something terrible happens when you do."

"Not the bargain, Linda. But suppose we were able to follow the Herald in somehow. Or, get out of him how to do it." Nick's plan was still only a suggestion to which his thoughts continued to turn.

"I don't believe you could." Linda replied so flatly he was momentarily deflated. Then he reacted to the deflation as swiftly, with the determination that he would at least try. But he would not give her the satisfaction of a protest. Instead he started eating.

"Are you going to try something like that?" His silence appeared to irritate her.

Nick shrugged. "How can I? At the present time I don't see any chance."

"Of course not! And there never was!" With that parting shot she arose and walked over to join Mrs. Clapp who was plucking the feathers from Jeremiah's addition to their larder.

Nick finished the stew, washed his bowl in the dribble of water that came out of the wall in one of the small alcoves cut in the cave, a dribble that found its way out again along a trough chiseled in the floor. But he set the bowl down there and did not return to the center portion of the cave. Instead he edged along through a narrow slit Crocker had earlier pointed out, one indeed too narrow for Stroud to negotiate, which led to another cave and a passage, and finally a very narrow opening on the world.

Just now Nick wanted no company, rather a chance to think without interruption. He had a puzzle. Perhaps it could not be solved, perhaps it could. But it must be faced and struggled with.

Nick worked his way up to that slit opening on the world. But, as he placed his hand on the side of the opening to steady himself, earth and a stone gave way under

his weight. He snapped on the flash from his belt and under its bright light he could see where other stones had
been rammed in to close an opening once much larger.
Those stones were no longer so well bedded, they could be
worked out with a little effort.

He began to pick and pull, laying the flashlight on a
projection of the wall to give him light. The barrier
needed only a little loosening. He would crawl out to
prove that and then wall it up more securely.

Nick thrust with his shoulders, kicked and wriggled.
Then he was out. It was only in that moment when he had
achieved his purpose that he became aware of more than
the action that had absorbed him. Crouched, his hands on
the ground, his back hunched, he looked down the slope.

A cloud shielded the brilliance of the sun. But it could
not dim the splash of color there. As he slowly rose to his
feet, Nick saw he had his perhaps dangerous wish. It was
the Herald.

◆ 10 ◆

Nick's first impulse was to dodge back into the cave. But it was already too late for that. He knew the Herald had sighted him. And he did not want to reveal even more this back door to the cave. Nick moved farther into the open to face the alien.

To his eyes this was the same Herald he had seen riding over the ridge to the city. The man (if man he really was) matched him in height, though his body was more slender than Nick's. His green breeches and undercoat were dulled by the brilliance of the stiff tabard with its wealth of color and glittering embroidery.

The tabard was divided into four quarters, each of which bore a different intricate device. Over each shoulder was a small half-cape with the same designs repeated in miniature. His four-pointed cap, beneath which his hair was so sleeked against his head as to appear painted on his skull, was stiffened by a band of gold like a small crown circlet.

His face was expressionless, impassive, and his skin very white so that the bracketing of moustaches about his mouth might have been drawn in ink. He did not move at once, but before Nick was more than three or four strides from the hole he was on his way to meet him, his walk an effortless glide.

Thus they came face to face with only an arm's length between them. And in all that time the Herald kept silent, nor did his set, smooth expression change. When he did speak it was startling, as if a painted puppet had been given a voice.

"I am Avalon."

There was a pause that he did not break. Nick gathered it was his turn for self-introduction.

"I am Nicholas Shaw." He stated his name formally, sensing the occasion demanded that.

107

The Herald made a slight inclination with his head.

"To that which is of Avalon, and of Tara, of Brocéliande, of Carnac, may you be welcome, Nicholas Shaw, if it be of your own will and choice that this be so."

So, this was it, the stating of the bargain. Nick thought furiously—he must stall, try to learn all he could without giving a quick denial. But to play such a game with this stranger would, he was sure, be very difficult.

"This is not a land to make one welcome." He sought for words that might in return bring some of the answers he wanted. "I have seen things here that are dangers past my own world's knowing." Even as he spoke he felt a faint surprise at his choice of words. It was as if he tried to speak a foreign language, yet they were of his own tongue, merely ones he would not naturally have selected.

"This is a land of strangers. Those who accept the land will find that it accepts them, and there are, then, not the perils you have seen."

"And the manner of this acceptance?"

Avalon slipped his hand beneath the stiff front of his tabard. He withdrew it, holding a small box, which he snapped open. The box was round, and nested in it was a single fruit, a golden apple, gold that is for the most part, but with a beginning blush of red on one side. From it, or the box that cradled it, came an aroma to entice the sense of smell, as it also enticed the eyes.

"Of this you eat, for it is of Avalon. Thus Avalon enters into you and you are a part of it, even as it is a part of you. Having so taken Avalon, you are a freeman of all it has to offer."

"I have been told"—Nick was cautious but hopeful of perhaps gaining a shred of answer—that if one does this thing, becomes of Avalon, one is then apart from one's past, no longer the person one was before—"

Still the Herald's expression did not alter. "One makes choices, and each choice changes one a little. This is the way of life, one cannot avoid it. If you fear what Avalon has to offer, then you make one choice, and by that you must abide. There are those who will not become a part of the land, thereby the land rejects them, and they shall have no good of it, nor any peace."

"There is peace then in Avalon?" Nick tried to get disbelief into his tone. "What I have seen here suggests that is not so. I have watched men entrapped by others, I have seen wanderers who cannot claim any portion of this world for home."

"It was their choice to reject Avalon, therefore Avalon rejects them. They remain rootless, shelterless. And the day approaches when they shall find that, without roots, shelter, they are utterly lost."

"Those truly of Avalon will turn against them?" Nick demanded. Was what he had just heard a threat or a warning?

"There is no need. Avalon is no man's enemy. It is a place of peace and safety. But if one remains without, then comes darkness and ill. This has happened before, the evil lapping at the land. Where it meets Avalon and Tara, Brocéliande and Carnac, then it laps against walls it cannot overflow. But for those without those walls there is peril beyond reckoning. Alternately that evil flows and ebbs. This is a time of the beginning of the flow."

"Is it this evil that brings such as me into Avalon in the first place?"

"Such questions are not for my answering, stranger. Accept of Avalon and you will understand."

"I cannot decide right now—" Nick fenced.

Again the Herald inclined his head. "That is understood, for your race are not of controlled thought. Clear decisions come hard for you. I shall see you again."

He closed the box, put it once more under his tabard, and turned from Nick, gliding away at such a pace Nick could not have matched unless he broke into a jog. But he was determined to follow, at least a little way. The Herald was not mounted, surely Nick could trail him—

With only that idea in mind Nick pushed through bushes, trying to keep in sight the blaze of that tabard. Meanwhile he thought about what Avalon had said. Apparently he called himself by the name of the land as if he were its official spokesman, identifying himself wholly with it. And had he threatened, or merely stated, that some great danger lay ahead for all those who were not protected by the People?

The mass migration of the drifters gave part proof. And what Nick had witnessed of the attacks from the saucers underlined the safety of the Herald and his city. On the other hand there was the manifest horror of his offer that the English displayed, though their reasons still seemed vague to Nick.

It was all—

Nick halted. The blaze of color had also stopped. Nick ducked into a bush. There was someone rising out of similar cover to confront the Herald, holding on high a pole topped with a cross of dull metal.

"Demon!" The figure used the cross-pole as a club, seeking to bring it down on the Herald's head. But Avalon was not there to take the force of that blow. Instead his body was well to one side. Again that wild figure, wearing a tattered and mud-bespattered brown robe, with gray hair matted about his head and a beard of the same on his jaw, tried to do battle. This time the Herald vanished from sight.

"Stay!"

From behind Nick came a gust of foul odor, with a sharp prick in his mid-back to reinforce the order. A moment later the same voice called, in a thick gabble he could not understand, some summons.

The Herald's would-be assailant was still moving about where Avalon had last disappeared, ramming the cross-pole into bushes, crying out in a high voice words Nick could not translate. His attitude was one of rage fed by bafflement.

At a second hail from behind Nick, he finally stopped beating the bushes and came toward the American in a lopsided gait that still let him cover the ground with speed.

His dress, Nick saw, as he came to a stop, leaning on the pole of his cross, was that of a monk. And the eyes in his grimy face were the burning ones of a fanatic.

"Up!" Pain in Nick's back. The American got to his feet, raging both at the man behind him and at himself for being so blind as to be so easily captured.

The monk thrust his face close to Nick's. His breath was foul and the rank odor of his body and ancient clothing was enough to sicken the captive. The fierce eyes swept up and down Nick.

"Demon!" He raised the cross and Nick thought it was about to thud home on his skull. He ducked and was rewarded by a cuff on the side of his head that sent him sprawling to his knees, his head ringing, half-dazed.

They gabbled over him, his captor and the monk. Hands caught and held him, one twisted in his hair so that he could not move his head. Again the cross loomed over him. And this time it was lowered so that its tip bit painfully into the skin on his forehead. The monk held it so for a long moment and then snatched it away, bending close to Nick to survey the result of that contact.

He grunted as if displeased, then gave some order to the other. Nick was pulled to his feet, his hands twisted behind him and secured there by a cord, which cut into his flesh. Then his hitherto-unseen captor came around to face the monk.

Though in build he was much like Stroud, he was far removed otherwise from the Warden in appearance. His face was largely covered with a greasy mat of beard, which climbed so high on his cheekbones that it was nearly entangled with brows as full and shaggy. On his head was a metal helmet, dented, rust streaked, which sprouted a piece to hide his nose. The rest of his clothing was in keeping, rusty mail over leather so old and filthy that it was near black. His slightly bowed legs were covered with tight-fitting, but hole-filled hose, and boots that were close to complete disintegration.

But he was armed. A sword was belted on, and a dagger nearly as long as Nick's forearm balanced that. Over his shoulder arose the curve of a crossbow. He had drawn the dagger and leered at Nick as he set it with the point aimed at the American's throat.

The monk shook his head with the jerky violence that characterized all his movements and spat some order. The other grinned, his mouth a broken-toothed gap in that noisome brush of beard. Seizing Nick by his shoulder, he gave him a shove after the monk who hobbled on, his cross-pole upheld as if it were both a banner and a threat.

That he had fallen into the hands of a drifter band was plain. Nick, shaken by his own folly in allowing himself to be caught, could not yet think straight. He doubted more strongly every minute that these people could in any way be appealed to as fellow refugees. The soldier, if soldier were his occupation, who kept him going with bruising slaps and punches, exuded such brutality as Nick had never before encountered. And the monk's attitude was, to his mind, no better.

They came into an open space by a small stream to meet the rest of this company. There were three more of the soldiers, as like his original captor as if they were all brothers. But the authority was not theirs. Rather it seemed divided between the monk and another who sat

with her back against a rock. She was tearing at a piece
of half-cooked meat from a supply speared on sticks and
set to roast at the edge of a fire.

Grease glistened on her chin, dripped to the front of the
laced bodice of her gown where it joined and reinforced
the stiffened evidence of many other such meals. Her skin
was gray with ancient grime, her hair braids lusterless
with neglect. But her features were those which, had she
been clean and well-cared for, might have made her a
beauty even in Nick's world. And her foully used dress
was patterned with what once had been fine embroidery,
just as her girdle and the rings she wore on each finger
and thumb were bejeweled. There was a gold circlet on
her head with a setting of a dull blue gem above her forehead. She was like some princess out of a fairy-book illus-
tration completely degraded.

At the sight of Nick she threw away the bone she
gnawed. Sitting up straighter, she pointed to him imperiously and uttered some command he could not understand.
Yet there were word sounds in it that were familiar. When
he did not answer, his captor cuffed him again.

But the monk waved the soldier away, voiced a furious
objection. The vicious amusement that had come into the
woman's face at her underling's correction of their
prisoner dulled with disappointment. She shrugged and
gestured. One of the other men hastened to uproot another spit of meat and take it to her.

However, the monk planted himself directly before
Nick and spoke slowly, spacing a breath between each
word. It was all incomprehensible and Nick shook his
head. Now his captor advanced again. He addressed the
monk with grudging respect, then he turned to Nick.

"Who—you?" The accent was very guttural but the
question made sense.

"Nicholas Shaw—and you are?"

The soldier grinned evilly. "Not matter. You demon
spawn." He spat. "We keep—demons see—They give us
sword—we give *you* sword!"

Now the monk broke into speech again, plainly demanding some response from the soldier. The woman, licking
her fingers, interrupted. At her words the four soldiers
laughed heartily. But the monk whirled to face her, waving his pole. She continued to smile but remained silent

under his spate of speech. However, the soldiers stopped
laughing.

Nick was jerked over to a convenient tree, his back
planted against its trunk and a length of twisted hide rope
used to anchor him securely. The monk surveyed the oper-
ation with approval and satisfaction. Then Nick was left
to his own devices and his thoughts, while the rest tramped
back to squat by the fire and eat.

The smell of the meat made him hungry. The stew
Linda had given him now seemed very far in the past. But
he was even more thirsty than hungry, and to see the rip-
ple of water beyond was an aggravation that increased as
the afternoon passed.

It would seem that this party was in no haste to travel
on. One of the soldiers (or, Nick decided, they might better be termed "men-at-arms" since their shabby trappings
were certainly more akin to that time labeled "Middle
Ages" than his own) went behind a screen of bushes to return leading a heavy-footed, uncurried horse, its ribs too
plain beneath its hide, and a mule with one lop ear. These
he guided down to the water and let drink, before herding
them back into the bushes again.

The monk stretched out on the ground well away from
the fire as the heat of the afternoon increased. His hands
were crossed on his breast, under them the pole of his
strange weapon. The men-at-arms, drawing away from
their betters, did the same, though they took turns on
guard, prowling in and out of the bushes.

Having finished her meal, the woman wiped her hands
on a tuft of grass, the first gesture toward cleanliness Nick
had seen her make. She went to the brook, drank from
her cupped hands, wiped them this time on her skirt. She
stood, eyeing the sleeping monk and the soldiers. Then she
gave a quick glance at Nick before returning to her rock-
backed seat.

But she did not settle to rest. Instead she lounged at
ease, playing with one of her long braids, humming. Now
and again she glanced at Nick meaningly, as he was fully
aware.

As he had felt the brutality of the men-at-arms, the raw
fanaticism of the monk, so the evil that was in her was
like a scent, rank and horrible. Nick's reaction to this
party he could not understand. Never before had he had
such an aversion to any person or persons, the sensation

that he knew their feelings. It was like his comprehension that Jeremiah could understand him, a heightened power of which he had never before been aware. And this added to his fear.

That he was in a very bad situation there was no denying. They would slit his throat with ease and needed no urging to it. In fact he would swear the woman would relish it. He could gather only one idea—that he was to be kept as a bargaining point with those they called "demons." And since the monk had screamed that at the Herald, it was the People with whom they intended to bargain, to so threaten by their usage of Nick. The thought was freezing. For what would the People care if he were murdered here? He had refused the Herald's offer—or at least delayed answer to it—so he was no concern of Avalon's. The terms had been made plain to him: Avalon defended its own, the rest could meet the fate they had chosen.

Now Nick wished he had answered differently. It seemed to him that the Vicar's talk of changing, of the wrongness of that choice, was as nothing compared to being in these hands. Yet—there was in him a stubbornness of which he was aware—he would not be forced to a choice he did not freely give.

This whole venture had begun because he had wanted to get away, to be himself without outside pressures, without interference. Yet he had met with nothing but that. He had been swung by duty into guiding Linda. After their meeting with the English party they had to conform to their type of existence, simply because he was not informed enough to take risks—

The monk was snoring, but his small snorts were nearly drowned out by the deeper chorus from the men-at-arms. Their comrade on guard duty came into view and the woman beckoned to him, gave an order. He touched his rusty helmet with a forefinger and went off in the direction of the animals. She watched him go, then arose and went to the stream.

Cupping her hands she dipped up as much of the water as she could, and came, swift-footed, with dripping fingers, to Nick.

"*Aqua*—" she held it out just a little beyond his reach. Latin! She had spoken Latin!

Her hands moved closer. His thirst was torment now

that the water was here. But he did not trust her in the least. He did not believe that she had a sense of compassion. This was a game she wanted to play.

The moisture dripped on his shirt, he could dip his head and drink. But something in him said "no," and he heeded it.

Her smile pinched into nothingness. She flung what remained into his face. Then she went back to her rock, to return as swiftly with a small whip, its stock tarnished but set with rough-cut stones. Raising it she struck him across the face, the lash as sharp as a knife stab, leaving a hot line of pain behind.

Now she laughed, for in spite of his control Nick had gasped, and stood flicking the lash back and forth, watching him to see if he understood the threat of that. But if she planned other mischief she was again defeated by the monk.

He had sat up, now he gave voice to what could only be a roar of rage. One so vehemently expressed that it brought the men-at-arms awake and their hands to their weapons, pulled their fellow back through the bushes at a run to join them.

The woman stood her ground, waiting for a lull in the monk's shouts. Then she replied with a matching sharpness. But she left Nick. Apparently the monk's wishes still ruled. Nick only wished fervently he knew what those were.

As the shadows of evening drew in he thought of the cave. They must have missed him by now, but even if they found his exit they would have no idea of where he had gone. And for their own sakes they would not venture into the open without a guide. He knew he could not hope for any chance of rescue.

He had been trying at intervals to loosen the ties about his wrists. But they were past dealing with. His hands were numb, and the lack of feeling was spreading up his arms. The support of the tree trunk against which he had been lashed kept him upright, but his feet were also numb. And he was not sure he could move with any speed even if he were now, by some miracle, set free.

With the coming of twilight the men-at-arms were busied. They had had one fire during the day. Now they were bringing wood, making a second some distance away. The monk labored with some lengths of dried branches he had chosen with care. He chipped away with his belt knife, used twists of grass in a way to suggest that he had done this many times before, and fashioned some more crosses of wood.

These in hand, he approached the tree and Nick and proceeded to set them in the ground, as if by doing so he erected a barrier about the captive. As he worked he muttered, and Nick thought that he recognized now and then a Latin word. Having set up the crosses the monk methodically paced along that line, touching each with the metal of the one on the pole, chanting aloud as he went. Behind him the others drew together and their voices were raised now and then in response to the ceremony he was performing.

They then lit the second fire, which gave a light that grew as the darkness increased. The horse and the mule were brought out, once more watered, and then tethered between the fires, while their guardian hung about their bony necks cords with bits of broken metal fastened to them. Into the light between the fires moved the whole company. The men-at-arms drew their daggers, kept them in their hands as if they settled in to await a siege. But the monk thrust the pole of his cross into the ground and stood not too far from Nick.

Their whole attitude was one of expectancy, and Nick found himself listening, though for what he could not imagine. From time to time the monk muttered, those between the fires shifted, or showed other signs of fatigue, but they lost none of their vigilance.

Nick became aware slowly of a foulness like the odor that wafted to him from the members of this camp. Only this was not a foulness born of the body, but rather of the spirit. That was another sensation he had never known, yet was able to recognize it for what it was. Just as the farmhouse wherein they had sheltered had been a haven of good, so did that which was closing in now advertise its threatening evil.

And the others must have expected its coming. It was not of Avalon, Nick was as sure of that as if the fact had been shouted aloud.

Dank, heavy, a cloud of corruption—Then Nick heard the rasp of something ponderously heavy moving through the brush—a panting breath.

Those in the firelight raised their hands—the iron they

held there visible. While the monk freed his cross-pole from the ground and made ready to use it, as he had tried to club the Herald.

Closer—Nick saw a bush quiver to his left. He turned his head to face what might issue from there. In the midst of the branches was a head. He made himself eye it, though fear battled his control and he shivered.

Gray white, bestial, twisted—it was obscene, the epitome of every night terror. It leered, showed fangs, was gone. A serpent, or something with a serpent's body, writhed out from another direction. It had a serpent's body, but the head was that of a woman. And, as the thing came, it called in a hissing voice words that those in the firelight must have understood, for with a cry of horror and hate one of the men-at-arms plunged forward, aiming at the creature with his knife. It sliced into the body behind the smiling head.

But there was no wound and the man cowered back, with a crowing sound, his knife forgotten, his hands before his eyes, huddling in upon himself, while the serpent woman coiled and reared—until the monk lashed out with his pole and she vanished utterly.

That was only the beginning of the siege.

There were monsters pacing on all fours, others humanoid
in shape. They leered, hissed, spat, called, menaced, only
to slip back into the shadows and let others come. So far
none of this hideous crew attacked the firelit party. But
their very appearance rasped the nerves, kept one tense.
And it was plain that the nerves of the party were already
badly worn, perhaps by earlier meetings with the same
threat.

When something with a goat's head but very human
body, save for a tail and hoofed feet, gamboled into the
light, prancing and beckoning to the men-at-arms, one of
them threw up his head and howled like a dog. The one
who had captured Nick rounded on his fellow and
knocked him flat. The man lay whimpering on the ground.
Goathead snickered, leaping in the air and clapping his
hoofs together.

The monk thrust out with the cross-pole and Goathead
uttered a thin scream, staggered back as if in that lay dire
threat. But there shot up in his place another with a human body that glowed with golden radiance, having white
wings stirring from the shoulder blades. Mounted on the
broad shoulders was the head of an owl. Its left hand lay
loosely on the back of a wolf as large as a horse.

"Andras!" The monk appeared to recognize this appari-
tion. "Demon!" Again he struck out with his weapon.

But this time his attack was not so efficient, for the owl
beak in the feathered visage uttered a sound. The noise
swelled higher and deeper, filling the night, one's head—
Nick flinched from the pain as that cry went on and on.

The agony grew worse, until he was aware of nothing
save that. And he must have been close to losing con-
sciousness when he saw, dimly, that those between the
fires had dropped their weapons, even the monk his cross-
pole. They were holding their hands to their ears, their

faces betraying their torment, and they tottered to their feet and staggered forward.

Not to meet the owl-headed one, for he was gone. No, they wavered and stumbled into the bushes, drawn by some force they could not withstand. Men-at-arms; the woman, stumbling in her long, dragging skirt; last of all, the monk, his face a tormented mask wavering out into the haunted dark. Nick felt the force, too, and struggled against his bonds, the cords cutting deep into his flesh as he sought to obey the command of that screech.

He fought desperately. There was no respite from the pain unless he obeyed that summons—he must go! Yet he could not. And at last he slumped, exhausted, only the punishing cords keeping him on his feet.

His captors had disappeared. The bony horse and the dejected mule remained. And both animals were attempting to graze as if nothing had happened. His own head was free of the pain, though he could hear, fading away that torturing sound.

What would be the fate of those answering it? Nick did not know. But that any would return to free him, or kill him, he did not believe. He was dazed from the assault upon his ears, but he began to realize he was still trapped.

Bright in the firelight lay the daggers they had drawn for their protection. But they were as far from his use as if they had been in his own world.

It was then that he became aware of a sound overhead, and pushed his head back against the rough bark, striving to find an angle from which he could see what passed there. Was it a flying monster?

He caught only a fleeting glimpse. But he was sure he had not been mistaken. One of the saucers was swinging in the direction of the fugitives.

Was that sound intended to drive or pull those sheltered here into the open where they could be taken? Those monsters—the people seemed able to identify them, he remembered the monk had named the owl head—what had they to do with this? But such could be used to disarm and break down the nerves of selected victims.

But if the saucer people made their capture they would learn about him! Perhaps they already knew and believed him safely immobilized. He had to get loose!

At that moment Nick feared the saucer people more

than any monster he had seen lurking here tonight. For the monsters could be illusions, but the saucers were real.

Get free, but how? The daggers— He had no possible chance of reaching those any more than he had of summoning Stroud, Crocker or the Vicar. Or of seeing the Herald—

The Herald!

Nick's memory fastened on the picture of the Herald as he had seen him from the cave entrance. The brilliant tabard seemed to flicker before his eyes. Slowly his fear ebbed. The stench of evil that had come with the dark was gone. What Nick now felt against his sweating face was the clean breeze of the woods, with it a pleasant scent.

But the saucer! Freedom before its crew could come here! He was too spent now to struggle against the cords that only drew tighter as he fought. His hands and feet were alarmingly numb.

The Herald—In spite of his need to think of a way of escape Nick kept remembering—seeing Avalon.

"Avalon!"

What had moved him to call that name?

The horse nickered. It flung up its head, called, was answered by a bray from the mule. Both animals ceased to graze. They stood looking toward the tree where Nick was bound.

Then—*HE* was there!

Another illusion? If so it was very solid-seeming.

"Avalon?" Nick made of that a question. Would the Herald release him? Or, since Nick had not accepted the bargain, would he be left to whatever fate the saucer people had in mind?

"I am Avalon." Nick could hear that.

"Can you—will you free me?" Nick came directly to the point. Let the Herald say "yes" or "no" and get it over with.

"Each man must free himself. Freedom is offered, the choice is yours alone."

"But—I can't move—even to take that precious apple of yours, if I want to!"

As before the Herald's features were untouched by expression. There was a glow about him that did not come from the fires.

"There are three freedoms." Avalon did not produce the apple. "There is the freedom of body, there is the freedom of mind, there is the freedom of spirit. A man must have all three if he would be truly released from bondage."

Nick's anger rose. With time his enemy, he had no desire to waste it on philosophical discussion. "That does not get me free."

"Freedom lies in yourself," Avalon returned. "Even as it is within all living things—"

He turned a fraction then, his level gaze moving from Nick to the horse and mule. For a space as long as several deep breaths he regarded the two animals. Then both of them moved their heads vigorously, certainly with more alertness than the half-starved beasts had displayed before.

They walked to the bushes and thrust their heads and necks into the foliage, turning, twisting with obviously intelligent purpose. Their motions snagged on branches the thongs about their necks that were hung with metal bits. Now each lowered its head and jerked back, so those cords were drawn off, left to swing there.

Freed they came directly to the Herald, lowering their heads before him. He reached out a hand but did not quite touch their halters. Those in turn fell away, giving them freedom from all man had laid upon them.

Yet they still stood and gazed at the Herald and he back at them, as if they communicated. At last the horse whinnied, the mule brayed. Together they turned and trotted off into the night.

"If you can free them," Nick said hotly, "you can do that for me."

"Freedom is yours, only you can provide it."

That there was some purpose in what he said more than just the desire to frustrate the captive, Nick now believed. The horse and the mule had had to rid themselves of "cold iron" that men had laid upon them. But all his struggles had only exhausted him. He could not free himself— that was impossible.

"How?" he asked.

There was no answer.

"You told the animals!" Nick accused.

Still the Herald was silent.

Freedom that only he himself could provide? Perhaps because he had not accepted Avalon's offer the Herald could or would not aid him more than in such oblique statements. Nick leaned his weight against the tree and tried to think. Undoubtedly there was a way. He did not believe that Avalon was tormenting him for some obscure reason. And if there was a way he must have the will, patience and intelligence to find it.

Futile struggles did not aid. He could not reach the daggers so tantalizingly within sight but not within reach. So—what remained?

Freedom of body he did not have. Freedom of mind, freedom of spirit—could he use either? Telepathy—precognition—there were powers of the mind—paranormal powers. But those were talents few possessed and he was not one of them.

The daggers—within his sight—freedom of mind—

Avalon waited. There was nothing to be gained from him, Nick was sure. What he had to do was wholly by his own will and strength.

The daggers—a use for them—

Nick stared with all the concentration he could summon at the nearest blade, the slender one the woman had dropped. Knife—cord—one meeting the other with freedom to follow.

Knife—cord— He must shut out of his mind all else but that slender, shining blade, red with the light of the now dying fire, the thought of the cord about him. Knife—cord—

Sweat trickled down Nick's face. He felt strange, as if part of him struggled to be free from his body. A part of him—like a hand—reaching for freedom. If he could not move the knife with his desire—what of his hand?

Nick changed tactics. A hand—an arm—free—reaching into the firelight. His body obeyed his mind in some things, would it now? Something was forming, thin, misty—touching the knife. So iron did not prevent this! Nick concentrated. A hand, five fingers—fingers and thumb to close about the haft. That grayish thing was there—clasped about the hilt.

There was the hand, but a hand must be joined to an arm or it was useless. An arm—he set himself to visualize a wrist, an arm. Once more there was the gathering of foggy material. It joined the hand, yet it also reached back to him.

Now!

He had never in his life centered on any act the intense will he now summoned. The long, long "arm" of mist began to draw back toward him. He must hold it—he must!

Nick's breath came in gasps. Back, draw back—he must bring the knife!

The blade was out of the firelight now, trailing across the ground in little jumps as if his energy ebbed and flowed. But it was coming! Nick knew no triumph, only the need to hold and draw.

Now the knife lay at his feet, misty hand, elongated arm collapsed, faintly luminous, coiled like a slackened rope. Nick was so tired—fatigue of a kind he had never before experienced hung upon him like a black cloak. If he let it get to him he was lost.

The knife must come up! The coiled substance thickened, loops melted into a stouter, more visible column with the hand at the top, the knife in it. Up! Nick's whole force of being centered to his desire.

By jerks the blade arose. Its point pricked his knee. He brought it higher to the first twist of cord. Cut! He gave the order—cut!

It moved slowly, too slowly. He almost panicked, and then firmed his control. Slow it was, but it moved—

Cut!

Feebly the blade sawed back and forth across the tough hide. If only the edge was sharp enough! Do not think of that—think of nothing but the action—cut—cut—cut!

A loop of hide fell at his feet. The column of mist collapsed, the dagger falling with it to the ground. Nick writhed furiously with all the strength he had left. His bonds fell away and he toppled over, to fall headlong, spent and breathless.

He turned his head to look for Avalon. But the Herald was gone. Nick lay alone between the dying fires, one of the wooden crosses standing in crooked silhouette between him and the limited light. He was free of the tree, but his hands were still tied and his feet numb, his body exhausted.

His hands—he must free his hands. There was the knife. Nick lay watching it. Once more he tried to create the hand. But the power, whatever power had worked in him to produce that, was gone. If he would help himself now he must do it by physical means.

Weakly he rolled over, hunched along until he could feel the blade. Wedge it somehow—but his hands were numb. Wedge it! Scrabbling in the leaf mold he dug the haft with the weight of his body into the ground. There was a stone, move that— Patiently he worked until he thought the blade secure. Up and down, Nick moved his wrists, not even sure the blade bit the cords.

He was not certain until his arms fell to his sides and the torture of returning circulation began. Then he pulled himself up onto his feet. He leaned against the tree that had been his place of bondage. The knife on the ground—iron. Stiffly, steadying himself with one swollen hand against the tree, Nick stooped to pick it up. Though the effort of putting his fingers around the hilt was almost too much, he managed to thrust the dagger into his belt.

Once more the danger of attack gripped him. He used the tree as a support, slipping around it, away from the fire. But his feet stumbled, he felt as if he could not walk. The bushes—if he could roll into, or under those—

Nick tottered forward. Ahead, only half to be seen in the gloom, was a thicker growth. He went to his knees, then lower, pushing, edging under that hope of shelter until he could fight no longer, his last atom of energy expended.

It was not real sleep that overcame him then, rather an exhaustion of body so great he could not lift his hand an inch from where it lay beside him. He was held in a vise of extreme fatigue but his mind was clear.

He could not yet understand what he had done. The mechanics of it, yes. He had brought the knife and freed himself. But how had he been able to accomplish that?

There were natural laws. He had been taught in his own world to believe what he had just done was impossible. But here those laws did not seem to hold. The Herald had spoken of three freedoms. This night Nick had used one to achieve a second in a way he would have sworn could not be done.

Nick closed his eyes. Do not think now—stop wondering, speculating. Close off memory. He needed release, not to think, concentrate, act—

A lulling, a slow healing— The evil that had been so thick was gone. The earth under him hollowed a little to receive his aching body, cradled him. Twigs and leaves brushed his upturned face, their clean scent in his nostrils. He was one with the ground, the bush—He was safe—secure—held— The sleep that came to him was dreamless.

He did not waken all at once as when one is shaken out of slumber by alarm. Recognition of reality was slow, gentle, sleep leaving him bit by bit. He could hear faint twitterings, rustlings—

Nick opened his eyes. There were leaves about him, very close above him, the tips of some brushed his face gently. He began to remember the how and why of his coming here. There was daylight around.

His body ached, he was stiff and sore, and there were rings of fire about his wrists, yet he felt wonderful, renewed, as if his body's hurts did not matter. And he was content not to stir as yet.

This was not the feeling of peace and security that had existed in the deserted farmhouse. It was alien, but it was friendly, as if he had been allowed a step inside a door that gave upon a new and different life.

Hunger and thirst awoke, flogging him into movement. Nick crawled laboriously out from his refuge. His hands were still puffed and the weals about his wrists raw. The stream must lie in that direction.

On his feet he lurched forward. There were the burned-out fires, two of the daggers, the cross-pole, now sun-bathed in the open. Nick passed the rock where the woman had sat, fell on his knees beside the water. Then he lay prone, to duck his face, lap at the moisture, dangle his hands and wrists in the chill water that stung his hurts. This roused him from his drowsy contentment.

By the strength of the sun he thought it must be close to midday. Could he find his way back to the cave? And had they come hunting him? Were the saucers out?

Gazing around Nick could see no evidence that the campsite had been visited after its people had been drawn away. He gathered up the other daggers, but left the cross-pole where it lay. Then he turned slowly, trying to guess the direction from which he had come, only to be baffled.

Trees would provide shelter from any hunting saucer, but woods also had strange inhabitants. He could follow the stream as a guide—but a guide to where? As far as he knew there was no such body of water running near the cave. And he was hungry—

The thought of possible fish in the stream was the factor in making his decision to travel along it. Though how he was going to catch any water dweller he had no idea. However, a short distance farther up he found berry bushes well loaded with fruit.

Birds whirred away at his coming, but settled again to their own harvesting. Nick pulled greedy handfuls of the well-ripened globes and stuffed his mouth, the dark juice staining his hands. Blackberries, he decided, and a growth of them that was very heavy. He rounded a bush, picking and eating avidly, and heard a snuffle. Farther along in this wealth of good eating a large brown furred shape was busy. Nick ducked back and away. The bear, if bear it *had* been, was fully occupied. Nick would keep to this side and let the woods dweller have that.

But in his sudden evasion he was startled by a sharp cry and jumped back. Fronting him, anger and alarm made plain was—

Nick blinked as the creature flashed away, was gone behind a tall clump of grass. He made no move to follow, he was not even sure he wanted to see more of what had been there.

Only, to prove that he had seen it, there still lay before him a basket. Nick reached down to pick it up. He could just get two fingers through its handle and it was very beautifully woven of two kinds of dried grass.

The berries that had fallen out of it Nick carefully returned. In addition he added enough more to fill it. And he looked toward the grass tuft as he set the basket back on the ground—in full sight, he hoped, of its indignant owner.

"I am very sorry." He kept his voice hardly above a whisper, remembering the bear.

Then, resolutely not looking back to see whether the harvester ventured out of hiding, Nick went on. His amazement had faded. The Vicar had spoken of legends come true here. And there had always been stories of the true "little people"—elves, gnomes, dwarfs—but the latter were supposed to live underground and mine for treasures, were they not?

Nick no longer doubted that he had seen a very small man, or a creature of humanoid appearance, dressed in a mottled green brown that would be camouflage in the forest. And surely that manikin was no stranger than anything else he had sighted here.

Dwarfs, elves—Nick wished he knew more. One should have a good founding in the old fairy lore before venturing into this world. Was Hadlett right in his contention that the People had somehow been able to go through the other way in the past, perhaps even been exiled in Nick's world, thus providing the seed from which the fairy tales had grown? Some of the legendary ones had been friendly, Nick remembered that. But there had been others—the black witches, giants, ogres, dragons—

The berries no longer tasted so sweet. He left the patch behind and forged ahead along the stream. But now he kept a sharp watch on the ground before him, as well as on the bushes. What was spying on him? Nick meant no harm, but would they understand that? And there might be drifters wandering here, such a vicious company as he had just escaped. Those would be enemies to the People he was certain, and could the People in turn tell the difference between a drifter of good will and one to be feared?

He hoped that they all had protection like the Herald's. His sympathy for the manikin and his kind was strong. The Herald—Where had Avalon gone last night? And why had he left Nick? Though he had given the American the advice that meant freedom, he had left. Did Nick now have knowledge his own companions could use in their defense?

Nick turned slowly, trying to sight something that he could use as a guide. He wanted to get back to the cave, to tell his story. And they must believe him! Surely, having faced all the improbabilities current here, what he had to say would not seem a complete impossibility.

He thought his way led left. And the woods seemed less dense in that direction. If he struck through there—resolutely he moved forward.

There were some more straggling berry bushes and he ate as he went, snatching at the fruit. But under the trees the bushes vanished and he hurried, trying to rid himself of the belief that he was watched, almost expecting to have some forester with an escort of outlandish animals confront him. But if Nick were paced by unseen company, they were content to let him go. And he chanced upon a path, marked here and there with deer prints, which ran in the direction he wished. So, turning into that, he made better time.

Nick came out on the edge of open country in midafternoon. He hesitated there, searching the sky for any sign of a saucer. Birds flew, a whole brilliant-colored flock of them, crying out as they went. They were large and their wheeling, dipping flight formed a loose circle out over the plain.

It was as if they were flying around and around some object. Prudently Nick took cover and continued to watch. The sun was bright but he could see nothing—

Or could he? Was something there, rising skyward like the towers of the wondrous city? But it was of such transparency that it was virtually invisible— The longer Nick watched the birds the more convinced he was that this was so.

Then the flock, which had been circling, formed a line and descended earthward, disappearing one by one as if winked out of existence when it reached the point where Nick was sure something did stand.

He rubbed his hand across his eyes. It was—it was becoming more and more visible. Towers—like the city—but smaller, fewer of them. Before his eyes they took on an opaque quality, gained substance. What he now saw was a towered, walled structure resembling a medieval castle.

⬧ 12 ⬧

To all appearances the castle was now completely solid, but lacking in the coloring of the city. No rainbow lights played along its walls, climbed the towers, glowed into the sky. It was gray white as if erected from native stone.

Though the birds did not reappear there was movement. A portion of the wall facing his hiding place descended slowly to form a drawbridge, as if the castle were surrounded by a moat. Over that rode a brightly clad party.

There was plainly a Herald as leader. Nick could recognize the tabard at a glance. Behind him were four others, riding the sky-mounting steeds, two by two. These wore tabards of the same cut as their leader but of forest green. And only a single emblem, which Nick could not distinguish at this distance, was on the breast of each.

They rode easily at what seemed a slow amble but which covered the ground with a deceptive speed so that they swiftly drew close to Nick. He did not now try to conceal his presence, sure he was in no danger. And he wanted to learn all he could of this company and their visible-invisible castle.

But the Herald and his party had no interest in Nick. They rode with their eyes forward, nor did they speak among themselves. There was no expression on their faces. But as they approached, Nick saw two had hair that brushed their shoulders and one of them was Rita. Their riding partners were not quite like the Herald but might have once been as human as the English girl.

Now that they were closer Nick could make out the designs embroidered in gold and silver glitter on their tabards. Each was the branch of a tree. The first male had what was unmistakably oak—leaves and golden acorns carefully depicted. With him was Rita with her apple branch. The next couple sported patterns Nick did not know, both depicted in flowers of silver white.

Their passage was noiseless since the paws of their steeds made no sound. And they might have been caught in a dream with their sight fixed ahead.

Nick first thought to force a meeting. But their aloofness was such as to awe him to remaining still and silent to watch them go.

Just before they reached the woods their long-legged beasts began to mount into the air. As if that provided a signal there came wheeling from aloft a pair of birds, white winged, huge. Twice these circled the riders, then forged ahead of them.

Nick watched them out of sight. Then he turned to look at the castle. He had half-expected it to fade from sight. But it was more solid-seeming in the twilight than before. Only the gap of the drawbridge had disappeared.

Curiosity worked in him. Enough to draw him to that structure? Nick hunkered down, his full attention on it. Was it real, or wasn't it? After his own experience he could not accept anything here without proof. Should he put it to the proof?

"Nicholas!"

The sharp whisper broke the spell. His hand was on the hilt of the dagger in his belt as his head jerked to the bush from which the sound had come.

"Who is it?" Nick had the blade out, ready, though never in his life had he used a weapon against another.

Cautiously a branch swung up and he saw the Vicar's face screened in the greenery. Nick pushed the weapon back with relief. He slid around his own cover and in a minute was confronting both Hadlett and Crocker.

"How did you find me?"

"Where have you been?"

The questions mingled together, Crocker's the sharper, with anger in it.

But the Vicar's hand closed about Nick's upper arm in a reassuring squeeze.

"How fortunate, my boy. You are safe!"

"Now," Nick returned. "If anyone can be safe here." It was growing darker with a speed he had not expected. A glance upward showed a massing of clouds. And in the distance was the lash of lightning fire, a distant rumble of thunder.

"What happened?" Crocker repeated his demand aggressively.

"I was caught—by some drifters—" Nick edited his adventures. With the Vicar he would be more explicit, but his past contacts with the pilot had not been such as to provoke confidences. He had not accepted the Herald's bargain, but he was just as sure that he was not the same person he had been in his own world. And if the English looked upon change as a threat and a reason to outlaw one of their own, there was no need to hand Crocker a good excuse to get rid of him.

There was a second deep growl of thunder, this time closer.

"It would be better to seek shelter," Hadlett said. "The storm is near."

"Over there?" Crocker pointed to the castle. Though it did not reflect light from its walls, there were sparks here and there along the towers as if lamps hung behind windows.

Nick wondered if the others had seen the castle materializing from thin air. Much as his curiosity was aroused, he was not drawn to this as he had been to the city.

"We can, I believe, reach a hollow I know before the rain comes." Hadlett ignored Crocker's question. "Providing we start now."

It was he, not the pilot, who led the way through the brush, edging west along the line of the forest. But the first of the rain hit with great drumming drops before they came to his hollow.

One of the giant trees had fallen long since and its upturned root mass had in turn been overgrown with vegetation. The curtain of this could be pulled aside to give on a sheltered place into which the three could crowd, though they must rub shoulders to do so.

A certain amount of seepage from the storm still reached them, but they were under cover. And they had no more than settled in before Crocker was back with his question.

"So you were caught—by whom?"

Nick obliged with a description of the band. Once or twice the Vicar interrupted him with a desire that he expand some portion of his story, namely when he spoke of the monk. But when Nick described the monsters that had held the camp in siege, he felt Crocker stir.

"Snake with a woman's head? Thing with an owl head? Do you expect us to—"

"Lamia—and Andras," the Vicar said.

"A what and who?" Crocker sounded belligerent.

"A lamia—a snake demon—well known in ancient church mythology. And Andras—"

It was Nick's turn to interrupt. "That *was* what the monk called him—or at least it sounded like that!"

"Andras, Grand Marquis of Hell. He teaches those he favors to kill their enemies, masters and servant. In the army of the damned he commands thirty legions." It was as if the Vicar read an official report.

"But you don't believe in—" Again Crocker began a protest.

"*I* do not, nor you, Barry. But if one did believe in a lamia come to crush one's soul with its snake body, or in Andras, Marquis of Hell, then what better place for such to appear in threat?"

Nick caught the suggestion. "You mean—the nightmares one believes in, those have existence here?"

"I have come to think so. And if that *is* true, the opposite ought to exist—that the powers of good one holds to will also make themselves manifest. But it is easier for a man to accept evil as real than it is for him to believe in pure good. That is the curse we carry with us to our undoing. To those poor wretches this is Hell but they have made it for themselves."

"They were evil." Nick used an expression that would not have come easily to him in his own world. "You didn't see them. That woman—she was—well, you might call her a she-devil. And the monk was a fanatic, he could burn heretics in holy satisfaction. The others—in our time they would be muggers—have their fun beating up people."

"Padre." Crocker might have been only half listening, more interested in his own thoughts. "If they thought they could see monsters and devils and did, do you mean we could think up such things, too?"

"It is very possible. But we come from a different age. Our devils are not born of the same superstition—they are not, as you might say, personal. Our evil is impersonal, though it is not the less for that. We no longer decry Satan and his works and emissaries. Rather we have the sins of nations, of wars, of industry, of fanatical causes. Impersonal devils, if you wish. We speak of 'they' who are responsible for this wrong and that. But 'they' seldom have a name, a body. Your monk was certain his devils had personalities, names, status, so they appeared to him in that fashion.

"We cannot summon our devils to plague us here because they lack such identity. There is and always has been great evil in our world, but its face and form changes with the centuries and it is no longer personified for us."

"What about Hitler?" Crocker challenged.

"Yes, in him our generation does have a devil. What of yours, Nicholas?"

"No one man, no one cause. It follows the pattern you spoke of, sir."

"This is all very interesting," Crocker cut in. "But how did you get away from that crowd? Did one of the devils cut you loose and then disappear in a puff of smoke?"

Nick was uneasy. This was getting close to what he hesitated to tell. One had to accept many improbabilities in this world, but would these two accept what had happened?

"Well?" Crocker's voice sharpened. "What *did* happen next?"

He was boxed into telling the truth, which meant bringing Avalon into it. And he had neglected to speak of his earlier confrontation with the Herald. That omission might make him suspect.

"You are troubled, Nicholas." The Vicar's tone was as soothing as Crocker's was a source of irritation. "Something has happened that you find difficult to explain."

Hadlett said that as if he knew it. And Nick believed that the Vicar would be aware of any evasion or slighting of the truth. He braced himself.

"It began earlier—" In a rush he told of his meeting with Avalon, afraid if he hesitated longer his courage would ebb.

"Repeat those names!" Hadlett's command brought him up short at a point which seemed to him to have little significance. But he obeyed.

"He said, 'Avalon, Tara, Brocéliande, Carnac.'"

"The great holy places of the Celtic world," Hadlett commented. "Places that are rumored even today to be pyschic centers of power. Though Avalon, of the four, has never been completely identified. In legend it lay to the west. Heralds bearing those names—yes, the proper pattern—"

"What pattern?" Crocker wanted to know.

"That of ancient heraldry. The heralds of Britain take their titles from the royal dukedoms—such as York, Lancaster, Richmond. The pursuivants derive theirs from the old royal badges. And the Kings-of-Arms, who command all, are from the provinces—Clarenceaux, Norroy, Ulster and the like. If Nicholas has the correct information, there must be four heralds here, each bearing the name of an ancient place of great power in our own world—perhaps once an entranceway to this. Tara lies in Ireland, Carnac and Brocéliande in Brittany—but all were of Celtic heritage. And it is from the Celtic beliefs that much of our legendary material about the People of the Hills and their ways have come. I wonder who is King-of-Arms here?"

"I don't see what that's got to do with us!" Crocker protested. "We all know what the Herald is and what he can do to anyone foolish enough to listen to him. You seem to have listened for quite a while, Shaw. What did he offer you—enough to make it interesting?"

Nick curbed his temper. He had expected the suspicion Crocker voiced.

"He offered me," he said deliberately, "a golden apple and the safety of this world. He foretold the coming of great danger; this has overrun the land periodically before, and is beginning such an attack again. According to him only those who accept Avalon will have any protection then."

"A golden apple," Hadlett mused. "Yes, once more symbolic."

"And deadly! Remember that, Padre—deadly!"

"Yes." But there was an odd note in the Vicar's voice.

"So you met this Avalon—then what happened? Did your men-at-arms grab him also?" Crocker brought Nick back to his story.

"They tried to, or to kill him—the monk did." He told of the fruitless assault with the cross-pole and the Herald's disappearance.

"So that was when they grabbed you. Now suppose you explain how you got away."

Nick went on to the sound that had been a torment and the disappearance of the drifters, the fact that he was left behind. He did not enlarge on his own fears, but continued with the return of the Herald, the scene with the horse and mule. Then, trying to pick those words that would carry the most emphasis, he told the rest of it.

They did not interrupt again but heard him out through his account of the rest of his wanderings until he had seen the castle materialize from the air and the emergence of the Herald and his four attendants.

It was then that the Vicar did question him, not as he had expected, concerning the actions he had been engaged in, or had witnessed, but about the designs embroidered on the green tabards of those who had accompanied Avalon.

"Oak and apple, and two with white or silver flowers," Hadlett repeated. "Oak and apple—those are very ancient symbols, ones of power. The other two—I wonder— But I would have to see them. Thorn? Elder? It is amazing—the old, old beliefs—"

"I find it amazing," Crocker said deliberately, "that you are still here, Shaw. You took the apple, didn't you?"

Nick had expected this accusation. But how could he prove it false?

"Do I show signs of the changes you mentioned, sir?" he asked the Vicar, not answering Crocker.

"Changes—what changes?" Hadlett asked absently.

"The changes supposed to occur in those who take the Herald's offer. I didn't. Do you want me to swear to that? Or have you some way of getting your proof? You have had more experience with this than I have. What happened to me back there—when I escaped—I cannot explain. The Herald told me about freedom, I just tried to use what I thought he meant. It worked, but I can't tell you how or why. But—I—did—not—take—the—apple—" He spaced the words of that last sentence well apart, repeated them with all the emphasis he could summon. Perhaps Crocker might not accept that, but he hoped Hadlett would.

"The changes," the Vicar repeated again. "Ah, yes, you refer to our former conversation."

To Nick he sounded irritatingly detached, as if this was not a problem that troubled him. But Nick believed he must have Hadlett on his side before he returned to the rest. Crocker's suspicions would, he was sure, be echoed by others there. Jean would support the pilot in any allegation he made. And Nick had no faith that Stroud would greet him warmly once Crocker had a chance to speak. But that the Vicar carried weight with all he was well

aware. Get Hadlett to stand by him and he would have
support to depend upon.

What he could do then, Nick had no idea. He did believe that the Herald spoke the truth when warning of
danger ahead. His own experience with the drifters and
their monsters, real or illusionary, as well as the threat of
the saucer people, argued in favor of investigating more
closely Avalon and its advantages. Safety, it seemed to
Nick, was what they must seek. He had no faith at all in
their plan to head down river. They did not even have
weapons to match those of the medieval group that had
captured him. Slingshots against swords!

"I believe you, Nicholas."

He almost started. That pause before Hadlett's answer
had been so prolonged Nick had come to expect the
worst.

"Also I believe that what you have learned during your
various encounters may be of future service to us all," the
Vicar continued. "I think we shall have to make the best
of this shelter until morning, but the sooner we return to
the cave and discuss your findings, the better."

Crocker muttered something in too low a whisper for
Nick to catch, even close wedged as they were. But he
was sure that the pilot was not in the least convinced.
Nick was, however, cheered. If he could depend upon the
Vicar's support he was assured of a hearing.

Outside, the storm was impressive, with an armament of
lightning, deafening rolls of thunder, and a curtain of rain.
They were damp, but the main pelting of the downpour
did not reach them.

Nick wondered about the Herald and his followers,
were they now riding the sky through this natural fury?
And the saucer people, how did storms affect their flyers?
The cave would be dry, and certainly the city a good shelter. The city—

His old half-plan of using the Herald to win a way into
the city and learn its secrets without surrendering to the
terms of Avalon— Could it be done? He was far from
sure, but he longed to try.

And the terms of Avalon— The Herald had saved him
in the forest, not by any direct aid, but by stimulating him
to save himself. Nick thought about that feat of concentration, and his hand went once more to his belt to finger
the hilt of the dagger he had drawn to his aid in such in-

credible fashion. If one could accomplish that by concentrating—what else might one do?

Hadlett said that his late captors had produced their own hellish monsters to harass them because they expected to see such. Therefore your thoughts had reality beyond your own mind. Those had expected Hell and its inhabitants, so that was what they had to endure and fear. In mankind was the belief in evil stronger than the belief in good, as the Vicar had also said?

If one concentrated just as strongly on believing in paradise here, would that be true? And would it hold? Nick remembered the intense weariness that had closed in on him after he had fought for his freedom. The mind could demand too much from the body. To sustain any illusion for a length of time might exhaust one utterly.

The monsters, Nick decided now, must have been unconscious projection on the part of the drifters. Perhaps, if you continued to expect to see the same thing, you added reality to it, more substance every time it materialized. Would it then sometime become wholly real? That was both a startling and an unpleasant thought. What he had seen in that night of horror must not obtain real life!

Real, unreal, good, evil— The little man he had encountered in the berry patch, the visible-invisible castle, Avalon himself—real, unreal? How did one ever *know?*

Nick longed to throw some of these questions at the Vicar. But not with Crocker listening. He would only provide the pilot with more evidence that he was a dangerously unstable person—someone who, whether he had had treasonous dealings with Avalon or not, was better exiled from their company.

Though the great fury of the storm ebbed, the rain continued to fall. Nick and his companions, in spite of their cramped position, dozed away the night until a watery, gray daylight drew them forth. Crocker took the lead, saying little, guiding them on a roundabout way, keeping out of the full embrace of the woods.

Nick wondered if the castle was still visible, but he had no excuse to linger to see. He must remain prudently quiet on such matters pertaining to the People until he was sure he was no longer suspect. If Hadlett had time to think things over he might be brought to consider invasion of the city—

Nick was not prepared to bring the women into any

council, though he knew that all three of the English party
would have a voice in any decision. To Nick, Margo's influence on his father had been a brutal shock. She had set
up barriers one by one so skillfully that it had been
months before Nick was able to realize what had happened. When he knew, it was too late to do anything. Dad
was gone, there was a stranger, friendly enough, but still a
stranger who spoke with his voice, wore his body— Just as
if Margo had manufactured an illusion to serve her purpose. That stranger made an effort now and then. Nick
could look back at this moment and understand those ad-
vances, tentative and awkward as they had been. But they
had meant nothing, because Margo's illusion made them.

And losing Dad, Nick had sealed off those emotions
that had once been a part of him. Sure, he had gone out
with girls, but none of them had meant anything. There
was always the memory of Margo, of her maneuvering,
her skill with Dad, to hold as a shield. Linda was a part of
the world in which Margo existed. She, too, was able perhaps to twist someone into what she wanted instead of
freely accepting him for what he was.

So Nick wanted now to argue out any decision, not
with the women, but with the men whom he believed he
could understand. And perhaps in the end he would find
more acceptance, he thought wryly, from Jeremiah and
Lung. Were animals more straightforward, less devious
than men?

They reached the cave as clouds were once more massing, threatening a second downpour. Lady Diana manned
the lookout.

"I see you found him. You don't look too damaged to
me, young man." Her voice was far from welcoming.

"Did you expect I might be?" Nick could not resist
countering. He had respect for her sturdy abilities, but he
could not honestly like her.

"The thought occurred to us, yes. Adrian, you are
soaked. You must have a hot drink, shed those shoes of
yours at once. Luckily Maude has just finished stitching up
a new pair. Linda," she called down into the cave. "Come
here, girl. They're back safe, and they have your boy!"

Nick stiffened. He was *not* Linda's boy! What claim had
she made on him to these others? But when she did appear in Lady Diana's place, Lady Diana herself laying

hands on the Vicar to urge him on into shelter, Linda did not look directly at Nick, nor did she speak to him.

He let Crocker pass him, wanting to say something in denial of any claim she had advanced. That this was perhaps not the time or place for that, Nick was uneasily aware, yet he was pressed to do it.

"You're not hurt?" Her voice was cool, he might have been an acquaintance about whom she was inquiring for politeness' sake.

"No." His wrists were still ridged and sore but one could not claim those as real hurts.

"You were lucky," she observed, still remote.

"I suppose so." He might not be hurt, but he had certainly brought back problems that might cause more trouble than physical wounds.

"You know what they think." A light nod of her head clarified who "they" might be. "They believe that you may have made a deal with this Herald. You sneaked out—without telling anyone—after you were warned. And you seem to know things—"

"Know things?"

"What you said about Jeremiah and Lung."

"You told them that?" He had been right in not trusting her.

"Naturally. When they started to wonder what had become of you. Believe it or not, they were concerned. They are good people."

"You are trying to warn me, aren't you?" he asked.

"To let them alone! If you've made some deal, live with it. Don't involve them."

"Thanks for the advice and the vote of confidence!" Nick exploded and swung down into the entrance of the cave. But why had he expected any other response? This was a typical Margo trick, one he had met many times in the past. He had been put in the wrong before his case had even been heard.

◆ 13 ◆

But they did not cross-question him at once. Hadlett was the center of attention, concern for him blotting out all else, though Jean brought Nick a bowl of hot soup, which he ate greedily. She, of course, made more of a fuss over Crocker, though Nick believed she tried to make those attentions not too obvious.

Nick was back safely, something he would have given much to achieve last night, or earlier yesterday. Now—he did not know. Though the others were within touching distance if he wished, he felt curiously detached.

But he had made no bargain. Unless—unless in following the Herald's hint he had somehow crossed a line between the old life and a new. Nick put down the empty bowl, studied his hands as they rested on his knees.

They were scratched, dirty, stained with berry juice. The rest of him was probably in keeping. But he was human still and not a creature of the People.

He was still hungry. But knowing the state of their supplies, Nick did not ask for more. As he leaned over to pick up the bowl again, he saw Jeremiah. The cat had appeared out of nowhere after the fashion of felines, and sat watching Nick with probing intentness that could disconcert a human at times.

Nick stared back. There was some reason for the cat's singling him out, he guessed. What did Jeremiah want of him? If the cat could communicate, he was not trying now. Nick disliked that cool stare, but he refused to let it ruffle him.

"How much, Jeremiah," he asked in a whisper, "do you really know?"

On Nick's knee, beside his hand, there was a shimmer as if the air took on substance in a small whirlpool of energy. It thickened, held so for a moment, then vanished.

140

But it had been there, and Nick knew he had in that moment seen a mouse.

Jeremiah! The cat could somehow use the same energy that Nick had tapped to free himself in the woods to materialize a representation of his most common prey. He was astounded. That an animal could—

Answering his astonishment came a cold thrust of near anger. Jeremiah's ears were flattened to his head, his eyes slitted.

"Animal? Who is an animal?"

The words did not form as such in Nick's mind, but some impulse brought them to the surface there. Indeed—who was an animal? In this place where all the old certainties had been swept away, could anyone make claims that could not be overturned?

Another idea came to him. Could—could Jeremiah's species (Nick tried to avoid "animal" and after all humans were animals, too) accept the Herald's terms? Was Jeremiah now a part of Avalon even though he stayed with Mrs. Clapp and the others?

Once more that swirl of air that was not air, the swift formation and disappearance of an object Nick had only an instant to sight—an apple! Then Jeremiah was— What? A spy?

Nick dismissed that at once. A guard? Against them? For them?

Jeremiah yawned, arose, and, with a flirt of his tail tip, which was firm dismissal of the whole subject, he stalked off.

"Now then." Mrs. Clapp came away from where she had settled Hadlett by the fire, his feet rubbed dry and newly fashioned moccasins on them. She stood over Nick, one of the handleless clay cups in her hand. An aromatic steam arose from it. "You drink this up! It'll roast the chill out. We want no lung fever hittin'."

She stood over him, in fact between him and the rest who were gathered about the Vicar, while he drank. And he found her gaze as searching as Jeremiah's had been. Did she know what her cat now was?

"You're a lucky lad, that indeed you are. With himself an' Barry out to hunt you."

Her voice was sharper than Nick had heard it before. He understood that, in her eyes, his late adventure was a disgrace, mainly because it had involved trouble for the Vicar.

"I know." Nick tried to be meek.

"Knowin' afterward is not doin't beforehand. I'm takin' it on me to say this—we've stayed together now for long an' we've managed. Because we think about how what we do is for all of us, not just for one. In this place you can set a foot wrong an' stir up trouble fast." The longer she spoke the softer her voice became. "There now, I've had my say. You'll hear it from the others without doubt, but they have a right to such sayin'—they knowin' all that's around us here. You— What in the wide world were you doin' to get that now?"

Her hand caught his, dragging it forward to bring his ridged, raw wrist into the full light.

"Oh, that happened when they tied me up." Nick tried to free himself from her hold, but she kept the grip with surprising strength.

"Raw that is—an' you could get a nasty infection. The other one is as bad, too. You stay right here 'til I get some o' my heal powder."

Nick knew it was futile to protest. He waited and she was quickly back with two large leaves on which was spread a greasy salve.

"Should have us some bandages, but we ain't got 'em. These leaves work good though. Now hold up your hand, lad—that's the way."

She was quick and deft, and Nick soon had two green cuffs about his maltreated wrists. It was not until she had finished he remembered his own first-aid kit in the saddle-bags. But already the stuff she had smeared over his abraded skin was drawing out the sting, and he was content with her treatment.

"Now." Mrs. Clapp tied strings of tough grass tightly enough to keep the wristlets in place. "You keep those on today an' tonight. Then I'll have another look at 'em. Should be as good as healed. Those there herbs worked into fat, they've got a lot of good in 'em."

She did not go away, but stood there, her supplies in her hands. There was no sternness in her expression now, rather a concern that made Nick more uncomfortable than her scolding had done.

"You've had a bad time—"

He summoned a smile. "You might say I deserved it."

"Nobody deserves bad, 'less they give it. To my mind you're not one of those who do. But you're young, you don't want to believe what you hear 'til you try it out for yourself—"

"And," he interrupted, "in that trying I might hurt more than myself next time?"

"That I said an' meant it." Mrs. Clapp nodded. "But I'm thinkin' you're not a stupid lad. You don't need no second lesson once the first has been swallowed down."

"I hope, Mrs. Clapp, that I shall deserve that confidence."

"Maude!" Lady Diana called, and his nurse hurried back to the group about the Vicar.

Nick sat down once more, his leaf-enfolded wrists before him. They thought that they were safe here, perhaps they were. But with their supplies dwindling they might be forced out. And he had no faith at all in the river plan. He had not seen Stroud since their return and wondered if the Warden still skulked about the site of their raft.

Stroud did not return until evening. And it was with news to dash their faint hope of making use of the river. The land was alive with bands of drifters and the sky with saucers whose crews preyed upon those in the open. The Warden had witnessed the sweeping up of two such parties, one being a squad of men wearing British uniforms of World War I vintage.

"Couldn't see their badges," he reported between mouthfuls of the nut-flour cakes Mrs. Clapp had ready for him. "But I remember m' Dad had him an outfit like that. Just a nipper I was when he had embark-leave the last time. Off to Turkey for the fightin', he was, an' reported missin' in action. We never had no more news of him, though Mum, she up an' tried to get some word hard enough. They kept tellin' her after the war was over the Turks 'd have to let their prisoners loose. Only after the war was over an' they did—m' Dad weren't one as they had any record of. Lot o' poor chaps never did get found.

"But I remember how m' Dad looked—an' these chaps those saucer tykes netted, they were wearin' the same sort o' gear, that I'll swear to! Could I have gotten close to 'em maybe we might've had a chance to get together." He shook his head.

"This migration and hunting has taken on unusual proportions," the Vicar observed. "Are the saucer people trying to make a clean sweep of the whole country?"

"Well," Stroud had finished eating, "there's that, of course. But I don't altogether think that's the right of it, Vicar. We've had hunts before, but not like this. I seems to me it's more like somethin' else started all these drifters on the move, something up north. They're comin' down from that direction an' they're not movin' slow at all, but pretty steady—like something was pressin' on their tails.

"Anyway, we'd best stay in cover, do we want to stay free. The saucers are takin' good advantage of all this movin'. To get out on the river in plain sight is as good as askin' to be caught."

"Nicholas." The Vicar summoned the American. "What did Avalon say when he warned you? Remember his exact words if you can."

Nick closed his eyes for a moment, summoning memory to provide him with the words Hadlett wanted to hear. He could see Avalon vividly. Now it was as if he could hear the Herald's emotionless voice so that he need only repeat word for word what the other had said.

"Avalon is no man's enemy. It is a place of peace and safety. But if one remains without, then comes darkness and ill. This has happened before, the evil lapping at the land. Where it meets Avalon and Tara, Brocéliande and Carnac, then it laps against walls it cannot overflow. But for those without the walls there is peril beyond reckoning. Alternately the evil flows and ebbs. This is a time of the beginning of the flow."

"Avalon?" Stroud repeated.

"The Herald." Crocker spoke up and there was silence. Nick knew they looked at him now, but he met no eyes save Hadlett's.

If the others accused him, and he thought that they did, that was not to be read in the Vicar's expression.

Stroud got to his feet and moved in until his weather-tanned face was not far from Nick's.

"You had words with the Herald now, did you?" To the Warden that fact must be of major importance.

"Yes," Nick replied shortly, adding no explanation.

"You was pally enough to have him give you a warnin'?" Stroud continued. All Crocker's disbelief was intensified in that red-brown face. The vast moustache bristled with antagonism.

"If you mean, did I accept his offer of safety," Nick returned, "I did not. However, he saved my life."

"That's not the way you told it before," Crocker cut in. "You got away by yourself—in a way that took some doing, too."

"He pointed the way." Nick kept the lid on his temper, but the irritation Crocker could ignite in him threatened his control. "If he had not—"

"It is all a very likely tale," Crocker snapped. "Let them listen to it—all of it—now. And see what they think of it!"

Hadlett nodded. "Tell them, Nicholas, from the beginning."

With the Vicar and Crocker listening, Nick could not alter his story, even if he wanted to. Which now he did not, that stubborn streak in him making sure that they must hear it as it happened and then believe or reject him.

Once more he told his adventure in detail from his first sight of Avalon to the meeting with Crocker and the Vicar. He had no more interruptions, but their full attention. As he finished, he waited for the voicing of disbelief, suspicion, complete rejection.

"You—you just thought—and you got that knife?" Stroud opened the examination.

Nick pulled the blade in question from his belt. He had already passed over to Hadlett and Crocker the other weapons dropped when the medieval band went to their unknown fate.

"I have this."

Stroud snatched it from him, studied it carefully, and then threw it to clatter on the rock floor some distance away.

"There's your miracle knife," he said. "Now let's see you get it back by thinkin'!"

A fair enough test, Nick gave him that. He turned to face the blade. Now he tried to set out of his mind everything but his need for the knife. He must have it— How had he done it before? A hand—a hand to take it up—and then an arm—

Nick concentrated on the need for the hand. But, though his mind ached under the lash of his will, nothing formed in the air. No mist thickened to put forth fingers closing about the hilt. He fought to produce that hand, but it did not come. There was something here that had not

been in the clearing, a barrier against which his will fruit-
lessly beat.

"I can't do it." How long he had struggled he did not
know. But something here short-circuited all his efforts.
"It won't work this time."

"Because"—there was triumph in Crocker's voice—"it
never did! That story was a lie from the start, I knew it!"

A hand grabbed Nick's shoulder with force enough to
hurt and swing him around before he could fight back.
Then Stroud's face thrust very close to his.

"You sold out to the Herald! Then you came back to
get us. Not openly the way Rita did—you crawlin' worm!"

Nick tried to dodge the blow. His effort was enough so
that Stroud did not knock him out, but sent him reeling,
half-dazed—to bring up against the wall. He was dizzy
from the force of the punch, only half-aware that Hadlett
had stepped between them.

"Sam!" the Vicar's tone was a command, which the
Warden answered with a growl. But he did not try to push
past to be at his victim again.

"He sold out, came back to get us," Stroud said thickly.
"You know that, Vicar."

"You are prejudging, Sam. All of you." Hadlett spoke
not only to the Warden, but to the others who had moved
in as if they were ready to join Stroud in whatever ven-
geance he proposed to take, their faces—ugly. Fear came to
life in Nick. He had heard of the hysteria that gripped
mobs. Was this the same horror?

"Listen to me carefully, all of you," Hadlett continued.
"This is of the upmost importance—not just to Nicholas
and to you because you propose to mete out what you
conceive to be justice, but because it may also determine
our future."

He was answered by a sound, not quite words of protest, but certainly expressing that. But they no longer
moved forward, and Stroud dropped his ready fist to his
side. Now the Vicar half-turned to address Nick.

"When you brought the knife to your aid you were
alone?"

"As—as far as I know." Nick tried to control his voice
to steadiness.

"There was no counter power of disbelief there,"
Hadlett commented. "But when you tried just now—what
did you experience?"

"It was as if there were a barrier."

"Just so. A barrier raised by disbelief. Or so I think. Do you understand that?" He asked his question not of Nick but of the others.

Nick saw Lady Diana nod her head, reluctantly, he was sure. And Mrs. Clapp's lips formed a "yes." The others stood stolidly. But someone spoke from Nick's right.

"If we believe in him, then he can do it?"

Linda moved out. On one side of her paced Jeremiah, on the other Lung bounced along, his silky ears flapping.

"Nick." She did not wait for Hadlett to answer. "Nick, take my hand!"

That was no request but an order, and, without meaning to, he obeyed. She drew him away from the wall, and the others fell back to let them past. Once more they approached the knife. But Linda did not relax her hold. Instead she said:

"Try it again—now!"

Nick wanted to resist, but that seemed petty. Somehow, a new confidence was flowing into him. The knife—to move the knife—

Concentrate—see only that sliver of steel—a hand—fingers to grasp the hilt—pick it up—

There was still the barrier, but also—a new strength flowing into him. That came from the clasp of hands, from others—Linda—the two furred bodies at his feet. Nick had a moment of wonder and then shut that out. All he must think of was the knife.

Once more he saw that thickening in the air. From it developed the ghostly hand, building up finger by finger, not misty now—seemingly solid. From the hand his thoughts went to an arm. That, too, appeared inch by inch, a chain reaching from him to the hand.

"Come!" He thought that order.

The arm shortened, drew in toward him, and with it came the hand, fingers laced about the knife hilt. It drew back to his feet and then was gone. The knife clattered on the rock.

Linda's hand dropped from his. But it was she who rounded on the others.

"You saw that!" she challenged. "And I have been under your eyes all the time, I have had no dealings with Heralds! But I loaned Nick my energy to combat the wall of your disbelief, and so did these two." She stooped to scoop up Lung, laid her hand for a moment between Jeremiah's ears.

"Do you now judge all of us liars?" she added.

"Jeremiah!" Mrs. Clapp moved forward. The cat had turned his head at her call. She lifted him as if she feared him injured in some fashion and he moved his head to touch her cheek with his nose. Then he stiffened his forelegs, pushing himself out of her hold. But he stayed beside her, rubbing against her skirts.

"The two of you—" Hadlett began, but Linda corrected him instantly.

"The four of us! And I believe you can all do this—but you haven't tried. Nick had to, to save his life, and now you want to punish him for it!"

"He did it all right." The Warden picked up the knife, weighed it in his hand as if to assure himself that it was just what it appeared to be. "I saw it."

"Yes, he did it," the Vicar agreed. "My dear," he spoke to Linda, "you may be very right. We have never been put to such a test ourselves, so how could we know. Are you really sure about the animals?"

Nick had regained some of the strength the concentration had drawn out of him. He was not as worn by it as he had been the previous time, perhaps because the others had backed him up.

"The animals—they know—" He was puzzled—what could he say for sure that Lung and Jeremiah knew? His only contact had been with the cat. Would they believe Jeremiah had materialized a mouse? As for Lung's abilities, he had only Linda's assurances as to those.

"They know," he began again, "a lot—how much I can't say. Jeremiah can materialize things." Nick again braved disbelief and told of the mouse. But he said nothing about the apple, having no intention of turning against the cat the fury he had earlier faced himself.

"*Jeremiah* did that!" Mrs. Clapp gazed down. "But how—how could he, sir?" she asked the Vicar. "He—he's a cat. I've had him ever since he was born. He's old Floss's last kitten. She had a bad time an' she died. I couldn't let him, too—the poor mite! I got me a little doll bottle an' fed him milk an' egg an'—an'—Jeremiah's a cat!" She ended explosively, as if to think any differently would mean an end to all security.

"Indeed he is, Maude." Lady Diana put her arm around

the bent shoulders of the older woman. "But it could be that this world changes animals somehow. See, he's worried about you now."

The big cat was sitting up on his hind legs, his forepaws reaching above Mrs. Clapp's knee, as he hooked claws in her skirt to balance himself. He opened his mouth in a soft sound that was not quite a mew.

"Jeremiah!" She hunkered stiffly down on the floor to gather him into her arms. This time he did not push against her to gain his liberty, but butted his head against her chin and sounded a rumble of purr.

"I don't care if he can do strange things," she declared a moment later. "He wouldn't do no harm, not Jeremiah. He did good—lettin' us know that the lad was tellin' the truth. Jeremiah's a good cat."

Hadlett and Lady Diana between them drew her to her feet, still holding Jeremiah.

"Of course he is, Maude. And like all cats," the Vicar continued, "he doubtless sees things in a more sensible way than do a great many humans. Don't you worry about Jeremiah."

Stroud brought attention back to Nick. "Look here, mate." He held out the hand which, fist hard, had left the darkening bruise on Nick's face. "If you want to dot me one for what I gave you, you're welcome to do it. I shot off then before I aimed. I'm willin' to say it."

Nick met the hand with his own. "No hard feelings," he gave ready answer. "I thought no one might believe me, I hardly believed it myself. And I don't want a crack at your jaw in return." He laughed a little too loudly in relief. "What I would like is for you, all of you, to listen to something I have been thinking about—"

Whether this was the time to be frank he did not know. But they were predisposed in his favor now just because they had been so quick to misjudge him. Suspicion might rise again and he had better make his plea while they still felt a little guilty and ill at ease.

"And what's that?" Crocker's voice was neutral. He, Nick guessed, was not feeling guilt.

"Just this—you heard me repeat what the Herald told me. Stroud has reported what he saw. You all know the drifters are on the move and that trouble seems to be coming from the north. There is only one place of real safety that we know of—the city."

Nick waited for their anger to rise again. What he was suggesting was opposed to all their ways.

"You mean—take the Herald's bargain?" Crocker asked fiercely. "I think not! You see what he's doing?" the pilot demanded of the others. "Just because he pulled that knife across the floor doesn't mean he didn't sell out! I say he did—let him prove otherwise!"

They had drawn away again. Nick had made the wrong choice after all. Would Stroud be as ready with his fists? And the Warden had a knife in hand—

"How can I prove it?" Nick countered.

Stroud was not looking at him but to the Vicar.

"Best have him do that, if he wants to, sir. It'll stop all the trouble—"

"Yes." Hadlett sounded tired. "If you will come with us then, Nicholas—"

He did not know what they wanted of him, but as Stroud had suggested, he wanted the matter settled. Either they accepted him now or he would have to clear out. And he found himself disliking the thought of exile very much.

Stroud and Crocker fell in behind as the Vicar led the way into the small cave they used for storage, though the supplies there now were pitifully few. Inside Crocker spoke.

"All right. You said you'd give us proof. Strip!"

"What?" Nick was confounded.

"There are certain physical changes. I believe I spoke of them to you, Nicholas," the Vicar explained. "They appear very shortly after the bargain is concluded. It has been well over two days since you admittedly saw the Herald. If you have accepted his offer, you will reveal these."

"I see." Nick began to pull off his shirt. If they wanted proof they would get it now.

expecting was exposed to all their ways.

"You mean—take the Herald's bargain?" Crocker said
fiercely. "I think not. You see what he's doing," the...
reminded of the others, "if we sense to be called that

◆ 14 ◆

There was a fresh wind blowing and the morning was clear. Nick longed for binoculars. He had won his way this much—with Stroud he was back on one of the ridges above the city. They had traveled by night to reach this point, in spite of the Warden's reluctance.

But conditions around the cave had worsened. They were virtual prisoners there as saucers clustered to prey upon the drifters. And the still hazy plan Nick advanced, of trying to discover the secret of safety in the rainbow towers, had won some support. Now he was trying to line up enough cover on the plain ahead to give him a chance to scout closer.

Grass grew there but he judged, and Stroud agreed, that tall as that was, it provided no safe cover. And whether his own plan had any chance at all Nick could not know. Only he could not stall here much longer. Let a saucer home in on the city as Stroud said they did at intervals and they might be pinned down here for hours.

"All right, shall I try it?" Nick got to his feet. So much depended upon him now, upon his ability to use that wild talent. He had practiced with it, but hardly enough—

"You do, or we go back," Stroud returned. "We came to do it."

Did he believe that faced by a final choice Nick would back down? Did he hope for that? If he did, his disbelief had just the opposite effect: Nick was forced into action.

The Herald.

In his mind the American built up a picture of the Herald. Then that was not in his mind at all. He had done it! He had actually done it! Not captured the Herald physically as he had first thought to do, but projected him—

"I got him!" Nick was exultant.

"So it looks," Stroud agreed. "But can you keep him?"

"I'll have to. Here goes—"

151

Nick swung down the slope. The Herald was gone, winked out when Nick no longer willed him. But when it counted he could produce Avalon again—he had to. Stroud would remain behind, watch him into the city. They had not been sure whether this illusion of the accepted guide would hold for two, and since Nick's was the talent he went alone.

Now as he slipped and slid to more level ground he was excited, tense as one is before any testing. In a way his self-confidence had grown from that moment in the cave when he had been able to prove that he was not a traitor to his kind and his power had not been fostered by surrender to the People. Two days more he had tested it, and the others with him.

The Vicar had some ability to project, oddly enough Mrs. Clapp even more—though she tired easily. Crocker firmly refused to try. His antagonism to Nick had increased, Nick was sure, instead of diminished. The talent flared higher in the women—Linda, Jean (though she showed the same reluctance as Crocker), Lady Diana, could all produce some phenomena. Linda had formed a linkage with the animals again and produced stronger and longer-abiding illusions.

But all of them found it impossible to hold such for long. And the more one struggled to do so, the more one's energy was exhausted. Nick was not sure now how long he could hold the Herald, even if he could use that illusion for a key.

He did not believe that the People were active enemies of any of the drifters. From Avalon's words it would seem that when refugees from Nick's world refused alliance they were simply ignored.

However, if he were able to break through the invisible defense, enter the city, and be discovered there as an alien, would that indifference hold? During the past two days Nick had prevailed on the English to pool all their observations concerning the People and the city, even though they had shied away from that before.

It was from the city, or cities (they had seen others), that the Herald, or Heralds, issued. There were others of the People, such as the Green Man of the forest—some of these lived in water, others on the land—and these did not appear bound to the cities at all. Yet all were native, Hadlett thought, to this world.

The Vicar drew, as he readily admitted, on the half-forgotten lore of his own native country for his identification and evaluation of those he had seen here. Perhaps his guesses were of little value, but they were all he had to judge by.

In addition to those of the People who seemed neutral, there were others who were definitely a dangerous threat. But these in turn were bound to certain baneful portions of the land. And if one avoided those sections, refused to be drawn by such lures as the singing Nick had heard in the rain, they were no great menace.

Nick reached the level ground. He wished he could work his way closer to the city before he produced the illusion. But he had no way of telling whether or not he was already under observation. He concentrated with all the power he could summon.

Once more the Herald appeared. Nick did not try to make every detail of the illusion sharply clear. It was enough that the general appearance of his "guide" tallied with the real one. With the thing born of his will ahead, he started at a swift pace to the towers.

Stroud had pointed out where he might expect to meet the unseen barrier, and he was doubly eager to reach that, to make his entrance. Yet most of his attention must be on the phantom.

They were past the barrier point—though he could not be entirely sure, because Stroud might have been mistaken. Nick refused any triumph yet. The strain of keeping the Herald was beginning to tell. What if he could not hold? Would he be a prisoner on the inside of the barrier?

Doggedly he fought his own weakness, holding the necessary concentration. Then—

The city—he was in the city!

The transition was quick, as if the buildings had risen about him. Buildings—Nick forgot the Herald, his need for the illusion.

There were buildings, yes, towering up and up, doors, windows, streets. But where were the people? The streets were deserted, no one walked the white-and-green blocked pavement, no vehicle moved there. The doors were closed; the windows, if they were open, still had the appearance of being shuttered. The walls about him had glassy surfaces as if they were indeed crystal, backed by some opaque material. And up and down them ran those opaline changes of color, green, blue, yellow, red and all possible shadings between.

Nick hesitated. There was no sound in the city. He could be in a ruin deserted centuries ago. Yet this was no ruin, there was no sign of erosion, nor breakage, cracking—

Slowly he approached the nearest wall. He held out a hand hesitatingly so that just the tips of his fingers touched its surface. Then he snatched it back again. For what he had fingered was not cold stone or crystal, rather a substance delicately warm, alive with vibration.

Energy, some form of energy was encased in the walls. That would account for the radiance. The whole city might be a generator or storehouse of energy.

The avenue on which he stood ran straight. If Nick did not turn into any sideway how could he be lost? Summoning his resolution anew, Nick began to walk forward. But it was all he could do to hold control.

For he knew, was as certain as he was of every breath he drew, that the city, or those who dwelt here, knew him for what he was—an interloper. Twice he came to a stop, turned to glance behind. But no new wall had suddenly arisen, no guards were in view to cut off his retreat. The street was as silent and deserted as ever.

Where were the people? Had the population shrunk so that only a handful lived here at its heart? Or was the city really a city? Perhaps those terms from his own world did not apply here. This vast site might have some entirely different purpose. But the Herald came from here, he had returned with those who accepted Avalon. Nick had seen that happen.

He sighted ahead an open space with something standing within, flashing a brighter light, so bright that it hurt Nick's eyes and he wished he had Linda's dark glasses. To escape that he moved closer to a wall, tried to look up. But the tower rose so high it made him dizzy to attempt to see its tip against the morning sky.

Now, a little daring, Nick set hand to the door in the wall. This had a different texture than the wall. It seemed a single slab of silvery metal. And at close inspection Nick could see it was engraved with a pattern of many lines in intricate design. When again he tried to touch it, there was no vibration, but as his fingers moved along those lines he perceived a meaning sight alone could not give them, and they were more visible than they had been before.

There were queer beasts, some like the ones he had seen in the woods, a unicorn among them, and creatures that were humanoid. Around them, encircling them, were ribbon bands that bore marks unlike any lettering Nick knew.

As his fingers passed he could see them plainly for a moment or two. Then they faded so they were discernible only as faint scratches.

Having tried one door he passed to the next and once more put it to the test of touch. Again he saw pictures, though these were different in both form and arrangement.

What lay behind these doors? Nick gently applied pressure. There were no visible latches, locks, knobs, or any aid for their opening. And they remained fixed, immobile, under all his strength.

Locked doors, deserted city. Nick returned to the middle of the street and forged ahead. Though the belief that someone—something—was watching him held, Nick had regained a little confidence. He sensed no threat in this place. If he had violated some sanctuary then as yet those who guarded it had not made up their minds whether he was a threat to their purposes or not. And the longer they held off the more confident he felt. That in itself might be a danger, he began to realize.

Nick advanced resolutely toward the flashing point ahead, shading his eyes to its glare. So he came out into what might be the heart of the city, though he had no way of knowing if that were so. This was an open space into which fed five avenues, like the one he followed. The shape he could see was that of a five-point star, one street entering at each point.

Now that he was close to that which flashed, it did not glare as much as earlier and he recognized its shape. For this he had seen in his own world, and that it had a very ancient significance he knew.

Set up straight in the middle of the star was a giant representation of the Egyptian ankh—the looped cross. It appeared to be fashioned, not of the crystal of the towers, but of a ruddy metal. And in the mid-center of the two arms, on the arms themselves, and around the loop were shining gems. But could those be gems? Whoever heard of

precious stones of such size they could not be spanned by
two hands together?

It was from these that the light flashed, green, blue,
white—but no red nor yellow. As those rays shot well
over the level of his head, Nick judged that the height of
the ankh was equal to that of a four-or five-story building.

From it came such a force of radiant energy that he
felt dizzy, weak. He staggered back. Was this the source
of the safety devices of the People? But what powered it?
He saw no evidence of machines. Or was it some receiver
or booster broadcaster?

Nick wavered. For the first time, stark fear broke
through his wonder. This—this was overpowering. His skin
tingled, his dizziness grew. He must get away.

But could he? The avenue— Somehow he managed to
turn, though the gem lights nearly blinded him. There—
get—out—

Nick broke into a stumbling run, heading for the opening to the avenue. But it was as if he were trying to wade
through deep mud. Something sucked avidly at his
strength, his very life-force. He *must* get away!

He stumbled, fell, but somehow pulled himself to his
hands and knees and kept on at a crawl. The buildings
rose on either hand, he was within the avenue. But not far
enough. And he was not going to make it—

Nick gasped, fought for breath. Now it felt as if the air
about him was being sucked away, that he could not get
enough into his lungs—he was choking.

He lay flat, his arms outstretched above his head, his
fingers still moving feebly, trying to find some crevice between the blocks of the pavement into which they might
fit and draw him forward, even if only for an inch or two.

"Come!"

Had he heard that? Nick still fought to move. There
were hands on his shoulders, he was being dragged away
from the star, down the avenue, out of the baleful influence of the ankh. He could not summon strength enough
to look up and see who—or what—had come to his aid.
Not the Herald—the Herald had been his own illusion.
Stroud? His thoughts were weak, slipping from him. He
no longer really cared who saved him.

The tingling in his flesh faded. But he was not regaining
his strength. However, the hold on him relaxed and he

made a great effort to roll over so he could see his res-
cuer.

She did not have that misty outline of light about her
this time but looked thoroughly solid and substantial. Nor
were there tears on her cheeks.

"Rita."

He must have said her name aloud. Or else, like Jeremiah, she could read his thoughts.

"I am Rita, yes." There was in her speech that same
toneless quality that marked the Herald's.

But her face was not as expressionless as Avalon's.
There was concern there, and something else. She studied
him, Nick thought, as one might study a tool before one
put it to service.

"You might have died—back there. You are not of the
Kin." She made statements, she asked no questions.

"Are you alone here?" he asked.

"Alone?" Plainly that had startled her. She glanced
from left to right and back again, as if she saw what he
could not and was astounded by his speech. "Alone—
why—" Then she paused. "You are not of the Kin," she
repeated. "The sight is not yours. No, though you do not
see, I am not alone. Why did you come if you would not
be one with Avalon?"

"To find out what keeps the city free from attack. Your
people—they are in danger. They need protection."

"There is no danger for the Kin. Safety those others
can have for the asking. It is so. I have gone to them and
they drove me out. They are blind and will not accept
sight, they are deaf and they will not hear. They—" For
the first time her voice trembled. "They will be lost because they choose it so."

"They say that you changed."

"Yes. I have become one with the Kin. See." She went
to her knees beside him and laid her arm next to his, not
quite touching.

Her skin was white, a dazzling white, and very smooth,
without any fluff of hair along its surface. Against it his
arm was coarse, rough, browned. She took his hand in
hers and the sensation of flesh meeting flesh was not as he
had known it before, but rather as if fingers and palm of
sleek marble had grasped him.

"Thus it is with the bodies of the Kin," Rita told him.
"That is how we go protected against the weapons of the

flyers, and against other dangers here. There are evils that can destroy us, but those are evils native to this world, and they reach us in other ways than by wounds of the body. If your people accept Avalon, then they shall become of Avalon, as I now am."

"You are—hard—" Nick could not find another word for the feel of her flesh. "Yet—when you were in the woods—I saw Linda's hand pass through your arm."

Rita did not answer him. Instead she said with the authority of one who did not imagine she would be disobeyed:

"You have come where you cannot stay. If you accept not Avalon, then that which is of Avalon can kill. You have felt the beginning of that death. Get you out—this place is not for you."

She touched his forehead in much the same place as the fanatical monk had pressed the cross so painfully into his skin. There was a chill to her fingers. But from them flowed into him a renewal of strength so he could stand again.

"You saved my life. Is there anything I can do for you?" Always, Nick thought, he would remember those tears and what lay in the eyes where that moisture gathered.

"What words can you use with them that I have not already spoken?" Rita asked. "Their fear lies so deep in them that they would kill before they will accept what I offer."

He expected her to stay, but, when unable to find words to deny the truth of what she said, Nick started away, Rita matched step with him.

"I will go out of the city. You need not trouble—"

There was a trace of a smile on her face. "To see you to the door?" she ended for him. "But there is a need. I do not know how you entered, but you, being what you are, cannot win free again save that the door be opened for you."

Not all the strength drained from him had returned. Nick moved slowly along the silent, empty street. But to his companion was it either silent or empty? He believed not. That he could see her might be because she was originally of his kind. Or maybe she willed it so because she still felt a faint linkage with those outside. She did not explain, in fact Rita did not speak again until they reached the abrupt ending of the avenue, the beginning of the grassy plain.

Then again came her question delivered with authority.

"How did you enter through the barrier?"

Nick wanted to dissemble and found he could not. With her eyes upon him he must speak the truth.

"I followed a Herald."

"That is—impossible. Yet, I see that it is also the truth. But how can it be the truth?"

"The Herald was of my imagining. I pictured him into life."

He heard a hiss of breath that was a gasp. "But you are not of the Kin! How could you do such a thing?"

"I learned how to save my life. And it was Avalon himself who gave me the clue as to how it could be done. The others are trying it too—"

"No!" That was a cry which carried a note of fear. "They cannot! It means their destruction if they have not the power of the Kin. They are children playing with a raw fury they do not understand! They must be stopped!"

"Come and tell them so," Nick returned.

"They will not listen—"

"Can you be sure? Having used this power I think that they understand more than they did before. The Vicar, I am sure he will listen."

"Yes, he has a deepness of heart and a width of mind. Perhaps this can be done. I cannot but try again. But they must not attempt to weave the great spell. It can kill—or summon up that which it is better not to see. Avalon has some life in it that can answer one's dreams in a way to freeze the very spirit."

Nick remembered the devilish things that had besieged the party in the woods.

"So I have seen."

Rita gave him a long measuring look and then held out her hand.

"Let us go."

As her cold, smooth fingers closed about his, Rita drew him along. So linked they went out into the open, heading for the ridge where he had left Stroud on watch. Would the Warden accept Rita? Had the prejudice of the party been so shaken by Nick's discovery that they would listen to the one they had cast out? Nick hoped so.

But he was not so sure when they did climb the ridge

and Stroud was not waiting. Nick found the flattened grass where the Warden must have lain in hiding to watch him enter the city. But no one was there.

"Stroud!" Nick called, but he dared not shout as he wished.

An answer came in a croaking caw, as a bird burst up from the grass, beating black wings to carry it skyward. Once aloft, it circled them, still calling hoarsely.

"He has—he is in danger!" Rita watched the bird. "The balance has been upset, the force thoughts have released evil. You see—" she turned fiercely on Nick, her composure broken. "You see what such meddling can do? The Dark Ones hunt, run he ever so far or fast. And he, not understanding, will lead them to the rest!"

"Lead who?"

"All those of the Dark who are not bound to any place of evil. And all those they can command among the sons of men! You played with the power, erecting no safeguards. And they who do so open all doors, many of which give upon the Outer Dark. We must hurry—!"

Rita gripped his wrist again, her grasp biting into the still tender flesh so that Nick winced. But she did not note that as she strode forward, dragging him on.

Instead of skulking under cover Rita made her way confidently along the shortest route, heading for the cave. It would seem she had no fears of this land. But Nick did not share her confidence. However, when he tried to free himself from her hold, he found that as impossible as if her fingers were a metal handcuff.

He came to a stop, jerking her to a halt.

"Tell me exactly what we may be facing, what Stroud may have done, or what might have happened to him."

"Do not delay us!" Deep in the eyes Rita turned upon him was an alien glow. "He has fled—but you saw the Cor-raven where he had been. That is the creature of the Dark. It was left to warn us. It so declared this was not a matter for the Kin."

"Yet you are making it your matter," Nick pointed out.

"Yes, but that I cannot help. I am tied, heart-tied, and I have not been long enough among the Kin that those ties are loosed. Still do I care for those of my old heritage. I am free in Avalon, free of choice. If I choose to go up against the Dark, then none will step before me to say 'no.' For I choose, knowing what may be the price. But we waste time. Come!"

That she planned to be an ally in whatever lay ahead, Nick had no doubt now. And her urgency aroused his fear. He hoped that he had recovered enough from his ordeal in the city to keep going, as she began to run and he pounded with her, heading for the cave and what might await them there.

◆ 15 ◆

The sky that had been so bright was now overcast. Though it was summer a chill breeze blew, bringing with it a faint, sickening scent as if it passed over some source of stale corruption. Rita ran easily wherever the ground was clear enough to allow it. But Nick felt the effects of what he had faced in the city and would have lagged behind, in spite of his efforts, had not her hold on him lent that energy of hers.

He could see ahead the rolling hills among which was the cave. And there darkness gathered, clouds massed. While the air was alive, not with saucers, but rather things that flew with flapping wings, some feathered, some of stretched skin. There was movement on the ground, also, though Nick could not be sure of what or who caused that for it did not show clearly.

Yet Rita took no care in her going, as if no hint of ambush concerned her. She was as impervious in her attitude as the Herald had been when under attack from the saucer.

Before they reached the approach to the cave entrance she slowed to a halt. About them now, though Nick could see very little, he was aware of that same miasma of evil he had felt on the night he had been captive. A black-winged bird, with eyes of glowing red, blazing points of fire set in a feathered skull, planed down straight for them, uttering a piercing cry. Nick's free hand went to his belt, drew the dagger.

The bird, with a second scream, sheered away. And there was a small sound from Rita.

"Iron!" She pulled a little away though she did not drop his hand. "Keep that from me—you must! It will serve you, but to the Kin it is deadly."

In this dusk, which was increasing abnormally fast, her body showed the radiance he had seen before, her eyes

162

were bright. There was an excitement about her as if just ahead lay an ordeal.

But he could also see that the ground, the bushes, around them were astir. Things peered at them in menace, yet did not make the attack Nick braced himself to meet. Rita still moved forward, now at a walking pace. There was a breathless quiet about them that those skulking around did not break. Were they real, or illusions? And if illusions, fostered by what enemy?

Ringing them around, moving with them as they advanced, were dwarfs. They were squat of body, furred with gray hair. They turned faces grotesquely human, yet so malignant of aspect as to be weapons in themselves, toward those they escorted, showing teeth that were those of carnivorous beasts in frog-wide mouths, which they opened and shut as if they spoke, or shouted, yet there was no sound.

Behind these stalked others man-tall, specter thin, their limbs mere bones covered with dry and dusty skin, their hairless heads skulls. Moldy tatters clung to them; they moved stiffly yet at surprising speed.

There were other things—some that might have been wolves yet had an obscene humanity about them, reptile forms, giant spiders—all things that might have haunted the nightmares of generations were here given form. But these were only the fringes of the company. And suddenly the air was split with shouts, arrows sang.

"Hurry now!" Rita cried, "I cannot hold double protection long."

Then Nick saw that the radiance from her body had spread to enclose him. Against that the arrows dashed, to fall. He heard more confused shouting. Other forms rushed at them, shrank from the bright mist.

There followed what could only be the crack of a rifle. Nick involuntarily ducked, but did not reach the ground as Rita's hold on him dragged him up and on. The mist was thickening but he was sure he could see through it men in black uniforms. They must be passing through a small army.

Evil it was, the loathsome scent the breeze had earlier hinted at was sickeningly strong. It formed a choking reek. But Nick could see dimly the rocks that were the outer guard of the cave.

There came the sudden chatter of a machine gun. On

either side, as the besiegers reluctantly parted to let them
pass, men fell. A machine gun! Where had the English ob-
tained that?

"On!" Rita sounded breathless.

They scrambled among the rocks, up to the higher entrance. The rattle of gunfire was now constant, deafening— Perhaps it was turned on them. Nick did not know.
But at least nothing penetrated the barrier Rita held.
Though he could see that it was thinning.

With a last effort they tumbled into the hollow of the
sentry post. The radiance dimmed. A man arose before
Nick, aimed at him pointblank with a handgun.

"Illusion!" Rita cried. "It is an illusion!"

Real! The death before him was real!

"No!"

Nick thought to feel the impact of the bullet, but that
did not follow. The man swung away from him as if he no
longer existed. He was a stranger in battle dress. There
were three defenders with a machine gun, aiming and firing at the Dark Ones. Nick stumbled after Rita, down into
the cave.

"You!"

They were all there, even Stroud, though the Warden
lay upon the floor, his coverall marked with dark stains.
The rest stood as might those determined to fight to the
end, meeting death but not capture.

It was Crocker who had cried out, his voice echoing
through the cave. For the clatter of gunfire was now gone.
Jean caught at the pilot's arm as he faced Rita, his eyes
wide, his hand holding one of the daggers. He might have
been warding off attack, though Rita had not moved. The
glow about her was only a lingering glimmer.

"No!" That was Jean. "The gun—we have to keep the
gun—"

Out of the shadows pranced Lung, heading straight to
Rita. He leaped and barked before her, trying with all his
might to gain her attention. If the others had no welcome,
it was plain the Peke did not agree. His joy at her coming
was manifest.

"Get out of here!" Crocker shook off Jean, moved
toward Rita, the knife out.

"Stop, Barry." The Vicar stepped between. He looked
to Rita, not the pilot. "Why do you come?"

"Do you not remember that I was once one of you?

Should I not try to aid you now? You have done that which has brought the Dark Ones; you have dabbled in things you do not understand, to your own undoing."

"She's one of them! She wants to get at us!" Crocker pushed against Hadlett, but as if he did not quite dare to set the Vicar aside.

"I am of Avalon," she replied. Once more her features were composed, she looked as emotionless as the Herald. "But you have opened gates, which are of the Dark Side, and you have not that in you which can close them again. You have used powers and you have no defense—"

"And while we talk here," that was Lady Diana, "those out there will attack. We have to hold—"

"Your illusion?" Rita interrupted. "But that, which you strive against, is no illusion. Do you not understand? We of the Kin have our enemies. You have raised those. But you have not our weapons to defeat them. Look upon you—do you not already weary? It drains the energy to build an illusion. Granted that you now unite to do this and with some success—but how long can you continue? For those without are not bound by time, nor the frailties of bodies such as yours. They can wait and wait until you are brought down by your own lack of strength. And I say to you—better that you be dead than alive at the moment they overrun you.

"This is the beginning of the time of the Running Dark. From all the places of evil will come forth that which has been lurking there. Those it enspells become wholly its creatures. Others seek to run before it—those you have seen. And in the end it will be little better for them, for the sky hunters will take them.

"But to you have come the Dark Ones ahead of time. Avalon will not protect you, for you have refused its freedom. Put your iron to your throats, but even so there are those who can pour into your bodies, inhabit them, use them as clothing—"

"As you use Rita's?" Crocker's eyes were fires of fury.

"I am Rita. I am more Rita than I ever was before I accepted the freedom. Then I was as one asleep and dreaming, now I am awake—alive! Yes, I am Rita, though you will not believe it. I think that you cannot, for there is that in you which wants me to be the lesser. Is that not so?

"This day I have said to him who came with me that I

was still heart-tied to you. Perhaps that was true—once. When I came to you before, my once dear friends, after my change, it was as a begger, asking for your alms. But in that I erred. For what have you to give me now?"

"Perhaps nothing." Hadlett, not the pilot, answered her.

She laughed. "How well you sum it up. Still—there are those here—" Rita glanced from one to the next. "You have such courage, even if it is wrongly rooted. I know you all well, even these two new ones come into your company. And, though you may not believe it, I wish you well. What I can do for you, that I will. But I warn you—it can be but little. You have not the freedom. And what you have provoked is very strong."

"It was Avalon who gave me the first hint of using the mind power." Nick spoke for the first time. "If this was such a wrong thing, then why did he do it?"

He thought Rita looked a little shaken. "I do not know. The Heralds have their purposes under the King. This is a change time—"

"So," the Vicar said, "a time of alteration may bring things out of custom to pass? Logos once more faces Chaos. And you say that our strength will not hold to protect us?"

Rita shook her head. "It cannot. We with the freedom draw from Avalon itself. Look—it can be thus with us." She stooped to set her hand to the floor. Under her touch the rock crumbled, leaving the imprint of her fingers. "That is no illusion, set your hand within if you do not believe me. But its like you cannot do, for your gift is small. Unite if you will, as you have, and there is still a limit, for the land will not nourish you."

Lung who had been crouched at her feet, leaped up again, and she smiled at his exuberance, laid her hand on his head, while from the shadows sped Jeremiah, wreathing about her ankles, purring so loudly they could hear. And for the cat, also, Rita had a touch. When she raised her head there was a faint trouble on her face.

"Some can accept freedom, others choose their chains. Why is it so?"

"Because," Crocker burst out, "we are ourselves! We don't want to be changed into—into—"

"Into what I am? But what then am I, Barry?"

"I don't know. Except that you are not Rita. And that I hate you for what you have done to her!"

"But I am Rita, the whole Rita. Fear walks with hate. You hate because you fear."

Nick saw Crocker's face go tight. A man might look so when he killed.

"You see?" Rita spoke to Hadlett. "His mind is closed because he wills it so. We build our own walls about us. What is your wall, Vicar?"

"My faith, Rita. I have lived with it as part of me all my life. I am a priest of my faith. As such I cannot betray it."

She bowed her head. "You are blind, but your choice by your own standard is just. And you, Lady Diana?"

"Perhaps I can also say it is faith—faith in the past, in what made up my life—" She spoke slowly as if seeking the right words.

"So be it. And you, Jean? Yes, I can understand what ties you to danger and darkness."

The other girl flushed, her mouth twisted angrily. But she did not speak, only moved a fraction closer to Crocker.

"Mrs. Clapp, then?" Rita continued. It was as if she must force a final denial from each and every one of them in turn.

"Well—perhaps its's because I've been a churchgoin' body all m'life. If the Vicar thinks this is wrong—then I'll abide by what he says."

"And you, Warden?"

"It's like Lady Diana said—you make your choice 'bout who you stand with. That's good enough for me."

"And you?" Rita turned now to Linda.

"If one chooses Avalon, is there any chance of returning to one's own time and world?" the American girl asked.

"That I do not know. But I believe that the will to remain will be stronger than the will to return. For one becomes a part of Avalon."

"Then I guess it will be 'no'! But has Lung chosen?" Linda's eyes were now on the dog crouched at Rita's feet.

"Ask."

"Lung—Lung—" Linda called softly. The Peke looked at her and came, moving slowly, but he came.

"They have their loyalty also," Rita said. "He will stay with you because he is heart-tied. Even as Jeremiah will share what comes to you, Maude Clapp."

She was going to ask him now. Nick braced himself, because he knew what he would answer and what would come of it. Why must he take on this burden? He had no heart-ties, as Rita called them, yet he must go against all his inclinations, and for no reason he could put into words.

"I stay," he said before she could ask.

Rita was frowning. "For you it is not the same. You say the words but something more may come of this. We shall see. However, in this much shall I aid you all now. That which waits without is but the first wave of what comes. Use your will with mine and I shall set a barrier—to hold for a little."

"We want nothing from you!" Crocker flared.

"Barry, this is for all to decide," the Vicar said. "I think, Rita, you mean this for our good. What say the rest?"

Crocker and Jean shook their heads, but the others nodded in agreement. So having decided, they linked their power, standing within the cave, not knowing what it wrought outside, but feeling, too, the fierce surge of energy from Rita.

"This will not hold. It will only afford you a brief respite."

"For as much as you have given us, we thank you," Hadlett answered. "And, my child, we wish you well."

Rita raised her hand and traced a design in the air that remained there for an instant, written in pale blue fire—the ankh.

"I wish you—peace. And that none may trouble you thereafter."

Once more she wept, tears on her white cheeks. Then she turned and went from them, the shining envelope of radiance closing about her so they could not see how she disappeared.

"She wished us death!" Jean exploded. "You know that, don't you—she meant that by her 'peace'—death!"

"She wished us the best she could foresee for us." Hadlett's voice was very tired. "I believe she spoke the truth."

"Yes," Lady Diana agreed heavily. She did not add to that but went to stand by the fire, staring into it.

But Linda came to Nick. "There can be a way back—" she told him, an eager note in her voice.

"Back where?" He was hardly aware of her.

"Back to our own world."

"How do you mean?" She had his attention now.

"If we can only get out of here—back to where we came in. Once there, why can't we make a door and go through? If we could make soldiers and a machine gun, as we did"—she waved to the cave entrance—"then we ought to be able to get back by willing hard enough—all of us together. Don't you see? It could work—it has to!" She ended as vehemently as if at that moment she could see such a door, the safe past behind it.

"Even if it would work," Nick countered, "how are we going to get back to the forest to try? If we leave here—do you realize what is waiting out there? We couldn't fight our way across country—not with those things waiting for us!"

"We can"—she was stubborn—"use illusions. Don't you see—it is all we can do."

"What is the only thing we can do?" Jean's voice, hostile in tone, cut in.

"We have to try to get back to our own world. I was telling Nick—we can do it! If we go back to where we first came through—to where the jeep is—then make a door—we can go through! It's a way we'll have to try. Don't you see, we have to!"

Her excitement grew as she talked. That she was wrong, Nick was convinced. But to his surprise he saw an answering spark arise in Jean.

"If it would work—" The English girl drew a long breath. "Yes, if that worked and he—we—could be free of everything here! It would be wonderful! That forest is a long way from here and with all that out there—"

"We've just got to try," Linda urged. "She—Rita—you heard what she said about worse coming. If we stay here we're caught. But if we can make it back—"

"Can't do it." Crocker had been drawn to their group. "If the country was free, yes, it would be worth a try. But we can't fight our way through now."

"So we just stay here"—Linda rounded on him—"and wait to be caught by those horrors? Is that what you want? There ought to be some way we can get through."

She looked eagerly from one to another. Perhaps in Jean she still had an ally, but Nick knew how impossible such a trek would be. He had come cross-country under

Rita's protection and he had a very good idea that had it not been for that he would not have lasted long no matter how stiff a fight he had put up. With Mrs. Clapp, the Vicar, the wounded Stroud, to slow them, they would not have a chance.

"We have to get back," Linda repeated. "I—I don't want to die. And you were right, Jean. Rita wished us to die there at the last. She—the People won't do any more to help us. We'll have to help ourselves and the only way is to get back to our own world. Maybe—maybe you don't have to go to the place you came through after all. Maybe we could make a gate right here!" Her words came faster and faster.

Nick walked away. He was tired with a weariness that weighed on him like a heavy burden. He did not believe that Linda's suggestion had any hope of realization. And he was too worn out to argue about it. He sat down on the floor and was only aware of Mrs. Clapp when she handed him one of the wooden bowls that held some liquid with a sharp scent.

"Get that down you, lad. It'll perk you up. An' I want you to tell me somethin' true—no fancying it up because I'm an old woman as should be told only good things. I'm old enough to know that there are some things that have no good in 'em at all. Those are made for our bearin' when the time comes. Do you think there is anything we can do—you have been out an' seen it all—to help ourselves?"

Nick sipped the drink. It was slightly bitter, which was in keeping with the situation at hand. But as it slid down his throat it brought warmth—though it did nothing to banish the inner cold rooted in his mind and body.

"I don't think there is any more we can do than has been done. She said that the Dark Powers can draw men to help them. And I saw some out there that might be such. I don't know how long the barrier will last."

She nodded. "It is not what you've said, but all you've not. Well, there were the good years. But you young ones—it would be fairer to you if you had had longer. I wish Jeremiah had gone with her, an' the little dog, too. It's not right that good beasts have to be with us." She sighed and took the empty bowl he handed to her.

Nick longed to go and stretch himself out on his scanty bed. But who knew when the protection Rita had raised would fail? It might be well to check on what was happening out there.

He dragged himself to his feet and went to the entrance, pulling up to the sentry station. No phantom machine gun was there now. But before him, about five feet away, a shimmering cloud, very visible in the gloom, made a curtain. If anything moved beyond he could not see.

Not that he doubted they were still there. And there they would wait until the curtain failed. When that happened—illusions that could not be held and—

Nick put his arm across a rock, laid his head on it, and closed his eyes. But he could not close out his thoughts. Rita and the Herald were right; these stubborn English, he, Linda, were throwing away life for nothing. He did not believe that Avalon was evil.

The power radiating from the ankh in the city had nearly killed him. But there was nothing of evil in it. It was only that he, as he now was, was too frail, too flawed a thing to hold such energy.

Now the Dark Tide swept the land. Only in the city, in those places with the freedom of Avalon, would there be light. And those who did not accept the light opened a door to the Dark. They had tried to use the gift of the light to their own purpose, and, in that, Rita said they brought worse upon themselves.

But why had Avalon, the Herald, given Nick the hint that had led him to the discovery of the power? Certainly there was a purpose in that, a test, perhaps—wherein he had failed by the way he had made use of his discovery. It could well be.

In any event he would now have to face what lay before him and make the best of it. Perhaps Rita was also right in wishing them a swift death as the best she could offer.

Nick thought about death. Was it an end or a beginning? No one knew, only hoped for the best with the part of him that feared absolute extinction above all else. Death could be peace, in such a land as this.

"Nicholas—"

He raised his head. By the glow of the wall he could see Hadlett, though he could not read the Vicar's expression.

"Yes, sir?"

"You were in the city, Sam told us. What is it like there?"

Wearily Nick spoke of the walls and streets, of those doors with their pictures that came alive at the touch, and, finally, of the great ankh and the energy that could slay when one was unprepared to face its force.

"The looped cross," said the Vicar. "Yes, the key to eternity, as the Egyptians called it when they put it into the hands of their gods. A source of energy that only those who have surrendered to it can absorb."

"They are not evil," Nick returned. "I have seen evil and it does not lie in the city."

"No. It is not evil, yet it demands the surrender of one's will, of what one is."

"As is also demanded by our own way of worship." Nick did not know from where he had those words.

"But that is an older way, from which we turned long ago. To surrender again to its power, Nicholas, is to betray all our own beliefs."

"Or to discover that there is only one source after all, but from it many rivers—" Again Nick was not aware of his words until he uttered them.

"What did you say?" Hadlett's tone was sharp, fiercely demanding.

◆ 16 ◆

Nick was not given time to answer. For, from beyond the shimmering barrier now came a sound he had heard before—the compelling, head-hurting summons that had drawn his former captors. He clapped his hands to his ears, but the sound was in his head.

Only this time it was not so severe. Nick gritted his teeth, braced himself against obeying the summons. In the faint light he could see Hadlett doubled up against the rocks, his hands also to his ears, his white head bowed.

Fight it! Nick marshalled his will to do that. He did not know in whose hand was that weapon, but it was evil. Then he was aware of someone pushing past him. He threw out his arm, tried to deter that other, reeled back from a blow.

He watched Crocker head to the barrier. Behind him scrambled the others; Jean very close to the pilot; Lady Diana, her face twisted, her hands to her tortured ears; finally Stroud lurching along, his gait that of a drunken man, or one so weak only intense purpose kept him going.

The four came to the barrier before Nick could move from where Crocker had shoved him, passed through, to be hidden from sight. Hadlett wavered forward, but this time Nick was prepared. He sprang to tackle the Vicar, bearing the old man with him down toward the cave entrance.

Linda, Mrs. Clapp—he must stop them if he could. He pushed and pulled Hadlett into the cave. The torment in his head continued but he could master that—he had to. This time he was not tied to keep him safe.

By the light within Nick saw a scene of confusion. Mrs. Clapp lay on the floor, struggling to rise. Linda knelt beside her, not striving to aid her but with both hands on the woman's shoulders, holding her down, while Mrs. Clapp writhed and flung her arms about.

173

Before them crouched the two animals. Lung snarled in anger, the cat growled and lashed his tail. Both of them faced the women as if at any moment they would join the struggle.

Linda's face was twisted with pain, her mouth ugly as she moaned and cried out. Mrs. Clapp uttered meaningless sounds.

"Help!" Linda gasped as Nick came, pushing the staggering Vicar.

He gave Hadlett a last vigorous shove, this time taking no care, only heading the older man toward the interior of the cave. Then he ran to Linda.

"She—mustn't—go—"

"No!" he agreed. But his help was not needed, for Mrs. Clapp with a last cry, went limp and still.

"No!" Now the protest came from Linda. She lifted the woman's head, held it against her, cradled in her arm, touched her face gently. "Nick she can't be dead!"

"I don't think so. Watch her." He returned to Hadlett. The Vicar had slumped to the floor, sat there with his legs outstretched, his head sunk on his chest, his arms hanging limp so his hands lay palm up on either side of his body. He was breathing in heavy gasps, but that was the only sign of life.

The clamor without was retreating. Nick could think more clearly, relax a little. The cat and the Peke were still alert, but had ceased their active objection. It was as if they were to be given a breathing space.

"She's—she's alive, Nick!" Linda glanced up from her charge. "But the others—they went out—where?"

"I don't know."

"That was—was more of the Dark Ones' attack?"

Nick had no answer to that either. "I don't know. It was what took the drifters who captured me. But I never saw what caused it—only them going."

"As they did here." Linda settled Mrs. Clapp's head more easily against her arm. "I wanted to go, Nick. But Lung tripped me, jumped at me. And Jeremiah pulled at Mrs. Clapp's skirt, tangled her up so she fell. They—both of them—helped me think straight, know that I mustn't go—she must not. But how did you and Mr. Hadlett get away, Nick?"

For the third time Nick had to admit ignorance. He only knew that, painful and compelling as that sound had been, he had been able to withstand it, not only that but somehow prevent Hadlett from being drawn also. He flinched away from imagining what might have happened to the others. For this moment it was enough to know that in so much they had beaten the enemy.

"Maybe because I heard it before and could not answer," he speculated. "It may lose impact the second time around. And Hadlett was with me. He did not move out at once, which gave me a chance to—"

"To save me, Nicholas." The Vicar slowly raised his head. His gaunt face was so haggard that he might have been mortally ill. As he spoke a twitch started beneath his left eye, a flutter of skin and muscle that drew his face into an unsightly grimace for a second. "To save me from the Devil's own work, Nicholas." He straightened and winced as if his body protested. "We must not allow the others to be taken by that—that thing! They are possessed—"

"Jeremiah!" Mrs. Clapp opened her eyes, looked up into Linda's face, her expression dazed. "Jeremiah—he jumped at me! My own old boy—he's gone mad!"

"No." Linda soothed her. "He wanted to save you, and he did."

The cat padded closer. Now he set both forepaws on Mrs. Clapp's breast, leaned down to touch her nose with the tip of his own. His tongue came out and he gave her face a small, fastidious lick.

"Jeremiah." Mrs. Clapp lifted one hand, laid it on the cat's head. "Why—"

"To save you," Linda repeated. "Just as Lung saved me, and Nick did Mr. Hadlett."

"But—" Mrs. Clapp struggled to sit up and Linda aided her. The old woman looked about. "Where're the others? Lady Diana—she was right here—and Jean—and Barry—"

"They have gone." It was Hadlett who answered. "And we have to do what we can to aid them, as soon as possible."

He struggled to his feet as if he would go running with the same unheeding recklessness as had taken the others. Nick moved between him and the entrance to the cave.

"We can't, not until we know what we're facing. It might be throwing away any chance we do have to just go blindly out in the dark."

For a moment, he thought the Vicar would give him a hot argument, even try to push past him. Then Hadlett's shoulders slumped and he answered dully:

"You are right, of course, Nicholas. But we must do something."

"I intend to." That was wrenched out of Nick. Again he was being forced to a decision he did not want to make, take a course he knew was dangerous. The sound had died away, his head was free of the pain. Did that mean that the menace had withdrawn with the prey it had so easily snared, or only that it had subsided to prepare for another and perhaps stronger assault? There was no use looking for trouble in the future, he had enough facing him now.

"Not alone." The force and vigor that had always been in Hadlett's tone was returning. "We must go together—"

"All of us," Linda broke in, "all together."

Nick was about to protest, and then he understood that perhaps she was wiser than he. To leave two women here alone, for he knew he could not argue the Vicar into staying, would be utter folly. When the barrier failed the Dark forces would overrun the cave. Linda and Mrs. Clapp would have no chance at all. And what he had seen of the besiegers made Nick certain that they must not face what had walked, loped, slithered out there.

Of course it was the height of stupidity to go out at all. But if he did not, he was sure Hadlett would set off by himself, or with the women. Nick must be as practical as this impractical situation allowed.

So he suggested that they make up packs, the heaviest to be for him and Linda, though both Mrs. Clapp and the Vicar insisted they shoulder their share. And the Vicar did offer experienced advice.

"Is there any other way out—besides the one I found earlier?" Nick asked.

"Along the stream, sir—" Mrs. Clapp looked to the Vicar.

Hadlett seemed doubtful. "That is a rough passage, Maude."

"Rough it may be," she answered stoutly, "but if it takes us out where those things ain't watchin', won't that be for the best?"

"I suppose—" But he did not sound convinced.

"Along what stream, sir?" Nick pursued the matter.

"An underground one. We never explored it far. But there is a place, Sam assured me, where one can scramble out. I believe some distance from this—" He gestured at the entrance.

"All the better." Nick was a little heartened. He would have suggested the back entrance he had found but he was sure that neither the Vicar nor Mrs. Clapp could make it.

If they only had in truth the machine gun of the illusion, or weapons from their own world. He had the knife, and now he found in his saddlebags the camp knife he had almost forgotten. Since Hadlett had one of the daggers, he gave this to Linda. Iron—little enough for defense. They might as well, thought Nick savagely, go barehanded.

Mrs. Clapp looked about her. She had quietly stacked the wooden bowls, folded up some crudely woven mats. It was plain she believed it would be long before anyone returned here.

"A rough wild place it is, but it's been good to us."

"Yes, Maude," Hadlett answered gently.

"Sometimes—sometimes I dream about walkin' up the walk—seein' the roses an' those lilies Mrs. Lansdowne at the lodge gave me the settin' of. There's m' own old door an' Jeremiah's sittin' on the step watchin' for me. I dream like that, sir. It's as real as real for a while—"

"I know, Maude. I wonder if that bomb did hit St. Michael's. Five hundred and near fifty years—a long time for a church to stand. It still stands for me."

"We got it all to remember, sir. That nobody can take away. An' you can close your eyes sometimes, when you're restin' like, an' see it as plain as plain. Maybe if we went back—Sometimes I think to m'self, sir, that I see it better'n it really was. You can do that, you know. Like lookin' back down the years to when one was a little maid—everything was brighter an' better then. The years were longer like, not all squeezed together like they seem to be now. An' there was a lot packed into every one o' 'em. Well, a clackin' tongue ain't goin' to get me, nor anyone else, goin'. But for all its roughness, this has been a good place. Come on, Jeremiah!"

Her speech ended on a brisk note. Linda moved closer to Nick.

"She makes me want to cry. Oh, Nick, I don't want to remember, not now. It does something to me, I get to feeling wild, as if I could just run about screaming, 'Let me out!' Don't you ever feel like that?"

"It depends," he answered as he shouldered his pack, "on what you have to go back to. Anyway there's no use looking too far ahead now. We had better concentrate on getting out of here."

"Nick," she interrupted him, "what can we do—to help them? Can we even find them?"

"I doubt it. But those two"—he nodded to the Vicar helping Mrs. Clapp over the rough footing in a side alcove of the cave—"won't give up trying. And we can't leave them to do it alone."

Linda caught her lip between her teeth, frowned. "No, I can see that. Will they ever admit it's hopeless? What do you think happened to the others, Nick?"

"Your guess is as good as mine," was the best answer he could give her. He was trying to control imagination which was only too ready to present him with horrors.

The way Hadlett guided them into was rough, and soon they had to go single file. Lung and Jeremiah had the best of it as they padded along with far greater ease than the two-footed humans and soon outpaced them. Linda called anxiously now and then, and was always answered by a single bark from the Peke.

After a very short time they hit a downward incline, dropping them well below the surface of the larger cave. Twice they had to stoop, proceeding at a back-aching angle. Nick's flashlight in Hadlett's hand lit up the worst of the obstructions.

Now they could hear the gurgle of water. And a last scramble brought them into a wider tunnel, one that water over the centuries must have carved for itself, though the present stream running along it was much smaller than the space through which it passed.

"This way." Hadlett turned left. Nick was pleased at that. Unless he was completely misled, any opening in this direction to the surface would be well away from the upper entrance. He wondered if the barrier there still held.

With that gone, would the enemy make a frontal attack? With no resistance they could enter the cave. At that thought, Nick turned uneasily to glance over his shoulder, tried to listen. But the sounds of the stream and their own journey effectively cloaked what might be behind. He wished that the Peke and Jeremiah had remained in closer contact. The animals had a far better range of hearing and could sound the alarm if it was needed.

Nick wanted to hurry, but he knew with Mrs. Clapp's stiff and painful legs and the Vicar's age, they could push on at no better speed than this. He drew his knife, always straining to hear any sound except that of the water and their going.

"Here—" Hadlett flashed the light to the left. There was a break in the wall of the tunnel. Then the light showed the surface of the water. They must splash through that to reach the cleft. Nick wondered how deep it was. He saw Jeremiah sitting on the other side. But Lung whimpered and ran to Linda, begging to be taken up. So the Peke thought the flood too deep or had some objection to splashing on. The cat must have jumped it. Nick took warning from Lung.

"Don't try to wade!" He crowded up beside the Vicar. "Give me the flashlight."

"You noticed Lung, yes." Hadlett passed over the light.

Nick squatted on his heels. The rest had flattened against the wall of the tunnel. He turned the light directly on the water. There were no signs of a swift current, and it looked shallow, but he was not a trained woodsman to know. The stream might be a trap the animals knew by instinct. Yet it was too wide for their jumping—they did not have Jeremiah's talents. It would be wade—

"Nick!" Linda dropped beside him. Now she swung her arm across his chest to point upstream.

The troubling of the current was plainly visible. And that was not caused by some rock nearly breaking the surface, for it moved toward them. Nick handed her the light.

"Hold that!" He was ready with his knife. For the sight made him believe he faced the alien.

The disturbance in the water ceased, but Nick breathed faster. That thing, whatever it might be, was not gone. Rather it had taken to what cover the water afforded.

"Nick!" Linda's cry scaled up to near a scream, but her quick reflexes saved them. The hand and arm flashing from beneath the water did not achieve its purpose. Webbed fingers grasped in vain. Linda now had the flashlight well out of reach.

The American stabbed down into the water with the knife. There was a flurry there. Then the head and shoulders of the being that had tried to rob them of light arose. This was no human. In the first place the creature could not be much larger than Jeremiah. Secondly it was covered with fur as might be an otter or seal.

It had great round eyes, a whiskered muzzle, a wild tangle of coarser hair like a mane reaching to its shoulders. The mouth opened, showing yellow fang-teeth. Then it snapped shut while it hissed much as might Jeremiah in a rage.

Nick advanced the blade he held. The water thing sputtered, made mewling sounds, but it retreated. This was one of the natives of Avalon he was sure. But it did not seem as one with the Dark forces. That it was hostile to his kind was plain, but it was not strongly evil.

"Wait, lad." Mrs. Clapp came forward. "Iron will keep that off, but there is another way also."

Nick glanced up in surprise as she fumbled in her bag and drew out a small length of branch. Solemnly, as if performing some ritual in the Vicar's vanished St. Michael's, she recited:

> "Nixie, pixie—
> The water is draining,
> Your fine home awastin'.
> Comes now th' cattle a-stampin', a-trampin'.
> Naught will remain.
> By th' elder, by th' ash,
> Begone—thrice!"

She struck the surface of the water three times with her branch.

The thing stopped in mid-hiss, watching her warily. But as she said "thrice," it gave an eerie cry and submerged. They could see it moving at lightning speed upstream. Lung ran along at the edge of the water barking furiously, while Linda called him.

Mrs. Clapp laughed. "There now, I never thought to say that in a lifetime. M' old Aunt Meg, she was a proper one—more'n my auntie she was really, 'cause she was sister to m' great-granny. But she lived a long time. A hundred 'n' more she was before she took to her bed the last time. She had the healin' an' the Second Sight. Folks used to go to her for wart charmin' an' the like, 'fore it got so the young folks laughed at such.

"Aunt Meg, she could see the Gentry—that was what we called 'em in our bit o' country in those days—though she never talked much of that. Offered me a bite of yellow cake stuff once when I was little. Said it was Gentry-baked. My Mum struck it out o' m' hand an' beat it right into the dust when I fetched it home. She said it was silly, but she knew right enough about dealin' with the Gentry.

"That there was a nixie. Auntie, she said they were mischiefmakers. Live in bogs, some of them do, an' lead people astray. She learned me that spell an' told me about usin' elder. There's nothin' like elder an' ash to stand up to them of the Gentry as is for mischief. Yes, she learned me that when I was goin' for the milk up to Barstows' farm an' had to pass over a bit of bog there if I took the quick way home. I was old enough to keep m 'tongue inside m' teeth, an' Mum never knew. Never saw a nixie, though, not there. But I always kept careful watch like Auntie said to."

"Will it be back?" Linda had caught Lung and was holding him.

"Not if we do it right." Mrs. Clapp appeared to have complete confidence in her method of routing the water thing. "First we see just how deep this is here." She used the elder branch for a measure. " 'Bout knee-high, I would say."

"Now," she continued with authority, "we'd best take off our shoes, an' pull up m' skirt an' your pants. We can take a wettin' better than our clothes can, dry off sooner, too."

"A very wise precaution." Hadlett was already pulling off his moccasins, rolling up his trousers.

"An' this"—Mrs. Clapp held out the branch—"I'm goin' to stick in so." She pushed it down into the water and it stood there upright. "That there elder is goin' to be a cover for us."

Splash across they did, though Nick kept watch for any telltale line in the water that would mark the return of the nixie. He was the last across and Mrs. Clapp yelled to him:

"Bring the wand with you, lad. Don't know when I'll get m' hand on another good bit of elder. Don't seem to grow too plentiful hereabouts."

He pulled the branch free, dragging it behind him through the water as an added precaution against an attack, to hand it back to its owner. Mrs. Clapp flipped it to shake off the droplets along it and stowed it briskly away as if her past performance was as ordinary as eating or sleeping.

Now they climbed at a sharper angle than they had descended. It was difficult for Mrs. Clapp. At times all three of them boosted or pulled. She breathed heavily but she never complained. Sometimes she even made some cheery remark on their aid or her own clumsiness.

"Just ahead now. I had better turn this off." Hadlett pushed off the flash button. There was instant and smothering darkness, and Nick began a protest, but the Vicar was continuing:

"Wait until our eyes adjust. It is night out there but there should be some light—moon—"

"Let me lead now." Nick did not want to do that, but he certainly was not going to stand behind two women and an older man. Something brushed past him and he nearly cried out. Then he knew it was Jeremiah.

Nick bumped into a solid surface with considerable force and realized there was a turn in the passage. Feeling his way with one hand, the knife in the other, he made the turn and indeed did see a pale spot ahead.

"Wait," he whispered, "until I make sure."

"Well enough," Hadlett agreed.

Nick took it very slowly. There was too much chance of tripping, or making some noise. If those who had besieged the other entrance to the cave had an outpost here they could be waiting.

That short advance was one of the hardest things Nick had ever forced himself to do. But at last he felt the cool night air, saw moonlight. He crouched and listened, wishing with all his might he knew what were the natural sounds one should expect to hear—and those that would mean trouble.

Then Nick sighted Jeremiah. The cat was in the open, his gray fur hardly distinguishable. And from him Nick gained one of those thought messages. There was no one threatening nearby—they had gotten free of the Dark Ones—for now.

Nick crept back to the turn and whispered the good news. The waiting three followed him. A moment or so and they were out of the slit into the night, standing under the stars, seeing the silver of the moon.

"Which way do we go now?" Linda wanted to know. She carried Lung, and Nick thought she did not trust the Peke not to run into some waiting danger.

"Ahead I would say." Hadlett held Nick's compass. "We should go east for a space before we turn south. Thus perhaps we can outflank those by the cave."

"If they are still there," Nick commented.

Having three prisoners, would they be waiting for the rest? He thought it more in keeping that they would only leave a token force and be on their way with their captives. If they were captives still and not—

He refused to accept what his imagination supplied. Not yet, not until they had proof, would he believe the others dead. They might lose time by following the Vicar's suggestion, but it was a sensible one. And the more they could avoid the ghastly crew he had seen the better.

Rita—had she returned to the safety of the city? She had made it clear she would not come to their aid again. But that was only just. They had refused what she had to offer. And what had they gained in return—the loss of half their company.

"Nicholas." He turned toward that half-seen form that was Hadlett, now hand-linked to Mrs. Clapp, who had admitted her night sight was poor.

"What is it?"

"We are no longer alone." That was the chilling information Nick had feared ever since they had emerged from the cave's back door.

• 17 •

Nick sensed it also—the presence, or presences—but not the evil that had been such a foul emanation from the Dark Ones. He heard a mewling cry from Jeremiah.

Then once more he saw the cat. With him was Lung who must have escaped from Linda. The animals stood together and before them was one of the weird forest beasts, larger than either, but bending its head to touch noses with first the cat and then the Peke.

It was the one—or like it—that Nick had seen with the Green Man—the creature Hadlett had named "enfield." In color this had a golden sheen, misted as the Herald and the People appeared. And that radiance made clear its fox head, greyhound body, the taloned, eaglelike forefeet, the canine hindquarters and wolf tail.

What manner of exchange passed between the animals they had no way of knowing. However, the enfield raised its sharp-eared head and gave a cry that was neither bay nor bark, closer to song. It was answered from the darkness about in various notes and tones, as if the human party was now ringed by strange and alien creatures.

The enfield turned its head to eye them. In its skull its eyes were small yellow flames. For a second out of time it studied them. Then once more it voiced the call. When it was answered, it was gone, winked out as might be the flame of a candle caught by a puff of breeze.

"What—?" Linda began shakily

But Nick knew, without words he knew.

"We have nothing to fear—from them," he said.

"The freedom of the woodlands," Hadlett added. "Perhaps we have not been given full seizing, that ancient right to estate under formal rule. But this much—"

"I don't know what you are talking about!" Linda burst out. "What was that—that thing? And, Nick, from the sound, they're all around us. What if—"

184

"We have nothing to fear," he repeated. "Not from them."

Could they dare to hope they had acquired an escort? Or would the unseen company of beasts merely remain neutral? He knew they were still there, though he did not sight them. And with the vanishing of the light radiating from the enfield he could no longer see either Jeremiah or Lung.

"We'd better get on," Nick added. What he did not say was that he wanted to see if the other company would move with them.

"Yes!" Linda was eager to push ahead. Undoubtedly she wanted to leave the unseen behind. "Lung," she called softly. "Here, Lung!"

The Peke came to her readily and she scooped him up, holding him as if she feared he might be snatched from her at any moment. Then Nick felt the push of a furred body against his legs, stooped and gathered up Jeremiah. The cat wriggled up, draped his body about Nick's shoulders stole-fashion. The American was a little uncomfortable under the weight, but knew that he must be content with Jeremiah's choice.

Guided by the compass, they went east, skirting the open where there was need. But their pace slowed. Nick knew without seeing or being told that Mrs. Clapp was lagging, and he suspected it was little better with the Vicar. They would have to rest.

When he suggested a halt there was no objection, and, using a bush growth for cover, they dropped to the ground. Jeremiah leaped from Nick's shoulders to disappear. There was no measuring how far they had come, but Nick wondered if they should not now turn south, strive to cut across the trail of the missing.

Morning light would be better for a tracking attempt and he pointed this out. To his surprise, the Vicar agreed. They planned to keep watch, the three of them, allowing Mrs. Clapp full rest, turn about.

Nick volunteered for the first sentry go. The moonlight somehow appeared dimmer and he had to depend more on his ears than his sight. He stuck the knife point down between his knees, resting one hand on its hilt, and tried to think.

There was, he believed, very little chance of them being able to rescue the others. But that fact they would have to prove to themselves. Afterward—what could they do? Would it be possible to slowly work their way back through a now totally hostile world to the place they had left the jeep and there try Linda's suggestion of opening a return door? Nick thought they might try, but the chances for success were close to nonexistent. What would remain then? A harried, ever-endangered existence as the prey of either the Dark Ones or the saucers. Perhaps they could get as far as that farmhouse again. But there was the matter of food— And life in a continual state of apprehension was no life at all.

The English had known that at home with the air raids, the constant threat of invasion. Nick had read about it, but that was all very far away and long ago. You could not understand such fear until you, yourself, were forced to live with it. And he and Linda, though the world they knew also had its violence, had not had to deal directly with it before.

The best answer was still the city. But if the Vicar and Mrs. Clapp continued to refuse—what then?

Nick tensed, jerking the knife free. He had heard nothing, he saw nothing—but there was something out there now. One of the alien animals? They had had an escort from that meeting, of that Nick was fully convinced.

Now he heard a small whine. Lung came from where Linda lay. His small body, when Nick laid hand on it, quivered as if he wished to run forth in greeting. Nick could sense no fear, only excitement.

There was a faint penciling of light in the air, outlining a figure. Nick arose to face who—or what—stood there. The light grew stronger, that figure more solid. Nick expected Avalon. But this was Rita!

"You! But—"

Then anger rose in him. "You gave us a very dramatic good-bye. Why return now?"

Her porcelain face was without expression. "For your purpose it will be enough that I have come at all. Those you seek have been taken by the flyers, not the Dark Ones. If you would have them forth, seek the sky hunters."

"Why are you telling me this?" Nick demanded. "By your own words you are apart from us, and Avalon cares nothing for us."

"True." Now there was a faint troubling of her expression. "But if you seek among the Dark Ones—then you shall be totally lost. I would have you save yourselves."

"And the others?"

Rita shook her head. "How can you save them? For those who have taken them are mightier than you can hope to be. They have weapons that are as far beyond those you have known as yours are beyond bow, sword, and spear. Those they take are gone, accept that."

Nick's anger, aroused by what he could not analyze, remained steady. At this point had Rita said the sun was bright, he would have denied it. At first he thought her information might be a trick. Then he was sure it was true.

"Was that sound one of their weapons?"

"Yes. It compels—draws—"

"Then why did it not take us all?"

"I told you—you are different. The Great Power touched you. Also he—and Maude—and the girl—they, too, believe, though they deny it. Maude and Adrian Hadlett have the old belief in their blood, their past. The girl—her dog has given her the open door. You each had a small defense against that weapon, and Lung and Jeremiah were fully armed. They are of Avalon in their own way."

He saw now by the glow of light about her that the cat and the Peke were seated at her feet, gazing up at her as if entranced. She stooped to touch fingertip to each furred head.

"Wise in their time are these," she said.

"Wiser than we?"

"Ask that of yourself, not me."

Her glow was fading, drawing about her. Nick moved.

"Wait!"

But she made no answer. Rita was gone.

"That's a good act." Linda was beside him. "Do you believe a word she says?"

"Yes."

"The trouble is, though I don't like her—in fact, if you want the absolute, down-to-earth truth, I think I hate her—I believe her, too. Which means what, Nick? Can we possibly help the others if the saucer people have them? I don't see any chance of doing that."

"Right now I don't either," he confessed. "They could have taken them anywhere."

"It is not as hopeless as it would seem." They were both

startled by the Vicar's voice out of the dark. "Yes, I have been awake, saw and heard our visitor. And I also believe her. But, remember, we were brought to this continent as prisoners of the saucer people. They had then a headquarters here, not too far from where we were wrecked and freed. Surely any prisoners they take will be found there."

"But we haven't a chance of getting in," Nick protested. "Rita was right, you know. They do have weapons beyond anything we know. They stunned those men we saw netted. And that sound—the rays they turned on the Herald. We have no protection against such. It's crazy to think we can get them away." But even as he protested, Nick knew that Hadlett would remain unconvinced, determined to rescue the others, be that possible or impossible.

"We seem to have a partial defense against the sound." It was as if the Vicar had heard nothing Nick said. "What was it that Rita told you—Maude and I, through our blood and the past—now what did she mean?" Nick thought he asked that question of himself rather than his listeners. "Maude is of Sussex, very old Sussex. She was a Boorde before her marriage. And you heard her speak of her great-great-aunt who had the Sight and the powers of healing. As for me—we have been ten generations in Minton Parva, squires or churchmen, and I know the old ways—

"The old ways," he repeated. "Yes, Avalon, and the People, I have long heard of them. Iron and the Church drove them out, but they lingered for a space. Perhaps in England they were in exile, perhaps they were colonists. 'The Gentry' some called them—because they were indeed 'gentle folk' in the old meaning of the word, fair to look on, courteous, sometimes helpful to man."

"They had their faults, too, sir." Mrs. Clapp had been roused. "They disliked those who spied on 'em, an' there were them as made trouble. But they was known, least-ways to the old folks. These here flyin' people, they're different, not like us at all. If they've got 'em—Lady Diana, Barry, Sam, Miss Jean—then how are we goin' to get them back, sir?"

It was as if her brisk question roused the Vicar from his thoughts.

"That will take some consideration, Maude."

"It will take more than consideration." Hadlett was not a man with whom to be brusque, Nick had known that from his first meeting with the Vicar. But he would not accept some unworkable scheme now. He worried too much about the powers of the saucers. Perhaps, in a way, he could understand those better so he really dreaded them more than the monsters he thought might be illusions, horrible as those were.

"You are right, Nicholas," the Vicar agreed.

"But," he continued, "we now know where we must search—to the north, not the south."

That he was going to be able to argue the English out of abandoning the search Nick already guessed was impossible. And to leave them—that he could not. It would be up to him to try to think up some telling argument, but at present his mind was a blank.

What he did do was question Hadlett methodically to learn all he could of what the Vicar had observed during their captivity in the saucer. That the flyers could stun their prey was the truth. Rendered completely helpless such prisoners were loaded into the saucers and it was some time before that effect wore off. When it did, they were locked into compartments meant to be prisons.

The escape of the English party had been a fluke which might happen perhaps once in a thousand times. Some motive power of the saucer had failed and it crash-landed. The door to their cell had been sprung and the English had found at least two of their captors dead.

"Their helmets were shattered," Hadlett explained. "It is evident that they cannot breathe this air without the protection of the snout-masks that are part of their headgear. That is one advantage for us—"

A very small one, was Nick's conclusion. How were they going to break helmets in any battle when the enemy could stand off and ray them down? The more he thought about it, the more he was convinced this was a suicide mission.

"Were they all killed?" Nick asked.

"Yes. Barry and Sam went back to the ship—Barry had some hope of learning their method of flight. But all he could discover was that the ship was locked onto some homing device. What had caused it to crash he could not discover. But the crew were all dead. They were very small—dwarfish—and their skins blue. Barry and Sam did not have time to learn much, for they found another machine broadcasting what Barry thought was a distress signal. We hurried away, which was prudent, for we saw in the distance later another saucer—perhaps hunting the wreck."

"Locked into a homing device," Nick repeated. Then if one had access to a saucer it would take one to their headquarters—perhaps.

"That has some meaning for you?" the Vicar began and then added excitedly, "But, of course, it would be the perfect way, would it not, to enter the enemy stronghold undetected."

"The perfect way," Nick reminded him, "to walk straight into a prison and whatever the saucer people have ready for those they capture."

"Perhaps, perhaps not. It is a point to consider, Nicholas. Yes, an excellent point to consider. Think of it this way, my boy—if we were not altogether affected by their sound weapon, then it could just be we could allow ourselves to be apparently captured, to turn the tables—as the old saying goes—on our captors."

Fantastic! Did he really think that? It was the wildest suggestion yet. Nick's penetration into the city was as nothing beside this.

"Could we do it?"

Nick nearly rounded on Linda hotly. Somehow he had unconsciously expected her to support him in any trial of wills in their small party, but listen to her now. "Could we use illusions for bait?" she continued.

Nick's annoyance faded. Though her face was only a blur in the dark he stared at her. An illusion for bait? Then perhaps an ambush of the saucer? No, it would not work—they had no weapons except their knives—

"Now that, m' dear, is right smart thinkin'. I do believe, sir, that Miss Linda has an idea that might just work—"

"And how do we jump them when they come down with the net?" Nick raised his voice in protest. Pressure— a sharp pricking against his leg. He exclaimed. Jeremiah had hooked his claws well into Nick, demanding attention.

"Jeremiah." Nick went to one knee, stroking the cat. "What is it?"

Foggy—like trying to see a picture through a dense mist—outlines that wavered back and forth, on which Nick tried to focus. Even when he concentrated, the pictures were odd, as if he saw through eyes that were not normal, having other qualities than his own. Lung—certainly that bouncing creature was Lung at his most exuberant. And there was the enfield, and behind it other weird, mixed things. The beasts of Avalon. Was Jeremiah promising now their help?

Yes! Thought answered his unasked question.

It would be a plan of many pieces, and much would depend on luck, on attracting a saucer, on timing thereafter. But maybe, just maybe, they could do it. And it was better than just blindly walking into trouble—which is what the Vicar might well do if Nick did not produce an alternate plan.

"Sir," Nick tried to bring all his powers of persuasion to bear. "Do you think a plan such as this might work?" As he continued, he thought of new details, added improvements (he hoped they were improvements).

Thus it came about that hours later found them in the hot sun on the edge of the open. Having set their plan they had rested and then, with the beasts of Avalon guiding, they had reached this point.

Now they were linked, men, women, dog and cat together, with an ingathering of power. Perhaps they were again misusing that as Rita had warned. But it was their only key. They lay in hiding, but out in the open two figures walked very slowly. There was a limit to their power of projection and Mrs. Clapp had suggested that instead of trying to reproduce their whole party they create only two illusions, that of the Vicar and herself. She and Hadlett had formed those figures, Nick, Linda, and the animals feeding them the sustaining energy.

Jeremiah and Lung were out there, pacing beside the slow-moving illusions. There were others concealed in the tall grass. Nick had suggested such were visible from above and there had been amusement beamed from Jeremiah. Perhaps the beasts of Avalon had some native protection against such sighting.

Now—all they needed was a saucer to take the bait. How long would that take? They might have to set this scene many times, for they could not hold any illusion long. How—

Not long at all! A saucer burst into view in one of those instantaneous arrivals. It swooped, to center over the staggering figures. Now! Nick gestured. The illusions slumped forward, lay full length. From the belly of the saucer the net broke, descending.

Nick could see twitching grass, the beasts were on the move. Surely the aliens would spot that suspicious movement! But if they did, they did not counter it. It was time for him to make his own move. He was sweating, and not from the heat of the sun. It all depended now on whether they *did* have any protection against the alien weapons.

He began to run, zigzagging as he went, though that might be no protection against attack. One of the suited crewmen was already sliding down the rope toward the inert bodies, a second swinging out of the hatch to follow him.

Then Nick was hit by a force from the saucer, as if a fist struck him. As planned, he gave way, falling—which was only too easy. They would think him a prisoner—perhaps he was. But he summoned up the strength of will that he had commanded in the woods. He *could* do this, his body was his own to order. He *could* move. And he did.

The grass was tall about him, hiding most of the scene around the net. Hadlett, Mrs. Clapp and Linda would hold the illusions of the inert figures as long as they could. If their plan was to succeed, they must hold until he reached the net. He saw now one of the aliens prepare to slip the net around the illusion of Hadlett. Behind the suited figure the grass moved. A small gray shape leaped, hit the shoulders of the alien, clawing at the helmet. It was joined by a flashing creature that could only be the enfield. The other alien, partway down the rope, turned to reclimb.

Out of ambush arose a thing to swing up the rope with the agility of its monkey body. Yet on its shoulders was an owl's head. With no difficulty at all it caught up with the alien, scrambling over his body, so the suited figure lost hold and fell back and down.

Nick was under the shadow of the saucer. The longer he had fought the force that tied his limbs, the easier it became to move. He reached the net. How many crewmen were still in the saucer? The owl-monkey scuttled over the ground leaving a crumpled body behind. The net was now burdened by a number of the beasts, weighting it down. With any luck at all they should anchor the saucer.

Up! Nick caught at the rope ladder. But the owl-monkey was before him, springing up as if this was a stairway. As it went, its outline blurred, it became one of the suited aliens. Nick began to climb. Was the party in hiding successful also? Was he now in the likeness of a helmeted dwarf? Up and up—he hardly dared believe he had made it this far. Now he was through the hatch, the owl-monkey-alien disappearing through a door beyond. Behind Nick came Jeremiah, able to use his claws on the ropeway.

Nick hurried after the beast. His impetus carried him into the control cabin of the saucer. Flame flashed, outlined the owl-monkey whose illusion had vanished. But the creature was as untouched as the Herald under the raying. Nick leaped—there were only two aliens, and the owl-monkey had beaten down the weapon of one, bearing him down into the seat from which he had half-risen.

With a crash Nick met the other alien, carrying the smaller figure back against the wall of the cabin. At the shock of being slammed against it, the alien went limp. Nick held him for a moment, making sure he was harmless. Then Jeremiah landed on the suited form, his snarling face pressed against the surface of the helmet. The eyes of the being inside were closed.

His fellow crewman was still struggling feebly but uselessly with the owl-monkey who proceeded to draw him back to the door opening into the hatch space. Nick, apprehensive, searched the ship. But the four beings they had already taken were the entire crew. Nick was shaking a little from reaction, unable to believe they had done this thing.

Now he feared that the saucer might as suddenly vanish with him. The two aliens, both still alive, Nick thought, were lowered to the ground. Of the two who had been with the net, one was dead with a cracked helmet, the other a prisoner. Nick could not kill in cold blood, but to maroon them in the open country, prisoners of the beasts, unable to summon help, was the answer. And the sooner he got his own party on board, the better.

Hadlett and Linda could climb. But they activated the net to raise Mrs. Clapp and Lung. Once that was inboard the hatch snapped shut of its own accord, and the saucer quivered to life.

Nick ran for the control cabin, forced his larger body into one of the seats. He could not hope to use any of the levers and buttons before him. Like it or not they were on their way, locked into an enemy craft, their destination unknown. And now that he had time, he began to worry again. Their amazing good fortune with the ambush could not continue to hold forever.

◆ 18 ◆

"This is our chance!" Linda tried to fit herself into the narrow neighboring seat.

"Our chance to do what?" Nick had prowled the saucer ship twice. He made several finds of what might be weapons, but he dared not experiment with them inside the cabin. The only chance he could see was one so hedged by threats it was nearer to an invitation to disaster.

"To get back to our own world." She was impatient. "These saucers must go through. People have seen them back there. We have only to learn how, then we're home!"

"That learning how," Nick pointed out, "might take some time. Time we don't have. When this lands—"

"We can use illusions again." Linda dismissed such details as unimportant, her own goal the real one.

"You mean, we hope we can." Nick found the flight pattern of the saucer made him queasy, he wanted nothing more than to be free of the alien ship.

"We can. And we can get back, too!" Her optimism remained high.

"You're forgetting the time factor, aren't you?"

"What time factor?"

"These others—they thought they had only been here a few years. But it's been thirty. How long have we been here—days—a week—I've not counted. But how long have we been *away?*"

What had happened back in the world of the Cut-Off? How long before they had been missed and the search begun? What about Dad and Margo? Who had been hunting Linda? She had said no more about her past than he had. Who was missing her?

"Nick—" Her eagerness was gone, he might have struck her in the face. "Do you think— But it couldn't be! We can't have been gone months, we can't!"

He could give her no reassurance. Before, he had not

195

really considered that point as it applied to himself or Linda. But now Nick faced it squarely and found that he really did not greatly care. All that had happened before their arrival in the forest seemed to be the past of another person and have very little meaning for the Nick Shaw that now was.

"Dave——" Linda stared ahead of her. "What will Dave do? What will he think?"

"Who's Dave?"

"My father, David. He's with NASA—on the Cape. I was staying with Aunt Peg for a vacation. But there's just Dave and me—we're a family!"

Linda hunched down in the seat her body did not adjust to. "Nick, we've got to get back. And the saucer people must know how."

"First things first——" Nick had only gotten that far, not knowing how he could make her see the impossibility of what she wanted, when the saucer began a vertical descent.

They had reached whatever goal had been set. Nick had had no control over that flight. Now it must be tested whether he had any defense over what they might encounter outside.

With a hardly perceptible jar the ship touched down and the vibration of its life ceased. Nick headed back to the area about the hatch. They had made the best plan they could and at least they would have surprise on their side.

Again he was to have the active part. The rest, using their combined concentration, would back him. As the side of the saucer now opened slowly to form a ramp, Nick drew a deep breath and walked forward.

He could not tell if his protecting illusion was in force, if he would indeed appear to anyone outside as a normal alien crewman. What he could see ahead was not too reassuring. There another of the saucer ships rested on stilt-legs, its ramp down. To the right was a section of ground in which huddled a group of drifters. Nick could see no walls, yet none made an effort to escape even though there were no visible guards.

To cross the space between the ship and the captives was an ordeal. Nick expected any moment to be challenged, or else simply rayed down. He studied the prisoners, tried to understand what kept them there.

Some distance beyond the captives a tall pole arose into the sky from a broad earth base. At its tip sprouted two fan shapes fashioned of glittering wires stretched over frames. Even as Nick sighted them they moved, the fans waving slowly upward until they joined above the tip of the supporting pole. Along the wires glowed light, deepening to a fiery red.

The air about Nick tingled with energy. It was like and yet unlike the broadcast of the ankh. Nick knew, without understanding why or how, some vast power was at work.

Now he saw those who controlled it. There were six of the suited aliens clustered about the base of the pole. What they might be doing there did not matter, the fact that they were so engrossed by it did, giving Nick a slender chance.

"Those we seek—there—" An impression from Jeremiah on his right side. Lung was to his left.

"Can't go through—a wall ahead—" For the first time he also caught the Peke's thought.

Nick walked forward with caution. Jeremiah moved before him, stopped, as if his nose touched an unseen barrier. A force field? One of the aliens need only look up—see him investigating it—

Though Nick put out his hand to touch what the animals said was there, he felt nothing—save that a bolt of energy nearly rocked him from his feet. With that how could the captives hope to escape? And how could he and his party hope in turn to reach them? If he knew how to control the ship perhaps they could lift it and drop it on the other side of the barrier. But that was beyond his skill.

The prisoners noticed him. He saw faces turn in his direction. Two of the disheveled figures got to their feet—Crocker and Jean. Did they see him as himself, or did the alien illusion hold?

Illusion—some wisp of thought he could not pin down exactly. What had Hadlett earlier said—that the illusions a man could produce were born out of his own particular thoughts and fears, that those from the medieval period who had taken him prisoner had seen the demons and devils of their own time. Demons and devils—what would be the demons and devils of the aliens? If he only knew more! Nick felt bound and helpless, with weapons just out of his reach, as he had been in the camp when he had first used the freedom of mind. He had no guide, no way of knowing what would serve as the proper demons and devils to evoke here.

Into his mind flashed a memory—that of the Herald riding unconcernedly along under the attack of the saucer. But he was no Herald, nor could he, Nick was sure, take on the seeming of one himself, even though he could create the image of one for a short space. He sensed that the Herald was too much of Avalon to be used here in human counterfeit. Also if this place was of Avalon, what had it to hold for these who were not subject to the People or their powers? What other fear or threat could he summon? Wait—there had been that time when another flyer of a different shape had attacked the saucer—

The cigar ship! Demons and devils! But could they produce that as an illusion?

In the prison compound Jean and Crocker were aiding Stroud to his feet with the help of Lady Diana. If Nick was right in his surmise he would have to drop his own cover, give all power to the illusion.

"Join!" Nick sent the message to Jeremiah in the linkage he could not hold direct with his own kind. The big cat crouched, his tail tip quivering as if he stalked prey. He did not glance at Nick but the man felt his message was received.

Lung bolted, skimming back to the ramp of the saucer. How long did they have? Nick fastened his attention on the sky above that pole, tried to draw there the demon of the aliens—one of the cigar-shaped ships.

He—his message had gone through! Jeremiah—Lung—those in the ship behind him understood. There was the enemy that the aliens knew, hovering over their source of energy. He heard no sounds from the crew working below, but saw them freeze for a moment and then scatter, heading toward positions in the grass. They were about to defend their post desperately, as if it were paramount to their existence.

In his hand Nick held one of the weapons from the ship. It was a rod about the length of his forearm, with two buttons at one end. Being hollow in part he equated it with some type of gun. What it might do he had no idea, nor even if he could fire it. But the action of the aliens was a clue. If the fan-pole was so important, for they were firing rays into the hovering illusion to protect it, then if he could destroy it. . . .

Nick began to run. There was shouting from the prisoner pen, but he paid no attention. The pole was the important thing now. He came to a halt, raised the rod and took a chance, pushing the nearest button with his forefinger, aiming at the fans overhead.

He thought he had failed. There was no trace that the weapon had fired. Then—

The red glow of the wires above flashed an eye-searing white!

Nick flung his arm over his eyes. Was he blinded? And that roaring—enough to deafen one. The ground shook under him, rolled as if solid earth had vanished. He staggered around blindly, trying to head away from that holocaust, back to the ship. But where was the ship?

He was finding it hard to breathe, as if the air was being drained away. Then he was crawling through a world afire. This might be the ancient Hell of human-kind—

Nick lay on the still trembling ground, pressed against it by a force like a massive fist weighing upon his back. He was being crushed and he thought he cried out feebly. Then came darkness in which the fires of Hell were quenched.

The ankh stood tall, glowing. From it streamed light, reaching out and out, and under that light was peace. The fan-pole stood and glowed balefully, it drew upon the life-force of Avalon, and the peace was broken. Things crept out of ancient places of the Dark to walk the land again.

Peace fled before the power of the pole, before the Dark, withdrawing into the city, into those places wherein Avalon nursed full strength. To and fro were harried those who were neither of the light nor the Dark—but were prey—

Little things, fleeing without purpose, pursued and attacked by their own fears made manifest and given foul life. They were blind to all but what they unknowingly summoned to their own torment.

The balance was disturbed. In the cities gathered the People. Rita, those others who had accepted Avalon. There stood the Herald who bore the name of this land, and behind him his four pursuivants, Oak and Apple, Thorn and Elder, each wearing the badge of his naming. To the fore of them all was Logos King-of-Arms. He was might, clad not in the brilliant tabard of a Herald, but in a robe of dark blue over which ran runes in silver that twisted, turned, formed words of deep wisdom, and then dissolved to form again. In his hands was a great sword, point down into the soil of Avalon from whose metals it had long ago been wrought. Up the blade of that sword were also runes. But these were fixed for all time, set in the metal by a forging of power in ways now long forgotten, even in a world where time meant little.

Two hands held the sword erect: wide shoulders held proud and straight, and above them a head— The face of one who could summon storms, bind wind and water to his will, yet who disdained to take power for his own desires. Silver hair, bright as the crawling runes. There was a name for this King, a very old name that Avalon knew, which was legend also in another world—

Merlin.

Now the Logos King-of-Arms faced outward from the city. His hands moved, uprooted the sword, raised its mighty weight with ease, pointing it out at heart level. His lips moved, but whatever words he spoke did not issue forth as sound—they were not for the hearing of lesser men or spirits.

The aliens' fan-pole lashed out with scarlet fire, which brought black smoke that settled to stain the land. Where those stains grew so did the Dark Ones spread, creeping toward the cities. And the drawing of the alien power weakened that of Avalon, so that life under it withered and lessened.

But—

There was a flare of force, so great that all that could be seen was swallowed up. All was red and then white. The world was gone, sight was gone. There was nothing.

"Nothing—nothing—" Nick heard that. Understanding returned sluggishly. "Nothing—nothing—" His own voice was repeating that.

He—he was Nick Shaw—and he was alive. But he did not want to open his eyes and see again the awful nothingness that had been the end of Avalon. How could he still live when all else, even a world, was dead?

"All dead—" He put this thought into words.

"No!"

He had not said that. Who was here? Who had escaped the end of Avalon?

"Who—?" he asked.

"Nick! Nick, please, look at me!" Someone—who?

"Who?" he repeated. He was not sure he cared, he was so tired—so very tired. Avalon was gone. In him there welled a vast sorrow. He could feel tears in his eyes, squeezing out under the lids he would not raise. He had not cried for a long, long time—Men did not cry, men could not cry. They could hurt as he was hurting, but they must not cry.

"Nick! Please, can't you help him. Do something—?"

"There is only what he can do for himself."

He had heard that voice before, long ago. In Avalon. But Avalon was gone. He had seen it die. No—worse, it had been his act that had finished it. Nick began to fit together painfully this scrap of memory and that, to form an ugly picture. He had fired upon the fan-pole with the alien weapon. There had been a vast explosion of power. And there had been the Logos King—Merlin—with the sword. But the blasting of the fan-pole must have overbalanced the energies on which Avalon existed. Avalon was gone and where he might be now Nick neither knew nor cared.

"Nick!" Hands were laid on him, their shaking hurt, but the pain of his body was less than that of his spirit, the knowledge of what he had unwittingly done.

"Open your eyes, see, Nick, *see!*"

He opened them. As he thought, there was nothing, nothing at all.

"There is nothing. Avalon is gone," he said into that emptiness.

"What is he talking about? Is he—is he blind?" There was dread in that voice from nothingness.

"He is blind in his own way." Again that other voice from the past.

The Herald! Avalon! But the land was gone, erased into nothingness. How did the Herald still exist?

"Avalon, Tara, Brocéliande, Carnac—" Nick said over those names that had once had great meaning and that he had rendered meaningless. "Oak and Apple, Elder, Thorn, and the Logos King—gone."

"He—he doesn't know what he is saying—" The first voice choked as if someone struggled against crying. "What has happened to him?"

"He believes, and to him what he believes *is*," Avalon replied.

"You are Avalon," Nick said slowly. "But that is not true—for Avalon is gone. Am I dead?" There was no fear in him now. Perhaps death *was* this—this nothingness.

"No, of course not! Nick—Please don't be like this! Oh, you can help him. I know you could if you would."

"He must believe."

"Nick, listen!" Someone was so close to him he could feel a stir of breath against his cheek. Breath was life—so that other must be alive. But how could one live in nothingness? "Nick, you are here with us. You somehow blew up that power standard, or whatever it was. And then—everything just happened. The prisoners were able to get out. And the aliens all died. Barry says the backlash of power did it. Their saucers were blown open. Then—then the Herald came, Nick, you must *see!*"

Something stirred in him. This was Linda. He could give a name to her voice. Linda and Avalon were here with him. He could feel her touch as she held his head against her, he could even hear the beating of her heart. A beating heart was life also.

And if Avalon existed for Linda, how could it be gone for him? Once more he opened his eyes on nothingness. But there should be no nothingness—there should be Avalon!

Nick drew upon his will of concentration. Avalon—let Avalon *be!*

Sight did not return as it had gone in a burst of fierce light—but slowly. He saw first shadows darkening the blank white of that place into which he had been exiled by his own desperate act. Then those shadows took on substance. There were figures. As he had concentrated on creating illusion, so he concentrated now on the return of a world. Was this an illusion also? No, he must not give room to such a doubt.

There was Linda, watching, concern on her face, in her touch as she supported him. There was Jeremiah, unblinking eyes regarding him, and beyond, standing, so he had to raise his head a fraction to see the better, the blaze of color that was the Herald.

Brighter, sharper, more real with every moment, the world came back. Had he indeed lost his sight so that it had made him believe he had lost all else into the bargain?

Nick did not know. All he cared about was that he had been wrong.

He was lying, he discovered, at the edge of what must have been a battlefield for forces, not men. Facing him, one of the saucers had flipped from stilt feet to its side, part of it plowed in a deep gash into the earth. The sight of that tore his mind from his deep self-consciousness to think of the others. He freed himself from Linda's hold, struggled to sit up and look around.

Linda was safe, and Jeremiah, and Lung, for the Peke was pressed close to the girl as if he feared they might be parted. But Hadlett, Mrs. Clapp—the prisoners in the pen—?

"The others," he demanded of Linda. "How are the others?"

She did not answer at once, only looked distressed.

"The Vicar—Mrs. Clapp?" What of those two who had shared this last adventure?

"Over—over there." She put out a hand to restrain him. But Nick pushed it aside and somehow got to his feet.

"Over there" was by the second saucer. There was a rent in its upper surface, its landing ramp was twisted. At the foot of it he saw Crocker and Jean. Mrs. Clapp and Lady Diana were on their knees beside someone stretched on the ground. Nick began to walk, though he felt very lightheaded and dizzy.

"Nick!" Linda was beside him. Before he could resist she had caught his arm, drawn it about her shoulders, steadying him. He did not try to push her away this time. If her help could bring him to the others sooner he accepted it.

He covered the gap, stood with Linda's support, looking down at the Vicar. Hadlett's eyes were open and when he saw Nick he smiled. "St. George," he said, "and St. Michael are supposed to be the warriors. I have never heard it of St. Nicholas that he went into battle, but rather that he was a giver of gifts."

Nick went to his knees. "Sir—" Until that moment he had not realized, though perhaps he had dimly suspected, how close were his ties with this man. Heart-ties Rita had called them. Now he could feel why.

"You won for us, Nicholas. And"—Hadlett turned his head just a fraction in Mrs. Clapp's hold—"I think it was perhaps a notable victory indeed. Have I the right of it, sir?"

Nick realized then that the Vicar spoke to someone behind, and he turned his own head to see that the Herald had followed them.

"He has won the freedom of Avalon, and not for himself alone."

"There was a danger then for you as well as us," Hadlett said. "Yet we were not allies—"

"Only in part. Avalon has its laws, which are not the laws of men."

Hadlett nodded, a fractional movement of his head. "That was—" He paused and there was a struggle on his face. "That was the truth that I had to abide by. Good may govern Avalon—but it is not—my—good—" A red bubble formed in the corner of his mouth. It broke and a trickle of scarlet came from it.

Nick turned on the Herald. "Help him!"

"No, Nicholas." It was not Avalon, but Hadlett who answered. "To every man his own season. And the season passes. You and I"—again it was Avalon he addressed—"know that. It is given few men to find peace. I am—content. You told me once, Nicholas, that there might be many rivers from a single source. That is also the truth, but we each choose our own. Now, let me enter into my own peace in my own time."

What he repeated thereafter were the words of his own priesthood and belief, the belief he might not surrender to Avalon. Nick could not listen. It was too unfair. The Vicar had given freely, and what came in return?

He pulled loose from Linda, moved away from the others, steadying himself with one hand against the bent support of the wrecked saucer. Before him stretched the open land with a crater rimmed in glassy slag to mark the site of the pole. Had that operated the gateway to the aliens' own world? If so it was closed, perhaps forever.

What would happen to him and his companions now? Would the Dark Tide Rita and the Herald warned of continue to flow? Or had his vision, dream, whatever it might have been, held the truth—that it was the force of the aliens that stimulated and released the Dark Ones, built up their power to spread over the land?

"Nick?"

He did not look around.

"You won't get back through any way of theirs now!" He struck out at her voice.

"No." But she did not sound crushed.

Nick turned his head. Linda stood there in worn and bedraggled clothing, her hair loose about her shoulders, a raw scratch on her cheek, Lung in her arms, as if he were now the only treasure she could ever so hold. She looked forlorn, lost.

"I hope—I hope Dave—" Her voice broke. "No—" She backed away as Nick took a step toward her. "Don't—don't try to tell me— We won't go back, ever. After awhile we're going to forget, I think. The past will all seem a dream. Maybe, Nick, I shall accept Avalon. I must! If I don't—I'll keep on remembering and that I cannot live with!"

"And what about them?" Nick gestured toward the others.

"The Vicar—he's gone, Nick." Tears spilled down her cheeks and she made no move to wipe them away. "And the rest—the Warden was killed in the backlash, as you might have been, Nick—as I thought you were at first." There was fear and horror in her eyes now. "The others—they know now what they must do. And you, Nick?"

"I always knew—after the city. There can be only one way of true life in Avalon. If we would be any more than those miserable human animals I saw in the woods, we must choose that."

He held out his hand, and Linda, cradling Lung against her with her other arm, let her fingers be enclosed in his. Together they started back. After all, Nick thought, in this choice the giving was not so much his. What he received was far the greater.

Avalon the Herald waited for them, the radiance about him very glorious indeed.